SOMETHING TO CROWE ABOUT

An Ill-Timed Truth is as Bad as a Lie

E.W. NICKERSON

Order this book online at www.trafford.com
or email orders@trafford.com

Most Trafford titles are also available at major online book retailers.

Printed in the United States of America.

ISBN: 978-1-4907-1273-4 (sc)
ISBN: 978-1-4907-1275-8 (hc)
ISBN: 978-1-4907-1274-1 (e)

Library of Congress Control Number: 2013915217

Trafford rev. 09/04/2013

 www.trafford.com

North America & international
toll-free: 1 888 232 4444 (USA & Canada)
fax: 812 355 4082

I would like to thank my wife Judy and
my friend Sue Manson for their help, assistance,
and direction in this my fourth novel.

This book is dedicated to my mother; E. E. (Mae) Nickerson (1909-1978). A woman of great strength and firm opinions, she resolved many matters over a cup of tea.

CONTENTS

CHAPTER ONE

SATURDAY, AUGUST 10ᵀᴴ 1985

"All hands on deck!" Pat called out from the helm of the boat.

Ed looked around. There were just the two of them. He looked at his hands, unsure what to say. Pat was taking her Captain's role seriously. He called back "Both hands on deck, Captain."

Pat looked at him questioningly. He held up both hands, grinning. She shook her head and continued. "Anchors aweigh," she shouted.

Ed walked to the back of the boat. The anchor was safely stored on deck. He waited for a few moments. "Anchor's on board," he called forward.

"Off to the blue yonder then," Pat called out as she put the motor in forward gear and slowly moved the boat away from the dock.

Ed grinned as he looked back. He called to Pat in full voice. "Should we untie the boat from the dock, Cap'n?"

"Oh damn," Pat said out loud, and put the engine in neutral. "Christ why didn't you say something!"

The owner of the boat stood on the dock, shaking his head. He untied the boat and threw the line into the water. Ed waved at him with a wink and pulled the line on board.

Ed walked to the helm where Pat was ready to commence their momentous trip. Ed smiled. "First, Captain, my name's not Christ. And secondly we ain't exactly heading into the wide blue yonder; we're heading down the Rideau Canal along with about twenty other boats."

Pat brushed him off with a wave. "Hey I'm the Captain, we use my language. I've been looking forward to this trip for months. I don't want a land-lubber like you spoiling it for me." She gave him a quick grin. "Why don't you go to the galley and brew some hearty coffee?"

Ed rolled his eyes. "Galley? Hearty coffee? This could be a long trip."

"You're the cook aren't you?" She didn't take her eyes off the waterway ahead.

"Sure I'm the cook," Ed agreed. "It seems I'm also the Chief Mechanic, the Sergeant at Arms, the late night watch, and the boiler stoker—and we don't even have a bloody boiler!"

She turned and kissed him on his cheek. "But you're also my First Mate." She smiled. "Get it? You're my first lover—my First Mate!"

Ed was tempted to say he hoped he'd 'get it', but thought better of the choice of words. "Aye, aye, Capt'n," he said, moving to head down to the galley.

She turned to him with a cheeky smile. "So what am I, your fifth mate? Your tenth mate?"

He smiled and winked at her. "You're my Captain. That's what counts here." He stressed the word 'counts'.

"Very clever," she smiled back. "And don't you forget it!"

"I'll go brew some hearty coffee."

Pat called after him. "Make sure the mess isn't a mess."

He turned back. "What?"

"You know make sure the mess, that's boating talk for the eating area, isn't a mess—as in untidy." She grinned, pleased with her play on words.

He walked down the stairs; now wishing he had taken the same Marine Training Course that Pat had taken. This was going to be a long one-week cruise.

The boat they had rented, that Pat had rented, was perfect for two people. The living area was high enough that Ed didn't have to walk about bent over, and the eating and sleeping areas were comfortably large. The fridge was small, but held enough basic food and white wine to get them through a couple of days. With plenty of shopping along the entire route, storage was not an issue.

Ed looked around. Pat had done a wonderful job of planning the trip—which was quite a distance—from Ottawa to Ed's hometown of Oakville. The entire length of the Rideau Waterway to Kingston and then along the shore of Lake Ontario, past Toronto, to Oakville was a challenge for two non-sailors, but Pat had worked hard and long to ensure their get-away cruise would be close to perfect. Everything was at hand. He put on a pot of coffee.

Ed had been impressed with Pat's organizational capabilities since they had met in May 1984 when they worked together on Operation Niagara. She had just a few days to convert him from a typical Englishman who knew very little of Canada, to a point where he could convince members of the Turkish terrorist party, the Kurdish PKK, that he was a Canadian immigrant from England, but one that had lived in Canada for four years. It had been a successful operation; Ed's first working operation with the British MI6, which had led him to move to Canada while still remaining a consultant with MI6. Ed and Pat's relationship had changed during the past fifteen months. They were lovers, with an agreed-upon understanding that it would lead no further. While denying she wanted to marry him, she knew in the depths of her heart she would gladly put up with a 'Delayed Pioneer', in spite of the fact that he constantly annoyed her with his penchant for correct English. Ed's love for Pat was what he described as a love with a small "L". It was real, but had its limitations.

Ed's true love was a senior MI6 operative Carolyn Andrews, daughter of MI6's Chief of Staff, Lord Stonebridge. In their less-than-normal arrangement they had agreed to live somewhat separate lives, with an understanding that Ed was going to ask Carolyn to marry him in October 1989, but with no understanding of how Carolyn would respond. It was imperfect but acceptable to both of them. In Ed's case, he had little choice but to accept the arrangement since it was better then no arrangement.

The coffee had brewed. Ed carried up two mugs of coffee to the Captain at the helm.

"Do I call these mugs, or is there a boating term for them?" he asked.

"You do indeed," Pat responded taking her mug and tasting the coffee. "Well done, mate." She grinned. "Get it? Mate the shipping mate and mate the English mate."

"If you don't give over with all these boating word games, I'm going to make you walk the plank and you'll end up in Davy Jones' Locker."

Pat grinned. "You mean *down* in Davy Jones' Locker don't you?"

"God help me," Ed groaned.

"Okay, okay," Pat laughed. "Truce!"

Ed leaned down and kissed her forehead. "Truce it is. Now what are our plans and where do I fit into our long-awaited cruise?"

"First," Pat asked, "do you like my cruising outfit?"

She was wearing a blue and white horizontally striped top and white shorts that just covered her cheeks. Her shoes were canvas topped.

"Very nice, and quite sexy if I may say so. You seem to have shrunk. Have you lost a couple of inches?"

"Don't be silly," she replied quickly. She didn't like people to make reference to her height. "I'm still five-two—and just as cute as I ever was. So there!"

"Yes you are cute, Pat." He kissed her forehead again. "It must be the plimsoles."

She frowned. "What's a plimsole when it's at home?"

"Your shoes. They're plimsoles."

"Don't talk silly English. They're cruising shoes."

"As you wish," he smiled, "but in England they're called plimsoles, and in Scotland they're called sannies. Mostly worn by girls. Only sexy girls of course."

She did a small curtsy. "Do you really think I look sexy?"

"Pat, would I lie?"

"Maybe."

"Trust me, you look sexy."

"Yeah, right." She stepped back and looked at Ed. "Have you put on weight?"

"Just a tad. Not enough sexual activity I suspect."

"Too much beer I suspect," Pat replied quickly. "I'll put up with our ten inch height difference, but I don't want a chubby lover. Understand?"

"I'm sure I can lose a few pound on this trip," he winked.

"I'm sure you can. No beer!"

"And lots of *activity* I trust." He looked at her again. "Are you wearing a bra?"

"Don't be impudent!" She turned her full attention to steering the boat. "But no, I'm not."

"Wow," Ed said, moving toward her. "Could I . . . I mean may I . . . ?"

"Certainly not," she giggled. "What kind of girl do you think I am?"

He kept his distance. "Well let me see. I think you are a very charming, intelligent, hard-working young lady. I think you put on a tough exterior sometimes, but in reality you are generous and kind hearted. You have to be nice if you like cats—it's the law. I think you are very sexy and I enjoy your company tremendously."

She held her head up, keeping her eyes straight ahead. "Really?"

"Really."

She ignored his comments. "If you'd turn you eyes to the starboard side of the boat, you will see the Parliament Buildings coming into view."

"Is that right?" he asked, enjoying his play on words.

She shook her head, deciding not to comment.

He walked over to her and kissed the back of her neck. "And what kind of a guy do you think I am?" he asked.

"The gothic looking building is the Library of Parliament," Pat pointed out. "Behind it is the Peace Tower."

Ed looked up at the impressive Parliament buildings, which were the centerpiece of the Capital. "It is very impressive," he said, taking a good look at the buildings that towered over them. They cruised past the buildings slowly.

"Over to your right," Pat said, pointing ahead of them "is the Chateau Laurier Hotel. We pass through the eight locks that start between the Parliament Buildings and the Hotel, and then in about eight kilometers we join the actual Rideau Canal at Hogs Back lock."

"I also think you are super organized," Ed said, lifting her hair and kissing the back of her neck. She shivered slightly at his touch.

She carried on as if nothing had happened. "When we get to Hogs Back lock we can pull over and I'll go over the week's planned cruising. We can go over the cooking and sleeping arrangements. I think I've got it all organized."

He stood closer to her. "Can we make love at Hogs Back lock?" he asked quietly.

"Can't you think of anything else?"

He reached in front of her and gently placed his hand under her top on her stomach. She took a deep breath at the feel of his touch.

"Okay," she said as he kissed her neck, "maybe we can."

"I do love you, Pat."

"Thanks, Ed. I like to hear that." She leaned back to kiss him. "Now will you get your land-lubber ass out on the deck and help me get this twenty-seven foot monster through the first eight locks without smashing into anything?"

"Aye, aye, Capt'n." He saluted her and headed out on deck. He leaned back into the cabin. "The Chateau Laurier Hotel is now on our port side, Captain."

"I'll drink to that," she replied with a grin.

"Oh God," he groaned. "I walked into that one!"

They managed to pass through the first lock with the help of the gatekeeper and other, more knowledgeable, sailors. They only once came close to throwing each other off the boat. By the time they had passed through the eighth and final lock, they were old hands at the process. They waved thanks to the other sailors and headed down the Rideau waterway to Hogs Back lock where they would join the Canal in its greater width and grandeur.

"Sorry about that," Pat said as they stood next to each other as she steered the boat slowly. "I guess I'm more nervous than I thought I would be."

He smacked her behind gently. "Not an issue, Captain. You're doing a fine job."

She turned to him with a wry smile. "That could be considered insubordination, sailor.'

He put his hand down the back of her shorts, under her panties and squeezed her cheek. "Now *that* could be considered insubordination," he quipped, removing his hand quickly.

Pat smiled and said nothing. She was tempted to increase the speed to arrive at Hogs Back lock sooner, but decided not to give Ed the pleasure of her desire to have him hold and kiss her. She maintained her smile as they motored slowly. She was happy, very happy. She wondered to herself if she would ever be as happy again as she was now. As if reading her mind, Ed leaned over and kissed her cheek. Pat gently moved the throttle forward to pick up speed.

As directed, Ed threw the 'thingies' over the side to protect the boat from banging against the wall of the canal. Pat jumped onto the canal walkway and secured the boat's front and rear ropes to the metal rings provided. With Ed's help she clambered back onto the boat and brushed herself off.

"Okay, all hands below," she announced. "The entire crew will meet below to discuss the week's planned voyage."

"Aye, aye," Ed saluted, and followed Pat into the cabin area.

Pat directed him to the table immediately to the right as they walked down the three steps. Pulling a file from the drawer in the kitchen, she opened it and spread the contents. She slid a package across the table to Ed.

"All hands present, First Mate?" she asked.

Ed looked at her and touched his head to make sure he was in fact in the room. "All both of us accounted for, Capt'n."

She giggled and rubbed her hands. "Thanks for playing along, Ed. I'm really enjoying this." She looked over to him. "I enjoy being the boss—just in case you hadn't noticed."

"It never crossed my mind," he lied.

"Yeah right!"

He shrugged and turned to the package in front of him.

"Page one," Pat said, now with real authority, "is the locations of where we will be docking each night. The second page outlines the events of the day, the shore excursions we'll be taking, and the locations of each meal. You will see that we will be eating ashore in several locations. This will give the Head Chef, that's you, a bit of a break." She looked up to make sure he was with her. He smiled his understanding. She continued on. "Page three is a list of all duties we must do, broken down by day and night."

He raised his hand.

"Yes, First Mate?"

"On page two," Ed asked, "what do the initials ML stand for?"

She licked her lips. "Make love."

"I see," Ed said, nodding his head and looking up. "There appears to be no ML on today's list of activities."

She held his gaze. "Captain's prerogative." Leaning over she took his page and wrote 'ML' on the top of the list for 'Hogs Back.'

"So do we vote on this?" he asked cheekily.

"My ship, my rules."

Ed raised his eyebrows and smiled. He reached over and taking her hand he stood, taking her with him. He turned her back to him, reached under her top and gently held her breasts. He squeezed her nipples and she shuddered slightly in delight.

"Can we muster in the bedroom, Captain?" he asked.

She took his hands from her breasts and turned to face him, looking up. She kissed his hands. "Ed, I know I'm kind of pushy, and I'll admit I enjoy being the boss, but when you have my breasts in your hands and we're about to make love I just want to be Pat, okay?"

He nodded. "Lift you arms, Pat." She did and he swiftly removed her top over her head. He lowered his head and kissed her breasts. Her back arched and she moved his head from nipple to nipple. Dropping to his knees he removed her shorts. Her panties were pale pink with a frilly edging.

"I wore them just for you," she whispered, looking down.

He lowered the front of her panties and kissed her softly. Standing, he turned her to the door that led to the berth at the front on the boat. "Go in, Pat, I'll join you in a minute. And keep a pillow free please."

She headed into the bedroom, knowing how he was going to use the pillow.

Ed pulled out his wallet and withdrew the aluminum foil ring that he carried. Originally made by Pat as a 'pinky' ring for Ed to make him an Engineer, they had subsequently used it as an 'engagement' ring which, while still strictly speaking was contrary to CSIS rules of 'non-associating' with employees within the organization or similar international organizations, they considered sufficient to allow them to make love. Ed pulled the curtains on all of the windows and then quickly stripped naked.

He entered the bedroom, now shaded by the drawn curtains. Pat smiled at seeing his erection. She was kneeling on the bed, her panties still on. She knew how much Ed enjoyed removing them. Leaning down, Ed took her left hand and slid the ring on her second finger. She smiled up in thanks. Before Ed had a chance to join her, Pat reached for his erection. She kissed it lovingly, looking up at him as she did. As he smiled down at her, she took his full erection in her mouth and slowly moved her mouth up and down his cock. When he was in danger of coming too soon, he joined her on the bed. They held each other tightly, forcing themselves to slow down their lovemaking.

"I do love you, Ed," Pat said, speaking into his chest. "I am so happy."

He reached down and slipped his hand into her panties. "Let me see if I can make you a little happier," he whispered.

She stiffened as he reached her moist area and gently caressed it. She clung to him, hoping the pleasure would never end. He moved gently out of her grip and slid his mouth to her nipples. Her body felt a warmth and lightness beyond any feeling she had experienced. She needed more.

"Please take my panties off, Ed," she asked, almost begging. Slipping her panties off, he lifted her lightly and slid the pillow under her back. In a moment he slid down her body and forced his tongue into her now wet mound. Her back arched in pleasure as he forced his tongue deeper and faster into her. She groaned in pleasure, squeezing his head with her hands to encourage him. When she could endure it no longer, she pulled his head up to her breasts. "In me, Ed. I want you in me. Please make me come . . . make me come!"

His cock entered her with full force and he thrust into her as hard and as fast as he could. Their bodies moved in motion as if guided by an orchestra. When neither could hold out any longer they both exploded in pleasure, perspiration covering their bodies and mixing as Ed fell into her arms.

Pat clung to him, her fingers digging into his back. She gulped to catch her breath, not sure that such pleasure was really hers to enjoy. She looked at him smiling. "Wow, Ed! If you'll excuse the language; fucking wow!"

Ed kissed her forehead. "May I ask a question?"

She nodded, grinning in anticipation.

He asked quietly, with a broad smile. "What's for lunch?"

She pushed him away, laughing. "You rotten bastard. You ravage my body, and then you're only interested in food!"

"Having sex is hard work," he commented. "If you'll excuse the pun."

She pointed to a ghetto blaster on the table by the side of the bed. "Would you press 'play' please? There's a song I want you to hear. Then come right back to me and hug me while we listen."

Ed leaned over and pressed the 'play' button, expecting to hear a Gordon Lightfoot song. As he moved back to her, Pat clung to him with her face against his chest. It was a Queen song: *One Year of Love*.

> *Just one year of love*
> *Is better than a lifetime alone*
> *One Sentimental moment in your arms*
> *Is like a shooting star right through my heart . . . .*

As they listened Pat gulped several times to the words and held on as if for dear life. Ed responded by kissing the top of her head and squeezing her tightly to him. He reached over and pressed the 'off' button when the song finished.

"Can you promise me one year, Ed?" She looked up as she asked, not letting go of him. "Can we go one year at a time? From now until my birthday next year—August 24th?" She smiled and reached up to cover his lips. "I know more about you than you think, Ed. One year at a time, that's my request. You don't have to give me an answer until we are having a glass of wine after supper tonight. Okay?"

Ed nodded. "Is this reciprocal?"

"No it is not! It's strictly one-sided. Remember I know you. If someone comes along for me, which I doubt, then I'll have to take that risk." She sat up, covered herself with a blanket, picked up her panties and moved to the door. "Now get your lazy ass out here and help me with lunch! Your mother doesn't live here." She closed the door as she left.

Ed sat on the side of the bed thinking. The door opened and his clothes were thrown in. "Move it!" Pat called in.

He couldn't believe that Pat knew of his intention to ask Carolyn to marry him in less than five years. Carolyn wouldn't have mentioned it, and he hadn't spoken of it; not even to his best friend Roy Johnston. He dressed in the confines of the small bedroom, surprised yet happy at her knowing whatever she knew or assumed. He opened the door as Pat once more called for him to get his ass in gear. "Yes, Capt'n," he called back. Pat smiled at his comeback as she worked on lunch in the galley.

Ed poured them a second glass of wine and carried them out to the seat at the rear of the boat.

They were now moored at the Long Island locks, Pat's choice for their first night on the Canal. It was just past seven in the evening, with several hours of sunshine left. They had passed through Black Rapids lock without any issues and had cruised at 5 knots an hour to Long Island. The view from the Canal was more beautiful than either had expected and although busy with other boats, it was relaxing and comfortable.

Pat joined Ed on the seat and toasted them. "Cheers."

"Cheers indeed," Ed responded. "Before we go any further, Pat," Ed said, putting down his glass, "I do want to say thank you for organizing such a wonderful trip, and as I had expected everything is so well organized."

She smiled her thanks. "And the answer to my question is 'No', correct?"

"No." He shook his head.

"Don't play word games with me on this, Ed. This is important to me."

He reached over and took her hand. "Pat, the answer is a definite 'Yes'. One year is fine and I'm honored you would ask me."

She gave a wide smile. "You and your fancy talk." She looked down at her left hand and twirled the aluminum foil ring, unsure what to do with it.

"Keep it on, Pat. Let's be engaged for the entire trip."

Her smile as acceptance was interrupted by the crackle of the radio in the cockpit.

"Base to Blue Heron. Base to Blue Heron. Come in please."

Pat rolled her eyes in disappointment. "Shit," she murmured and walked to the radio.

"Blue Heron responding," she answered.

The radio crackled back, "Message for PAW. Repeat, message for PAW. Phone home ASAP. Do you understand?"

"Understood and out!" Pat wanted to slam the radio back onto its clip, but laid it gently back slowly.

"Problem at home?" Ed asked.

Pat shook her head, now almost in tears. "No. That's the office code. Damn it!" She went below and collected her purse. "I have to make a phone call. There's a store not far from here."

"Figured you'd know that," Ed smiled.

"Yeah, Miss Organization, that's me!"

"Better a Miss than a Dis . . . ."

Pat chuckled. "Shut up, Ed. Get the music out. I'm sure we won't be leaving tonight."

"Aye, aye, Capt'n."

Pat left the boat and quickly walked away. Ed returned to the bedroom area. He collected the ghetto blaster and the tapes and straightened the bed covers, leaving the pillow he had slipped under Pat's back in the same position. He wanted to leave her a message.

Pat returned fifteen minutes later. Although she tried to hide it, there was a slight grin on her face and she walked more purposely. Climbing down onto the boat she sat on the rear seat, at the far end from Ed, and picked up her glass of wine. She took a slow casual sip and exhaled in comfort. Ed decided not to ask. He knew she was playing the game. She put her glass down.

"You are getting to be a pain in the ass," she smiled.

He rubbed his chin. "I am?"

"Oh yeah. A real pain in the ass!"

"Sorry about that. Can I ask what I did?"

"May I . . . ?" she corrected him.

"May I ask what I did?"

"You, Mr. MI6 Consultant, are to be in my boss's, boss's, boss's office Monday morning at eight sharp. We head back to my place tomorrow, and get a good night's sleep for your Monday morning meeting."

"Ouch!"

"You will then be connected to Lord Stonebridge at Stonebridge Manor by a secure phone line to get your marching orders. I assume you have your passport with you?"

"In my kit," Ed replied. Departmental rules required him to carry his passport with him if he planned on being more than an hour's travel distance away from his apartment where it was regularly carefully hidden.

She finished her wine and extended her glass, which Ed refilled. She toasted him. "Here's looking at you, kid."

"Look I'm sorry about this, Pat. Do you know what it's about?"

"No."

"Do you have any idea?"

"No."

"Would you tell me if you did?"

"No."

"Do you know who else will be at the other end of the phone call?"

"No."

"Did you ask?"

"No."

"Are you really, really pissed off with me?"

She shook her head. "No, Ed, I'm not. I'm terribly sad that our trip will end up as a two-day disaster, but probably more jealous that you'll be heading on a field trip and I'll be stuck in Ottawa."

"It may be two days, Pat, but it doesn't have to be a disaster." He slid over and put his arm around her. "What do you want to hear, Gordon Lightfoot or Queen?"

She looked about them. "Rideau Canal, Saturday night, lovely weather, and I'm here with my lover-boy."

Ed reached to the tapes. "Lightfoot it is then."

CHAPTER TWO

MONDAY,
AUGUST 12TH 1985
OTTAWA
8AM

Pat had introduced Ed to Ted Morden, Director, Canadian Security Intelligence Service and the three now waited for the phone call from MI6 chief, Lord Stonebridge. They chatted about the weather, not wanting to get into any real discussion. Morden was a big man, over six-four and heavily built. He had a distinguishing mustache that was large enough to match his size. For all of his presence, he spoke quietly and used facial expressions to readily reflect his thoughts. The phone rang and his eyes lit up in anticipation. He obviously enjoyed his role as head of the recently created CSIS.

"Morden," he announced into the speakerphone with his deep voice.

"Good morning, Ted," Lord Stonebridge responded. They chatted briefly about the weather. It was raining in England.

Lord Stonebridge moved on, explaining that with him was the General, who everyone recognized was Mr. Cooper's somewhat honorary title within MI6, and Miss Carolyn Andrews the recently promoted field operative. It needed no explaining that she was Lord Stonebridge's daughter—for this discussion that was of no importance.

Ted Morden announced that Pat Weston, Ed Crowe's contact in Canada, and herself recently promoted, was in attendance along with Ed. They all exchanged greetings in a flurry of words.

"If I may get to the point, Ted," Lord Stonebridge said, bringing the chatter to an end, "could I ask a few questions of Mr. Crowe?" He didn't wait for an answer, and Ed moved in closer to the speaker.

"Good morning, sir," Ed replied.

"Good morning, Mr. Crowe. How's your French?"

Ed cringed, and did his best. "Bonjour. Comment ca vas? Ouvrrez la porte. Qu'est ce c'est?"

There was a telling silence from the other end of the line. Carolyn finally responded. "Pretty bloody awful then, Mr. Crowe?" There was humor in her voice.

"Oui," Ed answered, pronouncing it as 'wee'.

Mr. Cooper spoke. "There are some in England that still believe that speaking French is conceding to the enemy, Ted."

Laughter broke out from both ends and it helped relax the conversation.

"We will have to work with what we've got," Lord Stonebridge chuckled. "How quickly can you make it over here, Mr. Crowe?"

Before Ed could answer, Ted Morden replied. "He's on vacation for a week and the plane is ready. He could be at the Manor by tomorrow morning." He turned to Ed. "Isn't that correct, Mr. Crowe?"

Ed nodded. "Yes."

Lord Stonebridge continued. "Then we'll see you tomorrow, Mr. Crowe, and Ted you'll sort out the other issue?"

"I'll get back to you on that today," he replied.

Everyone said their goodbyes and the line went dead.

Morden clasped his hands in front of him, looked at Ed and then at Pat. "I suppose you know what that other issue is?" he asked of both of them.

Ed shook his head. "No, sir, I don't."

Pat looked dejected and briefly closed her eyes. "Yes, sir."

Morden turned to Pat. "And?"

"Should I leave?" Ed asked, not wanting to interfere with what might be departmental matters.

Morden smiled and slowly shook his head. "Oh no, Mr. Crowe. Please sit exactly where you are."

Ed then understood the issue.

Pat thought carefully before she spoke. "You've raised the issue in a most generous manner, Mr. Morden, and perhaps I could respond in a similar but honest way?"

Morden waved her on.

"Mr. Crowe and I—Ed and I, were for a short while engaged. I understand the rules don't allow for different application given that, but . . . ." She let her comment settle in. "We are no longer engaged and are now just good friends. Ed stayed at my apartment last night as a guest and a good friend."

Ed nodded to confirm that fact. He hadn't understood her decision of the night before, but was now delighted to be able to confirm her careful but honest response.

Morden turned to Ed. "Do you know why I have to ask this, Mr. Crowe?"

"No, sir, I don't. But I do want to confirm Pat's comments."

"And very carefully worded comments, I might add." Morden nodded knowingly. "You, Mr. Crowe, do not speak French, while Miss Weston is most proficient in French. Are you with me here?"

Ed nodded.

Morden turned to Pat. "I am most reluctant to send you on this trip, Pat. Nothing to do with Mr. Crowe here, but this could be dangerous—and your first real field trip. I just don't know."

Ed decided to make a stand and rudely interrupted Pat's response. "Mr. Morden, sir, I have sat and watched Miss Weston shoot a man, and stood by as she was kicked in the face, only to get up and carry on like nothing happened. I'm unaware of the risks we're dealing with here, but . . ." He shrugged and let it go.

Morden raised his hand to stop Pat from responding. "I assume you want to go, Pat?"

"Yes, sir, I most certainly do. I can be ready to go and be at the airport by ten this morning." She spoke confidently and directly to Morden.

Morden stood and extended his hands to both of them. "Then go—as friends. And, Pat: keep in touch."

Outside of Morden's office Ed extended his hand with a grin.

Pat shook her head. "Don't even touch me, Mr. Crowe." Then with a mischievous grin she took off toward the elevator. "Let's go!" she called back. "Work to be done!"

"You're speeding," Ed said carefully, holding onto the safety handle above the passenger's side seat of Pat's car.

"Yes I know."

He swallowed hard. "No matter how fast you go, we won't have time to make love at your apartment before we leave for the airport."

Pat stepped hard on the brakes. "Are you out of your bloody mind?" She laughed aloud. "Hey, that conversation with my boss may have reduced your sex life, but it just eliminated mine!"

"Don't get personal," Ed quipped with a grin. "Just keep in mind the plane won't take off without us."

Pat nodded, and kept the speed lower than 'put-her-in-jail-and-throw-away-the-key' speed. "Thanks for backing me up, by the way."

"Thanks for not sleeping with me last night!"

"Well," she said flippantly, "you're not *that* good."

Ed rolled his eyes and gave up.

Pat drove carefully through the busy streets of Ottawa. Between thousands of tourists and even more government employees, the streets of the city were always crowded. As they drove out of the city into the residential areas the crowds were fewer and the summer drive was peaceful.

"So what do you think it's all about?" Pat asked.

Ed shrugged. "Something to do with your French language capabilities?"

"So what are you for? It can't be your good looks."

"Thank you very much, I'm sure. Maybe it's my perfect mixture of English manners and Canadian ruggedness?"

Pat shook her head. "Nah, I don't think so. Your manners are okay, but you couldn't build a canoe from a tree trunk in a million years!"

Ed laughed. "No, I haven't learned that skill yet." He paused. "So maybe it is my good looks?"

Pat looked at him sideways quickly. "No, definitely not! Not that you're ugly or anything, but you're no Sean Connery either."

"Then maybe it's the usual reason—my Canadian passport."

"Yep," Pat agreed, "that's it. Your good old Canadian passport."

"Well," Ed said quietly, "as long as I'm good for something."

Pat gently hit him in the arm. "You're good for several things, Ed." She winked. "Cooking supper for one!"

They shared a laugh as Pat pulled up in front of her apartment.

The eight-seat jet plane turned east and they looked down over the city of Ottawa.

"Nice location for a city," Ed remarked.

"We can thank the Americans for that," Pat replied thoughtfully. "The capital was originally Kingston, but being on Lake Ontario and close to the U.S. was too dangerous. Hence the move and hence the Rideau Canal!"

When the plane reached its flying altitude, Ed automatically moved to the table at the rear of the plane to make coffee. Pat remained in her seat thinking about what had happened over the past couple of days. Things were moving quickly and she relished the buzz of the activity. She went over in her head this morning's discussion with Ted Morden.

She was satisfied they had not lied. Not telling the entire truth was not a lie, of that she felt comfortable. Besides, Morden knew she and Ed had stretched the definition of being 'engaged'. She was wondering if that 'excuse' had been used before by others as Ed handed her a cup of steaming hot coffee. She thanked him and watched as he carried two more cups into the cockpit. He'd flown with the crew often enough he knew what they took in their coffee. She made a note in her head to learn their requirements. She hoped to fly often in the government jet. She followed Ed back to the table at the rear of the plane as he returned from the cockpit.

"So who's looking after Robin?" Ed asked. He liked Pat's cat. He was big and friendly.

"My neighbor."

"And you arranged this when?"

"This morning, before you woke up."

"Just like you half-packed before I woke up?"

She gave a quick shrug. "Yeah, sort of."

"Sort of?"

"Okay already, I was hoping to be part of the operation! Don't take it as a personal compliment. I am a field operative now you know."

"You are now, that's for sure."

Pat gave a wide grin and took a long sip of her coffee. "Yes, I really am aren't I?"

They sat back and relaxed, enjoying the smooth jet flight at forty thousand feet.

As the plane flew into the RAF airport northwest of London, they took their seats and buckled up. It was late evening and the sun was now far off to the west.

"So our arrangement for the year is finished I assume," Ed asked.

"Postponed anyway."

"So you've dumped me?" He turned to Pat as he asked, with just a small smile.

"I've never dumped anybody in my life," Pat replied quickly.

"You have now."

Pat thought about it as the plane turned and started its descent into the small, barely lit airport. "Maybe I have," she smiled. "I hope you don't mind being my first?"

Ed looked over to her and winked. "Not the first time I've been first is it?"

She returned the wink. "No it's not. But the other first felt a lot better than this."

The plane landed with a slight bump. It was just before midnight local time. They both understood they would now have to act entirely separately from each other, and this common understanding helped each of them feel relaxed and relieved as they entered into a whole new world of unknowns.

CHAPTER THREE

TUESDAY,
AUGUST 13ᵀᴴ 1985

The knocking on the door woke Ed from a deep sleep. It took him a few seconds to recall where he was. The night before, he and Pat had been driven down dark back roads from the RAF airport to The Inn . . . The knocking continued, louder now. He jumped out of bed and started pulling on his trousers.

"Okay, okay, keep your shirt on," he called out, walking to the door.

"I intend to," Carolyn said calmly as he opened the door. She was dressed in a dark business suit. She stood upright only four inches shorter than Ed, clearly inheriting her slim figure from her father. With her hands clasped behind he back she looked every inch a banker, not an MI6 operative.

"Carolyn! I'm sorry; I thought . . ." Ed mumbled, stepping back for her to enter. He closed the door.

"You thought it was someone else?" Carolyn asked demurely.

"Well I didn't think it was you, that's for sure." He now smiled and stepped back to properly see her. "You look great, Carolyn. You've changed your hair. It's shorter and I do think it suits you. May I kiss you?"

"No. Certainly not." She walked past him into the room and turned to face him. "Not now anyway."

"I love you, Carolyn."

"Yes I know."

"Later then?"

"Later." She walked back to the door and reached for the handle. "Pat has been up since five this morning bugging the staff about a cup of coffee. I think you should join her."

"I'll be there in fifteen. Can I ask you what this is . . . ?"

"Afraid not."

"Can I shake your hand?"

She held out her hand and he took it, keeping his eyes on hers.

"It's nice to see you again, Miss Andrews," Ed said, not letting go of her hand.

"And it's nice to see you again, Mr. Crowe." She slipped her hand out of his. "Fifteen minutes then." Against all of her natural instincts, she left the room and quietly closed the door behind her.

Ed looked at the clock. It was six-thirty.

Was this the third time, or was it the fourth; he had stayed at The Inn, he wondered. He knew its use was limited to MI6 and other similar or related departments and agencies. No doubt other people he had seen there were CIA, Mossad or other foreign intelligence operatives. But no one ever introduced themselves, it just wasn't done. It was a world unto itself, where all Inn employees were armed but only in the most discreet manner. No-one would let their gun show; that was simply unacceptable. About as un-American as you could get!

In less than fifteen minutes Ed joined Carolyn and Pat at their table in the large eating area. They were the only guests.

"Back together as a team," Pat said enthusiastically. Ed and Carolyn raised their cups of coffee to show their agreement.

Pat raised her purse from the floor. "I brought my gun, Miss. Will I need it?" She had used the code name they had agreed upon during their last assignment.

"Not sure, Boss," Carolyn replied, continuing to use their code names, "But I have Mister's gun in my purse," she added, looking at Ed, "just in case."

They all shared a high degree of confidence and respect for each other and while this was never actually spoken of, it was understood and now taken for granted. The remaining member of the team, the detail-oriented Sue Banks was with them in spirit. As if to confirm the point, Carolyn raised her cup of tea. "To Leader! To Sue Banks."

Ed and Pat raised their cups. "To Leader. To Sue Banks!"

Too excited to eat a big breakfast they collected their bags, threw them in the trunk of the limousine, and headed to Stonebridge Manor.

Entering the grounds of Stonebridge Manor was always a thrill for Ed. The grounds were large and beautiful and it was a full three minutes drive from the entry gate to the Manor. He knew there were security people throughout the grounds, but he had never seen them during any of his visits. Lord Stonebridge, as head of MI6, was protected at all times: that was a given. How, and by how many, was not the question to ask. Certainly not to be asked of Carolyn, Lord Stonebridge's daughter. While it was generally known that he was Carolyn's father, she went by her mother's maiden name as a form of separation. From Ed's perspective the process worked. Only a couple of instances during the times the three of them had been in the same room did the father-daughter relationship show, and even then it was only related to personal issues.

Pat was visibly excited as they drove through the grounds. She smiled and winked at Ed and Carolyn. Her enthusiasm was contagious.

The three of them were full of nervous excitement as the limousine pulled up in front of the main door.

Carolyn waved them in the foyer, not waiting for the maid to answer the doorbell. She motioned them up the stairs just as the door to the Library opened and Lady Stonebridge stepped into the foyer.

"Good morning, ladies and gentleman," she said, showing her authority and stressing the singular.

The three of them stopped and returned her greetings. She smiled and nodded to accept their greetings. "Perhaps a few words on your way out, Mr. Crowe?"

"Of course, Lady Stonebridge," Ed replied. He knew, and Carolyn knew, that she would want to speak with Ed. Carolyn and Ed were in love, and she knew it. Ed had told her of his love for Carolyn and she didn't need to be reminded that Carolyn had broken off a long standing relationship with her best friend's son to understand her daughter's feelings for Ed. She knew little about the details of her husband's job, but was not excited that her daughter had followed his career path into MI6. She was the mother of a strong willed daughter and her self-imposed role was to ensure her daughter was happy—but happy in a manner that reflected a full and comfortable lifestyle. And that meant children, or in Lady Stonebridge's case—grandchildren.

Carolyn knocked quietly on Lord Stonebridge's office door and entered not waiting for a response. They were expected. Lord Stonebridge and Mr. Cooper—the General—stood and welcomed everyone. Pleasantries were exchanged after which Lord Stonebridge motioned for everyone to take a seat. The chairs were situated around his large desk. At the center of the desk was a large speaker phone that included many buttons.

"New enough for me not to fully use all of its capabilities," Lord Stonebridge admitted. They were waiting for a call and they sat in silence until Lord Stonebridge broke the tension.

"You look considerably better without a black eye, Miss Weston," he commented to Pat.

Pat unconsciously touched her cheek. "Thank you, sir."

Lord Stonebridge turned to Ed. "And how are you, Mr. Crowe? Settling well in Canada?"

Ed nodded. "Very well. Thank you, sir."

A phone light went on, and Lord Stonebridge pressed a button. His secretary announced that his call was on line one. He pressed another button, and hoped. "Stonebridge here."

"Good morning, Lord Stonebridge. It is a fine day is it not?" The voice was undeniably obvious. Margaret Thatcher was on the line.

"Yes, Prime Minister, a very fine day. Our friends from Canada are with us and listening in on the speaker."

"Excellent, Lord Stonebridge, then let me commence." There was a slight pause. "Miss Weston, good morning."

Pat stood up in surprise and sat back down quickly, not sure of herself. "Good morning, Mrs. Thatcher. I'm . . ." She sat back in her chair without finishing her sentence.

Mrs. Thatcher continued. "Good morning, Mr. Crowe. We've rushed you back to the UK again at short notice."

Ed had time to think. "Good morning, Mrs. Thatcher. I trust I can be of assistance."

"I'm sure you will, Mr. Crowe. I'm sure you both will." There was a pause and everyone around the desk sat up straight to listen. Mrs. Thatcher continued. "As we all know this year is the fortieth anniversary of the end of the war. There have been appropriate recognitions of what terrible events needed to take place in order for us to enjoy our current freedoms, but there is one issue that still sits ill with me and I would like to do something about it." At 10 Downing Street, the prime minister lifted her cup of tea and finished the remains. She continued. "Mr. Crowe. What do you know of what is generally called Vichy France, alternatively referred to as the Vichy regime? Feel free to be honest with me, Mr. Crowe. I intend to be honest with you and everyone else."

Ed looked quickly around for help, but was offered only a friendly smile from Lord Stonebridge. He leaned closer to the speakerphone.

"Well as I recall the dates, in 1940 the French government conceded northern France to the German army and settled in Vichy to run southern France."

"Close, Mr. Crowe, and what else?"

"If you want me to be truthful, Mrs. Thatcher, then I would have to say that my mother speaks of the French surrendering without putting up much of a fight."

Carolyn rolled her eyes. Pat covered hers.

There was no response for several seconds, which seemed like forever. "Then I would have to say, Mr. Crowe, that your mother's opinion is quite widely held around the country and perhaps around the world. My own opinion is that while we had the fortunate circumstance at the time to have a leader like Mr. Churchill—who had many nay-sayers by the way—the French people followed the leadership of a very bad leader."

Ed grimaced. "Yes, I see."

"However," Mrs. Thatcher continued, "once in power the Vichy government more than crossed the line of general collaboration with the Germans. Indeed they assumed at least some of Germany's racist opinions. The result of which was the death of thousands of *undesirables*, including Jews, homosexuals, Gypsies, communists, and others. These people were French citizens! It is my belief that the general population of France shared many of these racist opinions, or at the very least nothing was said publicly in any way to question these policies. I think the world should be reminded of what happened in France."

Lord Stonebridge looked around, and spoke into the phone. "You have everyone's understanding and agreement, Prime Minister."

"Thank you, and thank you all. I will leave it to you to decide what actions to take, and please proceed with my full, if unofficial, blessing." Lord Stonebridge was about to end the call, but Mrs. Thatcher continued. "And, Miss Weston. I want you to know that I spoke with Prime Minister Mulroney yesterday to thank him for letting this go forward by using Canadian passport-carrying representatives. There is enough friction between France and the U.K. even at the best of time."

Pat leaned forward to speak. "Thank you, Mrs. Thatcher."

"And one more thing, Miss Weston. Since the British Official Secrets Act does not cover you, Mr. Mulroney did go on to say that if you breathe a word of this, the Toronto Maple Leafs will never again win the Stanley Cup."

Pat's eyes widened and she laughed. "Then you may rest assured I will take this to my grave."

As they shared a laugh, Lord Stonebridge pressed a button, ordered tea and pushed the phone aside. "Well, ladies and gentlemen, while we wait for tea perhaps a suggestion for a name for this operation. It must be decided here since this is a most unofficial operation."

Pats hand shot up, and she then slowly lowered it. "Sorry about that," she said, "but I have a suggestion."

Mr. Cooper spoke for the first time. "The floor is yours, Miss Weston."

"November 11th!" she stated. "In the U.S. November 11th is Veterans Day, and here in the U.K. it's Armistice Day. In Canada we call it Remembrance Day. So I'd suggest we name it Operation Remembrance."

"Excellent" Lord Stonebridge said.

"Absolutely," Carolyn added.

"Terrific," Ed said, pumping the air with his fist.

"Then Operation Remembrance it is." Mr. Cooper made it unanimous.

Lord Stonebridge's secretary wheeled in the trolley of tea and everyone helped themselves. After a brief break they resumed their seats.

"Then to Operation Remembrance," Lord Stonebridge announced. "I will give a brief update of what the goal is and then the General will provide a goodly amount of information on Vichy France."

The air took on a more business-like approach as they settled in to listen and to learn.

Lord Stonebridge continued. "The goal is simple in nature but will prove to be more complex than it sounds. All we really want to do," he shrugged to signify its simplicity, "is to bring to the attention of the French public and to a lesser extent the world, a reminder of what resulted from the implementation of the Vichy government and its relationship with the German military. We don't want to stir up any nastiness in the process, but clearly we want those people who think of France in the Second World War only as a network of French Resistance fighters doing *their bit* to fend off the German army with the help of all French citizens, to more fully understand the truth and its final implications. And the truth isn't nice. In fact the truth is nasty. This is not, by the way, to say there were no French Resistance fighters, because there were. But contrary to what we see on television, they were few and far between and very decentralized. Our message would be to recognize their valuable input, especially as the war drew to its conclusion when their numbers increased dramatically."

Mr. Cooper interrupted with a chuckle. "That's being damned by faint praise, if I ever heard it!"

Lord Stonebridge nodded with a grin. "I've been too close to too many politicians for too long!"

"And *that* is intended as a compliment, sir?" Ed asked.

Lord Stonebridge accepted both comments generously and proceeded. "Please keep in mind that this is very much Mrs. Thatcher's idea. She believes the lack of discussion on the entire Vichy France issue demonstrates France's collective amnesia. This operation, Operation Remembrance, has not been approved, or even run by, the Cabinet."

"Does that make it any less authorized?" Pat asked.

Lord Stonebridge shook his head, "No, just more secretive. If something goes wrong there are fewer people who would have to cross their fingers when they said they knew nothing of it, while stressing how important Anglo—French relations are."

"And what could go wrong?" Carolyn asked, knowing the question needed to be aired.

Lord Stonebridge shrugged. "Nothing serious I suspect. Perhaps Mr. Crowe and Miss Weston might get thrown in jail for a couple of days for disturbing the peace." He looked around the room. "I understand the food is very good!"

"What a charming thought," Pat chuckled. "That gives an 'evening in Paris' a whole new complexion."

Carolyn smiled at the comment. The three men missed the point.

"No doubt it will be somewhat disturbing," Lord Stonebridge added, withdrawing a sheet of paper from his deck drawer, "given that the two of you are on your honeymoon."

"Our what!" Pat exploded. "My what?"

Lord Stonebridge didn't respond to her, but shared with her the photocopy of her and Ed's Marriage Certificate. "Congratulations. You were married this last Saturday, August 10th 1985." He offered a fatherly smile.

Pat grabbed at the certificate, glaring at it in detail. She pushed away Ed's hand as he reached to take it.

"Courtesy of Prime Minister Mulroney," Mr. Cooper added.

Pat looked up at Ed who remained frozen in place, waiting for her response. "Not even a church wedding you cheapskate!" She handed the certificate to him, only then grinning at the turn of events. "Well I'm keeping my name," she huffed. "I have no intention of being an old Crowe!"

"Good for you, Pat," Carolyn said.

Ed looked at the certificate without comment. The circumstances were far too messy to contemplate. He looked around. They were waiting for his response. He thought for a moment.

"Was there a dowry?" he asked.

If looks could kill; he was dead. Pat's forehead narrowed to the point it nearly disappeared. She grabbed back the certificate, folded it deliberately into four and put it in her purse. "Just you wait until the divorce!"

With the tension broken, Mr. Cooper moved his chair closer to the desk and picked up a file folder. "Let me give you a summary of Vichy France, and then we can determine what plan best fits into our goal. I am old enough to have lived through its existence during the Second World War but, like most people, knew little of its details until quite recently." He opened the file and proceeded.

"Vichy France, which took its name from the City of Vichy where the government's administrative center was located, came into effect in July 1940 shortly after the lightning defeat of the French army by Germany. Its official name, in English, was French State, succeeding the Third Republic. The government was proclaimed and voted into effect by the National Assembly. There has been a historical argument since the end of the war as to its true legal status, but that is for another day's discussion. Marshal Philippe Petain was appointed both President and Chief of the French State. At the time he was 84 years old and a hero from the First World War. The French agreed upon a proposal to seek armistice arrangements with Germany with several conditions, one of which was that Germany would not require the French Navy to stand down or be taken over Germany. That condition was met and the Armistice was signed on June 22nd, six days after Petain had assumed leadership. On June 23rd, Paul Laval joined the government, and he was the main architect of the Vichy regime. The National Assembly approved the entire French State legislation on July 10th 1940."

Pat raised her hand. "Why did Hitler go along with the deal if it was recognized that France had lost the war?"

"The exact reasons aren't documented," Mr. Cooper continued, "but several reasons can be assumed. Firstly, it resulted in the end of fighting in France, which allowed Hitler to turn his guns on Britain. If the French had continued fighting they would have re-grouped in the then held French areas of North Africa and Hitler would have armies on three fronts; the Soviet Union, Britain, and the French in Africa. Secondly, and this is important, it eliminated the need for his armies to spend their resources on the administrative functions in France. What isn't generally understood is that the Vichy Government was responsible for almost all of France and not just the south that was not occupied by Germany. They had responsibility for the north of France, which was, of course, now occupied. The only areas that were not under French administration were two areas on the eastern borders and a fifteen-mile area along the French coast from Belgium to Spain. These strategically important areas were German controlled."

"It is extremely important to keep in mind," Lord Stonebridge added, "that having only two battle fronts was of huge military importance to Germany. Their armies in the north were now dedicated to the inevitable battle that was to take place against their enemy across the English Channel . . ."

"Dear Old Blighty," Carolyn mused. "I suppose the British people at the time were pretty annoyed at—how does one say this nicely—the lack of fighting spirit emanating from the French?"

Mr. Cooper laughed quietly. "That would be the understatement of the year, Miss Andrews."

"Then having set the stage, as it were," Lord Stonebridge said, "why don't you continue, General, with the resulting collaboration with the then German ideals and practices that has Mrs. Thatcher so determined to bring the Vichy government's actions fully into the light of day?"

Mr. Cooper flipped through papers in his file folder. "To expand on Mrs. Thatcher's comments concerning the actions of the then new Vichy government, let me summarize what are well documented occurrences. And in doing so it is important to keep in mind that the Vichy government, and therefore France, was officially neutral in the war. Shortly after the government was in place, it took actions against those who were considered 'undesirables', or sometimes referred to as 'internal foreigners'. As Mrs. Thatcher mentioned, these included Jews, Freemasons, communists, Gypsies, and homosexuals. The goal was to revive the 'French race', and this was to be accomplished by removing the 'undesirables'." Mr. Cooper took a long sip of his tea, and then continued. "One method used was accomplished by setting up a Commission whose role it was to review naturalizations granted since 1927, at which time a new law had been introduced. Between 1940 and 1944 some 15,000 people, mostly Jews were denaturalized. They were initially interned in camps that had been built as prisoner of war camps—that is to say for German prisoners of war. Subsequently they were shipped to concentration and extermination camps in Germany and elsewhere. Bear in mind, ladies and gentlemen, these 'undesirables' were arrested and interned by the Vichy police: the official French police! To address the French population of Jews that were not denaturalized the government introduced a 'Statute on Jews', which resulted in all Jews being considered an underclass, and made mandatory the wearing of yellow badges by Jews. Additionally Jews were barred from the armed forces, all forms of entertainment, the arts, and professional roles such as teachers, lawyers, and doctors. In 1942 the police confiscated all radios and telephones from Jews and enforced a curfew on them. It was also on July 16th, 1942 that the French police arrested nearly thirteen thousand Jews, including four thousand children and imprisoned them in the Winter Velodrome in Paris. From there they were transferred to a German run internment camp, and then on to the Auschwitz concentration camp. Some of them became the first Jews to die in the Auschwitz gas chambers. This one action represented more than a quarter of the French Jews sent to Auschwitz in 1942. The French abbreviated name for the velodrome is Vel' d'Hiv, and since then this incident has been referred to as 'Rafle du Vel' d'Hiv'."

Carolyn interrupted. "The Winter Velodrome round up!"

Mr. Cooper continued with a nod. "Or 'The Big Round up'. Exactly. Of the more than forty-two thousand Jews sent to Auschwitz, only eight hundred and eleven returned after the war." Mr. Cooper sat back in his seat, visibly disgusted at what he had reported.

The room fell silent as his words were absorbed. Lord Stonebridge motioned to the tea trolley, and they silently re-filled their cups.

"Well I have got to say," Pat spoke carefully, "that I am amazed I didn't know that this happened. Of course we are all aware of what the

Germans did to people, mostly Jews, but the French?" She shook her head. "It's so hard to believe."

"Mrs. Thatcher's point exactly," Lord Stonebridge said turning to Pat. "So we have a job to do, yes?"

Pat nodded. "Yes, sir, we do."

Lord Stonebridge stood and stretched his arms. "Why don't we take a break and order lunch. I think I need to get rid of the taste of the Nazis."

Carolyn stood and walked to the door. "I will order sandwiches, and perhaps, Ed, you should visit Lady Stonebridge?"

Ed stood and started walking to the door.

"Before we break, however," Carolyn said with a smile, looking to her father, "perhaps, sir, you could tell us why we use the word German, and you use the word Nazi?"

Lord Stonebridge mulled over the question. Mr. Cooper raised his eyebrows and turned to Lord Stonebridge. Ed and Pat kept straight faces, as if the question was of no importance.

Leaning back against his desk Lord Stonebridge took a deep breath before he replied. "Perhaps," he pondered aloud, "the advent of age renders in us a softer, more understanding approach to life. At least I would like to think of it that way. Youth, on the other hand, provides the ability to more readily challenge the past in a way that suggests their generation will make no mistakes."

Carolyn smiled. "Thank you, sir. I understand."

As Carolyn and Ed left the room, Pat leaned to Mr. Cooper and asked if she could read his file in more detail. He was happy to oblige. Lord Stonebridge remained leaning against his desk, wondering if he had given a completely honest answer.

"You're tough," Ed remarked as he followed Carolyn down the stairs.

Carolyn turned to Ed as they reached the library. "He's more than capable," she smiled. Kissing him quickly on his cheek, she opened the door and ushered him into the room. "Mr. Crowe, Mother," she announced, and closed the door behind him.

"Why, do come in, Ed," Lady Stonebridge said. She was seated on her usual sofa and, as was her style, dressed as if the Queen were about to appear unannounced. Ed took a seat and waited for the inevitable questions. This was now his fourth such visit and unlike on several other visits he now felt comfortable with Lady Stonebridge. They had agreed to refer to each other as Ed and Mrs. S., but only when they were alone.

"Your mother had a fine visit with us earlier this year," Lady Stonebridge said.

"She was most excited about it when she updated me. I think she was a tad surprised at the size and grandeur of Stonebridge Manor." Ed grinned.

"You didn't tell her where we live?"

"Oh no! That would have ruined all the fun."

Lady Stonebridge was taken aback. "Well, Ed, I am . . ."

Ed interrupted. "Believe me Mrs. S., either she wouldn't have believed me, or more likely she wouldn't have visited."

Lady Stonebridge nodded her understanding, and continued. "Are you still in love with my daughter?"

"With all of my heart."

"I see," she said quietly. "It would seem to me if such were the case, one might expect a more—should I say—active and closer relationship. What with you in Canada, and Carolyn . . . well, God knows where . . ."

Ed was about to mumble something but was interrupted by Carolyn entering the room. "Having a good old chit-chat are we?" she asked cheerily.

"No, we're not having a good old chit-chat," Lady Stonebridge replied coldly. "I was just asking Mr. Crowe . . ." Ed quickly interrupted.

"Your mother was reminding me that she was born and raised in Neasden and has easily grown accustomed to the countryside, its character, its more relaxed way of living, and its surroundings: so different from busy, bustling London. Accepting matters for what they are, and not fighting against them, might summarize your mother's comments."

Carolyn clasped her hands together, not understanding the message at all. "I fully understand," she said. "Should I leave?"

"Certainly not," Lady Stonebridge replied standing and walking to the French doors leading to the garden. "How much time do you have before you are required upstairs?"

Carolyn looked at her watch. "No more than five minutes, Mother."

"Then I shall return in exactly three minutes," Lady Stonebridge said stonily, and entered the garden.

Carolyn cringed. "Bad timing on my part?"

"Perfect timing, Miss Andrews."

She smiled. "I like it when you call me that."

"Yes, I know. And I love you, Miss Andrews."

"Yes I know," Carolyn said, extending her arms to Ed. He walked into her arms and they held each other tightly.

"I want to kiss you," Ed whispered.

"Then do," she said, turning her face up to his.

They kissed, gently at first and then passionately, holding each other as if for the first time.

"I want to marry you," Ed said as he pulled back and looked at her lovely eyes.

Carolyn closed her eyes and looked down. "Ed, we agreed . . ." He put his finger to her lips and kissed her forehead.

"I'm not asking you to marry me, Carolyn, that will be for another day . . . one thousand-five-hundred and sixty-eight days from now to be exact, but then who's counting? However since I plan on asking you to marry me, surely I can remind you that I want to marry you?"

She looked back up to him and kissed his chin. "You and your play on words! But thank you for saying that. It means a great deal to me."

Holding each other their time together passed quickly. Just as Carolyn stepped back from Ed, Lady Stonebridge walked in from the garden holding a bouquet of freshly cut flowers. After laying the flowers on a side table, she turned to Carolyn and Ed. "My only care is for the love and safety of both of you," she said smiling. "If that results in my appearing nosey, then so be it. But rest assured that is not my goal. Now please return to your work with my sincere best wishes."

Carolyn stood motionless for a second, a trifle shocked at her mother's change in attitude. She was tempted to give her mother a hug, but chose not to. "Thank you, Mother. Mr. Crowe and I—that is Ed and I, share a special relationship that, if I may use a colloquialism, works for us. It's very special."

Lady Stonebridge smiled. "Yes my dear and we wouldn't want to confuse it with that boring old word 'love' now would we?"

Carolyn accepted the comment. She and Ed excused themselves and headed upstairs. They entered Lord Stonebridge's office just as lunch was being served.

After everyone had eaten, Lord Stonebridge took his seat behind his desk, a message the business meeting was to resume.

"With the limitation that no-one be hurt physically in the process," he started, "does anyone have any ideas as to how we should proceed?"

Pat, who still had Mr. Cooper's file in her hand, broke the silence. "I have an idea, but it depends on where in Paris Boulevard de Grenelle is."

"Just south of the Eiffel Tower," Carolyn said. "It is a major access road that leads from the south to the River Seine." She grinned. "Lots of good shopping if you're interested?"

"Well perhaps a bit of shopping and Operation Remembrance," Pat replied. She held up the file folder. "According to the General's information Boulevard de Grenelle was the location of the Velodrome d'hiver where the fifteen thousand Jews were interned, and while the Velodrome is gone, there is a plaque marking the 'Rafle du Vel' d'Hiv'—The Velodrome winter round-up—at 8 Boulevard de Grenelle to this day. So I was wondering . . ." She stopped at the sound of Lord Stonebridge hitting his desk with his hand.

"Excellent idea, Miss Weston, excellent!" Lord Stonebridge stood from his desk obviously excited at the yet-to-be fleshed out idea from Pat. He knew enough of what she was thinking to know that it made sense. Start Operation Remembrance at the location in Paris where the issue at hand is commemorated. "Yes, yes, yes," he said enthusiastically, then sat back down. He spoke quietly. "I'm sorry, Miss Weston, please proceed."

Pat moved in close to the desk and outlined her idea. For an hour each of them offered ideas and suggestions. Everything was challenged as to its contribution of bringing to the mind of France the actions of the Vichy government. Finally they agreed upon an outline of Operation Remembrance. After Carolyn and Ed had read Mr. Cooper's file it was destroyed, along with any notes or documentation. The operation's plan was complete. Documentation was not needed. The operation was simple and quick; at least that was the goal.

Lord Stonebridge turned to Carolyn. "What arrangements are now in place, Miss Andrews?"

"The plane for Paris is ready to go," Carolyn responded. "All we need do is get the three of us to the airport. Hotel arrangements have been made in the name of Mr. and Mrs. Crowe at the Hotel Moderne at the Republic Square for tonight through to Friday." She smiled. "A short honeymoon I'm afraid."

Pat rolled her eyes but said nothing.

Carolyn continued. "I have sleeping facilities at the British Embassy—out of sight and out of mind. A 'war-room' has been set up in the embassy from where I will assist Mr. and Mrs. Crowe," she smiled again, "and be in touch with you on an as-needed basis, sir."

Lord Stonebridge nodded. "Any questions?"

"Just one, sir," Pat said. "My passport is in the name of Weston. Could that be a problem?"

Mr. Cooper tapped his nose. "Hence the Marriage Certificate, Miss Weston."

"Of course," Pat muttered. "Our Marriage Certificate!"

"Always wanted to spend my honeymoon in Paris," Ed said flatly.

He got the look he expected from Pat, but it was short lived as Lord Stonebridge stood to finalize the meeting.

"There are two things I think you should know as you head off," Lord Stonebridge said. "The first is that other countries did a good job of protecting Jews from similar atrocities. Denmark, while occupied by Germany, with the full support of King Christian smuggled some seven thousand Jews to neutral Sweden. And Italy, under the fascist Mussolini, refused to send Jews abroad, although this was changed once the country was occupied by Germany in 1943. Further, keep in mind that General Petain was tried and found guilty of Treason after the war, as was his Prime Minister, Paul Laval. They were both given the death penalty, although General de Gaul commuted Petain's sentence. Laval, who was clearly pro-Hitler—to the point of saying he hoped Germany won the war, in a newspaper article—was executed by a firing squad."

"And the second thing?" Ed asked.

Lord Stonebridge nodded and spoke carefully. "The second thing, and this is very important for you to know but not speak of, is that the current President of France, François Mitterrand, was an official at Vichy and was decorated by Marshal Petain." He paused to let the importance of his comments have their full effect. "Good luck on Operation Remembrance everyone. Mrs. Thatcher is relying on us!"

After packing their bags in the boot of the limousine, Carolyn, Pat, and Ed scrambled in and the driver pulled away quickly and smoothly. Lady Stonebridge hadn't emerged from the library. Her point had been made and clearly absorbed. Lord Stonebridge and Mr. Cooper waved them off.

"I'll give you your gun when we get to the airport," Carolyn said, looking at Ed. "Probably won't need it, but departmental rules must be followed." She turned to Pat.

"In my bag," Pat said. "Never thought I'd need it on my honeymoon!"

"I'll keep that in mind," Ed said.

"I don't shoot my subordinates," Pat replied, keeping a straight face. "I just tell them what to do, and they do it."

Ed looked at Carolyn and motioned at Pat. "Took a Human Resources course at University, she did."

Pat grinned with a wink. "Got an 'F'. Too nice."

They laughed together, happy to be on their way.

Their plane took off within minutes of them arriving at the RAF airport and headed southeast towards Paris. It was to be a short flight, barely enough time for a cup of coffee and a quick review of the plan for Operation Remembrance.

The plane taxied to the southwest quadrant of Orly Airport and the engine was turned off. Waiting for them were two taxis and a Custom's Officer. Carolyn lied to the Custom's Officer explaining all three were British Embassy employees. The man shrugged, accepted the comments and drove away satisfied.

Carolyn wished Pat and Ed well as they took separate taxis. "Don't forget to phone me at the embassy every so often," Carolyn reminded them, giving each of them a business card and three hundred French Francs, "and have a nice honeymoon, eh?"

Pat ignored the comment and got into the taxi. Ed waved and winked goodbye to Carolyn and then entered the taxi. Pat gave the name of the hotel to the driver in French. He nodded, happy to be spoken to in French by a foreigner.

Ed registered at the Hotel Moderne. The male receptionist looked at their passports and then at them. It was not a friendly look. Pat quickly showed him their Marriage Certificate, and that cheered him up considerably. He handed them the key with a knowing smile and a slight bow.

"Cheeky bugger!" Pat said as the elevator took them to the fourth floor.

Like a good husband, Ed carried both bags to their room. "Should I carry you across the threshold?" he asked.

Pat leaned close to him. "Two words, Ed, just two words—and they're not 'let's dance'."

"Gotcha." He opened the door and they entered their honeymoon suite.

The room was immense. Three windows faced the square, which consisted of a park with a large statue in the center, which they were later to find out was dedicated in 1883 to celebrate the new Republic. Flowers were everywhere throughout the square and the seats of the square were mostly filled with people of all ages. The bathroom was equally large. Ed noted that the bathtub was large enough for two, but said nothing.

Something was upsetting Pat. Ed could sense the concern in spite of her outwardly cheery mood. As they unpacked he wondered how to address his feelings and decided to raise the issue head on, well almost head on.

"Can I take you out for supper tonight?" he asked.

Pat didn't bother turning to him but kept unpacking. "Nah, it's okay. Let's just grab a bite here."

Ed took a seat at the table by one of the windows. "Can we chat, Pat?"

She kept unpacking. "Sure," she mumbled, "what about?"

"About world fucking peace, Pat. What the hell do you think I want to talk about?"

She threw the clothes she held into the drawer, slammed it shut and joined him at the table keeping her eyes down. "What?" she asked bluntly.

He waited. He wanted to reach over and take her hand, but he knew better than to do that. Not looking at his watch he counted thirty seconds. She finally looked up. "Okay, I'm sorry. What?"

"Look, Pat, if I've done something wrong or said something I shouldn't have for God's sake tell me. Please tell me what is bothering you?"

She shook her head in disgust. "Are you stupid, Ed? Are you brain dead?" She sat up straight, ready to fire from all barrels. "I'm here in

Paris with the man I love. The only man I've ever loved. The man that made love to me just three days ago, and now the man I can't touch and he can't touch me. The man I don't want to marry, but guess what? I've got a Goddamn Marriage Certificate in my purse that says we are married. This lovely room, this lovely city—the City of fucking Lights—and I'm with a man who wonders why I'm not the happiest bloody woman in the world. Were you in hiding when they gave out feelings, Ed? Surely you can't be that stupid?" She took a deep breath, determined not to cry.

The blood drained from his face and his jaw dropped. "Oh," he muttered, "I see. I thought . . ."

"That's just the point, Ed, you don't see. And I don't give a rat's ass what you think. Okay?" She stood and returned to unpacking not waiting for a response.

"So is this our first marital spat then?" Ed asked.

Pat froze in her place. She couldn't believe what she had heard. She turned to face him ready to scream, but Ed was now standing in front of her only inches away. He reached for her, but she backed away. "Fuck off, Ed, just fuck right off."

As Ed moved forward she backed into the chest of drawers. He stopped, their clothes touching. "Let me hold you, Pat. I won't try kissing you or anything, but let me hold you."

He took her lack of response as a yes, and reached out and took her in his arms. Motionless for a few moments, Pat then put her arms tentatively around him.

"I apologize profusely, Pat, I really do. Perhaps I was bunking-off, or playing truant as you call it, when they gave out feelings. It would certainly appear so." He stepped back and took her hands. "Please let me take you out tonight. Let it be a way of my showing you how much you mean to me, and I promise I'll only ask you to let me hold your hand. What do you say?"

She held back a tear. "Okay. But holding hands only and that's required because we're on our honeymoon and have to play the part."

"Playing the part, no other reason," Ed agreed. He walked to the door. "I'll go try my French on the Concierge for a nice restaurant. You take your time changing into something nice and I'll be back in thirty."

Pat smiled to herself as he left the room. Smooth talking Limey, she thought, but a smooth talking Limey whose company she enjoyed! She started looking for an appropriate dress. Having brought only three didn't allow her a lot of choice.

Ed returned half an hour later with a grin on his face and single rose. He handed the rose to Pat with a slight bow.

"Why thank you, kind sir," Pat curtsied. "You bought this just for me?"

"Actually I got it from the square. Helped myself, so to speak."

"Well it's lovely, and thank you," Pat said, putting it in a glass from the bathroom. "And for supper tonight?"

"I spoke to the Concierge. Just down the street is a KFC, and around the corner is a McDonalds."

"And your point is?" Pat asked.

"I made a reservation at the Sur les Quais," he said proudly. "You'll never guess the view from the restaurant."

"Well it can't be the ocean, but something close?"

"Where were we a couple of days ago?" Ed asked.

"On the Rideau Canal."

"Well this restaurant is on the St. Martin's Canal. How's that for good planning?"

She smiled. "I suppose you mean the Canal St-Martin?" she asked pronouncing it in French.

"Same place," he grinned. He looked at her, admiring her dress. "You look quite lovely, Pat."

"Thank you," she said, spinning around. "Notice anything different?"

"Er, let me see . . ." he mumbled.

She held out her left hand. On her ring finger was a gold ring, studded with several diamonds.

"Wow. That is beautiful. Where did you get . . ."

"Lord Stonebridge. It was his mother's wedding band."

Ed took her hand and examined the ring. "Are they real?"

Pat nodded. "The General whispered that it's worth about ten thousand!"

"Dollars?"

"Pounds."

"Bloody hell. Now for sure I'm going to hold your hand."

Pat held her hand out in front of her, admiring the ring. "Imagine that," she mused, "given a wedding ring from a Lord, and going out on a date with a commoner—a bloody Londoner yet!"

Ed sighed. "Ah, what one has to do to play the part!"

The restaurant was just what they needed. It was a short walk and Ed had booked a table on the patio. Taking their time and talking of nothing but idle chatter, they may well have been honeymooners in Paris. Waiting for the meal, Ed leaned across the table and took Pat's left hand. "It suits you," he commented about the ring. "It has class and is not too flashy." Pat squeezed his hand in response.

After a wonderful meal, they sipped on the last of their wine. The menu allowed Ed to order food he would never normally think of ordering, but permitted them to have fun in seeing what he would end up eating. More importantly it allowed Pat to relax and make fun of Ed's choices. He managed the Escargot appetizer, as Pat called it, but only with her help and by swallowing them with his eyes closed. She was now visibly relaxed and offered him several nods and winks of thanks. "If you're interested," Ed said, pointing to the canal. "It was Napoleon in 1825 that ordered the canal to be built, and it heads north to join the Seine a couple of miles from here."

"And you learned this from the Concierge?"

"I muddled through," Ed replied, feigning indignation.

"He speaks English then?" Pat asked.

"What are you implying, young lady?"

"No implication, Ed. In law it's called a statement of fact. Your French is all but non-existent."

"Well sacra blur, I must say!"

"Blur's the word for sure," Pat laughed, standing to leave. "Please walk me home, Ed. That was more than wonderful."

They held hands all the way to the hotel room. Pat let go as soon as they entered the room and had closed the door.

"Okay, Mister," Pat said slowly, now using Ed's code name, "while you were arranging our evening's meal, I spoke to Carolyn. She will be here tomorrow morning at eight sharp with lots of copies of the questionnaire. In order not to be involved, she will deliver them by taxi and we'll take them from her. Then she'll return directly to the British Embassy. Questions?"

"Just one," Ed said, looking around the room. "Do you want me to sleep in the bathtub?"

"Don't be silly," Pat chuckled. "Have you seen the size of the bed here? It's huge. Plenty of room for both of us—with space in between that is."

"As long as you can control yourself, Boss!"

"Oh, I'll do my best. Just one thing, Ed. Please keep your underwear on. I need my report to be both accurate and acceptable." Picking up her bag, she walked into the bathroom.

Pat returned several minutes later wearing a long cotton nightdress with pictures of cats on it.

"Now that is not sexy," Ed admitted.

"That's the goal." Pat got into bed, sticking close to one edge and turned her back to him.

Ed turned off the lights, undressed to his underwear and got into the bed on the far side from Pat. "Good night, Boss."

"Good night, Mister," Pat replied. "Nice evening. Enjoyed holding hands. Usual rules; I'm first in the bathroom."

"I'll order the coffee."

They fell silent. Neither fell asleep for some time.

CHAPTER FOUR

WEDNESDAY,
AUGUST 14ᵀᴴ 1985

P at was gone from the hotel room when Ed woke, and didn't return until he had cleaned up and ordered a pot of coffee from room service. As they sat to enjoy the coffee it was just past seven. Pat spread a tourist map of Paris in front of them and outlined where she had walked that morning.

"Up early then?" Ed remarked.

Pat chuckled. "Awake at five listening to you gently snore. It was either wake you up to make love, or go for a long walk. Sorry, you lost. Or perhaps I should say I lost?"

"Let's say we've lived up to departmental rules, and that can't be all bad."

"Okay, let's say that then." She finished her coffee and topped up. "Just one more thing before we turn to the operation. I want to apologize for telling you to eff-off last night. I know you don't like to swear. So I apologize."

"Understood and accepted."

"To work then," she said. "Let's go over the plan again between the two of us, and be ready to meet Miss downstairs at eight sharp!"

The taxi with Carolyn in the back seat pulled up at the hotel entrance at exactly eight. Without speaking, Carolyn passed Ed a large package and was gone. Returning to their room, the package was quickly unwrapped. As was expected there were five hundred legal-size single sheets with French on both sides.

Ed picked up a sheet. "Questions," he said, and turned the sheet over. "Answers!"

"You know your French," Pat quipped. She looked at the side of questions and translated for Ed. "The header reads 'Vichy France—a History Lesson'."

"Question One," she started. "What is the significance of 'Rafle du Vel' d'Hiv' and how does it relate to the Velodrome d'Hiver that was on this location?"

Ed smiled. "Good opener."

"Question two, how many Jews and other 'undesirables' were held at the Velodrome d'Hiver in 1942 before they were sent on to German concentration camps?"

Pat looked at Ed, and she continued.

"Question three, how many of them were children?"

Ed shook his head in disgust as he turned the page to see the answer; 4,115.

"Here's a good one," Pat said. "Question fifteen, what was the name of the Vichy Police whose only goal was to find and arrest members of resistance groups?"

"*The Malice.*" Ed answered more to himself that to Pat. "Oh God," Ed gasped. "Don't go on. I get the point."

"Doesn't mince words, does she?" Pat asked, turning the sheet over to review the answers. "I think these will make the point."

"Or start a war!" Ed said.

"Well that last one didn't last long for Vichy France did it!"

"Careful now, Boss. There was de Gaulle. Let's not forget him."

"Oh sure I know de Gaulle all right. He peed on Canada's parade in 1967 when he called for a 'free' Quebec. I'm glad we had the honor as a nation of sending him home early."

"That's not our fight here, Boss," Ed reminded her.

"True. I just wanted to get in a fighting spirit before we hit the streets."

"Then let's go!"

Pat asked the taxi driver to take them to 8 Boulevard de Grenelle via the Eiffel Tower. Without comment the driver pulled into the traffic and headed west. They crossed the Seine close to Notre Dame where there were already hundreds of tourists. Driving on the south side of the Seine along its banks allowed 'the honeymooners' a brief opportunity to catch the sights. Passing the Eiffel Tower to their left, they were only minutes away from their destination. Pat mouthed 'Good luck' and took the fare money from her purse, pushing her gun into the side panel and zipping it closed.

Ed leaned forward checking the gun attached to his left ankle, pulling his trousers down to make sure it was not visible.

It was a warm summer day. The crowds of shoppers and tourists were enjoying Paris. Many smiled at Ed and Pat as they passed them. Locating the plaque recalling the 'Rafle du Vel' d'Hiv', they started handing out the questionnaires. It was just before nine o'clock.

The lady that took the first questionnaire smiled at Pat and stopped to read. Flipping the page quickly from on side to the other, her smile disappeared and was replaced with a look of disgust. She screwed up the page, threw it on the ground and marched away. Her action attracted other passers-by and several reached out to see what had so upset her.

A young couple arm-in-arm read the questions and answers in full, letting go of each other as they read. The man looked to Pat shaking his head. "Non. Impossible!" he said in French. "Fausse, fausse!"

Pat spoke to the couple in French. She spoke calmly, not reacting to the girl who was now in tears and had covered her mouth with her hand. Pat finished speaking with a Gallic shrug and nod confirming in her gesture that it was not good, but it was true. The couple continued their look of disbelief, shoving the page in front of an old man who was watching them. He read briefly both sides of the page. Looking to the young couple, he nodded. His face and age confirmed their worst fears—he had been there, he knew the history. He knew the truth. He shook his head gently and continued on his morning walk: slower now, and sadder.

A crowd had now gathered. People were arguing and gesturing amongst themselves. Ed was worried some might come to blows, but thankfully it didn't. Pat spoke to several of the gathered, answering questions or defending the questionnaire's accuracy. It reminded Ed of playtime in school: almost a fight at any moment, with reason finally winning over. The difference, however, was that now there was no teacher to blow a whistle and call them all to class. People started taking photos, resulting in scuffles from those not wanting to be photographed. Pat wandered back to Ed who was now standing by the side of the building beside the plaque.

"Seems to be working," Pat said, motioning to the crowd. "Thought we were in for a fight for a while, but hopefully it's just the French style."

"Perhaps a coffee is in order?" Ed asked.

Pat agreed. The crowd was thinning. Picking up everything that had been dropped or thrown on the pavement, they crossed the street and turned down a side road toward a bistro with a patio.

Pat ordered two coffees and moved close to the table to provide an up-date. "Now nowhere on the sheet is Marshal Petain's name mentioned," she said, rubbing her hands together, "but I can tell you his name came up several times and it was not in a complimentary fashion. In fact one older lady all but spat his name. I felt bad for her since she reminded me of my grandmother, but my God, was she angry."

"Do you think she was Jewish?" Ed asked.

"Given that she crossed herself when she swore like a drunken sailor; I'd have to say not!"

"Yes, that might be bit of a clue. What else?"

"I suppose," Pat replied, finishing her coffee, "that what we expected actually happened. Young people didn't know the facts, or not the nasty details. Older people either agreed with the first old lady, or defended the decision to end the war and in doing so, save thousands of lives."

"Should we touch base with Miss?" Ed asked.

Pat thought about it and shook her head. "Nah. It's going as planned. We'll give her a call after we take a break for lunch." She stood, leaving money for the coffees. "Let's get back and hope we do as well this time."

The area by the plaque was now back to normal. People walked slowly, enjoying the warmth of a beautiful August day. Ed felt almost guilty as he started handing out the questionnaires, but also felt it his duty to spread the knowledge of the actions of Vichy France. Once more the reaction to the questionnaire was a mixture of surprise and disgust. Pat addressed any reasonable questions that were raised, while Ed continued the distribution. Suddenly, and unexpectedly, everything changed. Television cameras and commentators started reporting on the event, first using the crowd gathered as a backdrop but then the cameras moved in closer and microphones were held to capture anyone's point of view. Pushing and shoving got worse. Fingers and shouts were directed at Ed and Pat. Fearing danger, Ed took Pat's arm and pulled her toward the building for safety. She shook him off, and continued discussing, but now arguing, with those that shouted to her. Clearly no one was going to win this argument.

Ed leaned over to Pat, keeping his eyes on the crowd. "Calm it down for Christ's sake. If they start something, we'll be picked up and carrying guns ain't the norm in France!"

Reluctantly she agreed and took a deep breath. "Okay, good point."

Two television crews now moved in on them, the commentators asking a barrage of questions all at the same time.

Ed turned to Pat. "What are they asking?"

She rolled her eyes. "Well it's not the time of day is it?" She took a small step forward and raised her hand in order to speak and be heard.

Not understanding what she was saying, but knowing what the plan was; Ed nodded every so often, agreeing with what was said.

To Ed's left a new camera crew moved in and a microphone was shoved inches from his face. "No parli French," Ed smiled.

"That's okay, mate," the commentator replied with a grin, "we're with the BBC. So what's this all about then? You're stirring up a hornet's nest here y'know?"

Ed was shocked and pulled his head away from the microphone. "You don't sound like the BBC to me."

The commentator smiled and spoke into his microphone. "So tell me, sir," he said in a BBC accent, "what is your intention of distributing these materials and creating a considerable level of indignation in doing so?" He finished with a grin.

Ed took a breath and told the story. "We are simply taking the opportunity of our visit to Paris to remind people of what happened in France during the Second World War."

"And why would you do that, sir?"

"Because," Ed continued, now feeling more comfortable, "two of the young lady's uncles fought in the war, one landing at Juno Beach in Normandy and the other fought through Italy. They were both aware of the atrocities practiced by Vichy France and she promised both of them that she would remind people of what happened. It's that simple."

The man thought for a moment. "Does that make her a Canadian?"

"That is correct. As am I."

"You'll excuse me, sir, but you don't sound Canadian."

"Then you don't know much about Canada if you think we all speak with the same accent."

Shouts and screams from Ed's right grabbed everyone's attention. Walking into the crowd, jeering and shouting were three skinheads.

Covered in tattoos and dressed in the recognizable fatigues and heavy boots they were a menacing sight. Each carried a placard, which they waved and taunted everyone with. Ed leaned over to Pat. "What the hell do the placards say?" He asked in a voice loud enough to be heard over the shouting around.

"Shit!" Pat replied shouting. "They want all foreigner workers out of France, especially Turks!"

"Fuck!" Ed muttered as he turned away, only to find the BBC microphone inches from his face.

"Don't worry," the man holding the microphone said cheerily, "that's just between you and me." Ed acknowledged the comment with a quick nod. "So tell me, sir," the man continued, "is this what you were expecting?"

"Of course not," Ed answered. "They're the sorts of people that we are reminding the public to be careful of. They have swastika tattoos for a reason, don't they?"

The BBC man turned to the skinheads and the cameraman turned with him. "You can see, ladies and gentlemen, those extreme points of view by people known commonly as skinheads are not limited to the U.K." He walked away from Ed, heading toward the skinheads who were now standing in front of Pat blocking her from the television cameras.

The jostling got worse and Ed headed toward Pat. He wanted her out of there quickly. He was not quick enough. Pat grabbed a placard from one of the skinheads, threw it on the ground, stepped on it, and spat on it. For a moment there was silence as the crowd watched her. Then all hell broke loose. The crowd turned on the three skinheads shouting, punching and kicking at them. The three punched and kicked back. An old man fell to the ground bleeding from his nose. It turned worse with purses and walking sticks flying. Out-numbered and bloodied the skinheads ran shouting and threatening as they ran. A sound of a police car brought everything to a stand-still. People brushed themselves off and helped the old man on the ground to his feet. He shook his fist at the now disappearing skinheads, apparently his feelings hurting more than his nose.

Ed pulled Pat away from the center of the action. She faced Ed with a quick grin. "Got him, didn't I?"

Ed nodded, not wanting to get into the details of who got whom. Turning to make an escape, they bumped into the BBC crew. The commentator lowered the microphone. "Got it all we did," he laughed. "The last few minutes we were live!" He looked at Pat. "You're famous. You were just watched by five million viewers and tonight on the six o'clock news, by twenty million more." He looked at Ed. "You too, son. We'll even see if the CBC wants to pick it up. Can I get your names? Your family will be proud of ya!"

Ed looked back at the now quite crowd. "Yeah, that's something to crow about isn't it?" He led a grinning Pat away, heading for the safety of a bistro and a cup of strong coffee.

"So that went well, eh?" Pat asked, having ordered coffees and sandwiches.

"Marvelous, just bloody marvelous," Ed groaned. "That was the BBC for crying out loud."

"So?"

"So the first B stands for British; you know as in England? You know, where my mother lives?"

"Hmm, that is interesting." She chewed on her cheek, thinking. "No matter. We'll come up with a story if your mother sees it." She took a sip of her coffee. "Coffee's good!"

Ed ran his fingers through his hair. "Thank God I didn't tell them we were on our honeymoon."

"Oh oh!"

"You didn't?"

Pat shrugged. "Of course I did. That was part of the plan!"

"Being on television wasn't part of the bloody plan!" He held his head in his hands. "Christ, I can see it now. *Two Canadians stir up a mini battle in Paris over the French involvement in the Second World War!"*

Pat shook her head. "They don't know we're Canadian."

Ed looked at her and then looked back down again.

"Oh shit," Pat groaned.

Ed sat up and reached for his coffee. "Oh shit is right," he said. "Look who's joining us?"

The three skinheads were walking toward them, no more than fifty feet away. Without speaking Ed and Pat jumped up and ran down the side street away from the now shouting skinheads. As they reached a main road, they nearly ran into two Gendarmes who were lazily strolling their patch. Pat started talking to them as Ed waved down a passing taxi. They jumped in the taxi and watched as the skinheads walked quietly passed the Gendarmes as if nothing were happening. What they didn't see as their taxi turned a corner was one of the skinheads wave down a taxi and all three quickly get into it.

As soon as Ed and Pat entered their hotel room, Pat dialed the number Carolyn had given them. A female answered with "Hello" and Pat asked to be put through to Miss. After a short delay, Carolyn came on the line.

"Bon jour."

"Bon jour yourself," Pat answered, nodding to Ed that they had reached Carolyn.

"You had me worried," Carolyn said.

"We had an issue."

"So I saw, on TV."

"Worried we were rushing off to Hollywood?"

"Or the WWF perhaps?"

"Yeah, right. Look, Miss, we're okay, a bit shaken up perhaps. We were followed by those men you saw on TV."

"That's not good. You had better both come in. I think we've got our point across."

"Cancelled after one day? Half a day even?"

Pat could hear Carolyn take a deep breath. "I don't think you realize what's been going on. The television stations have been showing the footage every ten minutes. The questionnaire is everywhere. Politicians are raising hell, wondering why two 'foreigners' are creating a very divisive issue, resulting in your skinhead friends getting free television time to promote their type of hatred."

"Oh boy!"

"Exactly," Carolyn agreed. "And I've just got off the phone with 'C'. It's all over the BBC. Apparently Mister has been quite a hit based on the hundreds of phone calls into Broadcasting House."

"Not all bad then?"

Carolyn chuckled. "Not all bad at all, but let's manage it from here a bit more tactfully."

Pat nodded. "Okay, we'll be there within the hour. Put the kettle on." She hung up.

Ed had listened to the one side of the conversation and had taken the time to make a pot of coffee. They sat and Pat outlined the conversation in detail. Ed rolled his eyes when she mentioned the BBC. He knew he would have to phone his mother as soon as he got to the British Embassy and received the appropriate approval. Their story now had to fit with the morning's events.

"This is all too sad," Ed said glumly.

"What's so sad? It all worked wonderfully."

"Such a short honeymoon." He grinned.

Pat 'shot him' with her finger. "Move, Mister. Let's get out of here."

Packed and ready to go in fifteen minutes, Pat had to explain to the hotel Manager that their early departure was not a reflection of the hotel's service. Her explanation satisfied him and he hoped they would return some day.

"Obviously he's too busy to watch TV," Ed whispered as they walked to the curb to hail a taxi.

Within seconds of reaching the curb a rusting blue van pulled up in front of them and the side door slid open. At the same time two men closed in behind them pushing Ed, Pat and their luggage into the van. The driver was one of the skinheads and he grinned nastily at Pat. A second skinhead followed them into the back of the van, holding a gun on them. The third, who gave orders and appeared to be the boss, climbed into the front passenger seat. He held a second gun on them. The van pulled away at a speed and angle that had it almost tipping over. The boss screamed at the driver, and the van slowed to a more manageable speed. The man in the back threw the luggage and Pat's purse to the rear of the van, moving behind Ed and Pat to ensure there was no escape from the rear. Pat sat up, leaning against the wall of the van. The only movement Ed made was to rearrange his legs in such a way that his gun holster was not visible. With Pat's gun safely in her purse he now had the only weapon, and he had no intention of using it while in the van.

"Parle vous Anglais?" Pat asked the apparent boss.

He grinned. "I sure as fuck do, lady. Better than you!" His accent was northern England. He spat out his words.

"On vacation, are we?" Ed asked.

The boss turned his gun on Ed. "You can shut the fuck up anytime you like, you cockney bastard."

Ed nodded, deciding not to tell him that he wasn't born within the sound of Bow bells and as such was not really a cockney. Perhaps another time he thought. "So what do you want from us? We were just leaving the country."

The boss laughed. "Sure as fuck you were, just as soon as your Jew friends paid you off. You're a disgrace to the color of your skin, and a fucking disgrace to England."

For the first time in his life, Ed now felt guilty for being English. For his country to raise an adult like the man in front of him was sickening. What kind of upbringing could result in hatred such as this, he wondered. He shook his head in despair.

The man wasn't giving up. "What the fuck are you shaking your head at? You've left the fucking country haven't ya? You're nothing but a fucking hypocrite you are!"

Pat interjected. "That doesn't answer the question of what you want from us does it?"

"Don't be stupid you silly cow!" the man shouted. "Money! That's what we want. And we want it from the fucking Jews."

"Any particular fucking Jews?" Pat spat back.

The man turned his gun to Pat. "Don't push it. Just because you're female means fuck all to us. You're a fucking Jew lover, that's all that counts." He moved the gun closer to Pat's face. "Israel. That's where the money will come from. One hundred thousand fucking pounds! They pay us and you live. They don't . . . you die. Easy come, easy go!" In better French than Pat would have given him credit for, the boss updated the two other skinheads of what he had said to Pat. They both laughed, the driver banging the steering wheel with his hand in excitement.

The van bumped along. More relaxed now, the driver turned on the radio for music. Ed and Pat shared eye contact but didn't speak. Pat finally broke the silence.

"The government of Israel doesn't give a shit about us y'know? I did this, we did this, because my two uncles fought in the war and saw what happened here. I know it sounds stupid, but I promised them I would try to raise the issue of the Vichy government."

The boss turned to her. "I don't give a shite about your uncles and I don't give a shite about you." He looked around. "I don't give fucking shite about the bloody French either."

Pat looked genuinely surprised. "Then why . . ."

He grinned. "Because if we don't stop the foreigners here, then next they'll be crossing the Channel and we'll be full of them won't we? Look at them," he motioned outside, "Turks, Poles, Croatians, the whole fucking pile of them. Lazy, filthy foreigners the lot of them."

"What's that got to do with Jews?" Ed asked.

"Are you blind as well as dumb? It's their money that's bringing them all in. They run the world, the Jews. They run America and the fucking Yanks are too stupid to see it." He grunted. "They'll pay-up for you to live. Don't worry about that."

Ed shook his head, but held his tongue.

The boss laughed. "Then you'll both die on your honeymoon won'tcha?"

The van pulled up in front of a large wooden garage set of doors. The driver got out, unlocked and opened the doors. He got back into the van and drove it inside.

The garage had once been a working automotive garage. Three cars were parked inside with mechanics' tools and car tires and spare parts spread across the floor and hanging on the walls. It looked and smelled filthy.

Ed and Pat were pushed into a corner along with stacks of old car tires. They didn't speak, nothing needed saying. Both of them knew they had to get away on their own. No one was going to save them. No one was going to pay a hundred thousand pounds, not the British government, not the Canadian government, and certainly not the Israeli government. Without a warning to Ed, Pat walked forward toward the three men standing together fifteen feet away. Ed was tempted to follow her, but stopped as the boss raised his gun at Ed's head.

"Look," Pat said, keeping her hands in the air, "let's see if we can negotiate something here. My father has a few bucks . . ."

The boss spat at her. "Fuck off, lady. Go back to your coward husband."

She kept walking toward the men, faster now. "You go fuck yourself," she shouted. "Maybe I'll tell your friends here that you don't give a damn about then. It's all about you and jolly-old fucking England."

Ed couldn't understand what she was doing and took one step to bring her back, but was too late. Pat was head butted by the boss. He hit her on her forehead with a loud sickening thud. She staggered backwards falling in a pile on the floor. The two French skinheads were as shocked as Ed and started screaming questions at what happened. With the three of them arguing, Ed slowly and carefully reached down and dragged Pat back to the safety of the corner. He laid her head on a pile of filthy rags and stood with his legs apart between her and the men. His temptation to reach for his gun was great, but with Pat unconscious it was too great a risk.

The argument leveled off and the three men now carried on a lively conversation. Every so often the boss would point to Ed and Pat, apparently giving orders. Almost hidden by tools and tires, a phone on the wall rang. The boss picked it up and spoke for several minutes in French. Nodding in agreement as he spoke, he hung up the phone. Pointing to Ed and Pat, he gave what appeared to Ed as more orders. The three shook hands and handing his gun to the driver the boss got into a small car. The garage door was opened and he drove away. With the gun held on them during the departure, Ed held his ground. Pat didn't stir.

Ed knew the odds were better now there were only two of them, but they both had guns. He looked behind, down at Pat. She was breathing and thankfully wasn't bleeding. And then she winked. It wasn't a blink. It was a wink. Keeping a straight face he turned back to the two men. He backed up slowly just a few inches: closer to Pat. The men spoke in gestures, each swinging the guns they held as if they were cigarettes. Several minutes passed and their gestures showed they were now in agreement with what their next actions would be.

At a speed that was hard for Ed to believe, yet seemed to take forever, Pat pulled up Ed's pant leg, grabbed his gun and shot both men. They didn't have an opportunity to react. They were both thrown back against the wall and they slumped together down the wall. Tools and tires fell around them.

Pat jumped to her feet holding the gun on them, shouting to them in French. Ed took both of their guns, tossing them into the van. The van was their only escape. He turned to see Pat take the keys from the driver who was now awake and bleeding badly from a wound in his stomach. He spoke to Pat, almost in a whisper.

"Got the address," Pat said handing Ed his gun, which he held on the two men. It didn't seem to be needed, but it was the thing to do.

Pat was on the phone dialing as quickly as the old phone would allow. "Give me Miss, quickly!" There was very brief pause, and then she continued rapidly. "Miss, take down this address and get an ambulance here right away." She read off the address and the driver nodded his head. "Two men, both shot. Not us. I'm not sure exactly where we are, but we're going to head for the Eiffel Tower . . . half an hour . . . see you there, south side . . . we need to dump our transport." Another pause. "Will do." Ed and Pat jumped into the van.

Leaving the garage door open, Ed backed the van into the back alley and drove off in the direction they had arrived. Turning north on a major road, he headed for the Eiffel Tower, the only tall structure in all of Paris. Behind them they heard the sound of an ambulance. The sound faded and then ceased. Pat looked at her watch. "Eleven minutes. Not bad. I hope they live."

"How's your head?" Ed asked, keeping his eyes on the road and the Tower.

"Now that you mention it, it hurts like hell."

He leaned over and lightly kissed her forehead. "Better now?" he asked.

"Pain all gone," she laughed. She moved quickly from the passenger's seat into the back of the van, returning with her purse.

"Your gun?" Ed asked.

"Our Marriage Certificate." She searched through her purse. "And lipstick!"

Ed didn't try to understand. He drove with only one thing on his mind. Get to the Eiffel Tower as quickly as possible.

Pat found the certificate and lipstick. Turning the certificate to its blank side, she wrote an address in lipstick.

Ed looked out of the corner of his eyes. "Shopping list?"

She laughed. "This is the address where," she looked at her watch, "in two hours all hell is going to break loose."

"I'm listening."

"Your friendly English asshole is meeting at this address with a group of likeminded assholes and they are planning a massive attack on the Turkish area of Paris tonight. Knives, guns, Molotov cocktails, the works."

"Shit," Ed exclaimed, picking up speed.

"Slow down, Ed. Carolyn's last words were, and I quote, 'For Christ's sake don't speed'. The cops will throw you in jail and toss away the God damn keys!'"

He slowed down. "Flipping heck. Such language!"

"Wait 'til I tell her father."

Ed chuckled. "Wait 'til I tell her mother."

At a red light Ed leaned across and, holding her head, kissed her fully on the lips. "You done good back there," he said.

"You're not supposed to do that ya know?"

"That was a 'thank you' kiss, not a romance kiss."

"Hmm."

Keeping his eyes on the road with the Eiffel Tower as a guide he continued the careful drive. "So tell me," he asked, "what made you act when you did?"

"Simple. They were going to tie us up—arms and legs."

He nodded his understanding. "They'd have seen my gun."

"Exactly. And I figured that would've raise the stakes to a point where they'd have done something more, shall I say, dramatic?"

"We'd be dead!"

"That would be dramatic."

"Perhaps I owe you more than a 'thank you' kiss?"

"Just drive. We'll sort out compensation later."

As they approached the center of Paris, the traffic increased and their nervousness of being identified by the police intensified. The two men would surely have given a description of the van to the police, and Paris seemed to have police officers on every corner. Their luck held and forty-five minutes after telling Carolyn they would see her in half an hour, the Eiffel Tower was only two city blocks away. While Ed searched for an appropriate spot to park the van, Pat slid into the back and wiped down any area where their fingerprints might have been. Finally she wiped clean the two guns that belonged to the skinheads and hid them under a pile of rags. Slipping back to the passenger's seat she wiped the rear view mirror, front and back.

"Good thinking," Ed said. Seeing an empty spot he quickly drove to it and parked the van. He parked outside a Café by gently using the cars in front and back as 'feelers', shrugging a 'what else can I do' to Pat. As if planned, each grabbed their own bag from the van in their left hand leaving their right hands free for access to purse or ankle. Guns were now part of their lives—their security blankets. Pat wiped down the inside and outside doors handles for good measure, and placed the cloth in the closest garbage container. "Gotta be a good tourist," she said, and they quickly headed toward the Eiffel Tower.

A five-minute walk got them to the south corner of the tower. Assuming Carolyn would be coming from the north they waited on the western curb, acting as if they were waiting for a taxi. There was no need to wave a taxi down; there wasn't an available one to be seen.

A stretch limousine pulled up to them, resulting in a storm of honking from the cars behind. Quickly and without looking inside, Ed and Pat opened the door and clambered in. Not waiting for them to get seated the limousine took off and entered the traffic heading south.

Carolyn, seated in the forward seat, watched them sort themselves out and smiled a welcome. "Interesting day?" she asked.

Ed combed his fingers through his hair to settle in. "That could be the word."

Pat got straight to the point. "Are they alive?"

Carolyn nodded. "They were twenty minutes ago, although one is in pretty serious condition."

Pat shook her head slowly. "Shit. I couldn't aim at their legs for Christ's sake. They both had guns."

"It was them or us," Ed added, hoping to soften Pat's concern.

"We'll get more information when we get to the embassy, and then we'll get you both on a plane to England. The police are working with us, although they're pretty annoyed themselves. Don't like shootings."

Pat looked up. "It's not that easy. There's action going down tonight, and it ain't going to be nice!"

Carolyn thought for a moment. "We're minutes from the embassy. Update me when we get there."

Carolyn listened to Pat's story with her eyes closed. She wanted to catch every word. The three of them were in Carolyn's 'War Room' which in addition to regular office facilities included a bed and a television. The room was accessible from the parking area at the rear of the embassy and there was no need for them to be in the public areas of the embassy. When Pat had finished Carolyn opened her eyes and raised both eyebrows. "You're sure of the time and address?" she asked Pat.

Pat opened her purse, withdrew the Marriage Certificate and handed it to Carolyn. "Came in handy," she said.

Carolyn looked at her watch. "So the meeting starts in less than forty-five minutes. Not a lot of time is there?"

Ed spoke for the first time since they arrived. "Surely they won't all be there on time? They're French aren't they?"

"Yes, you're right," Carolyn said enthusiastically. "So allowing time for late-shows and then a bit of time to get organized, we've got an hour, hour and a quarter?"

Pat and Ed nodded in agreement.

Carolyn picked up a phone and dialed. "Mr. Ambassador, could I see you please? Top priority."

Two minutes later Sir Peter Edington joined them in the War Room. He looked at Ed and extended his hand. "Mr. Crowe," he said, "wasn't expecting to see you this time."

"No, sir. Change of plans."

Ed had met Edington the previous time he had been in Paris. The visit was intended to be personal, with Ed arriving without Carolyn's prior knowledge of either the visit or the fact that Lady Stonebridge had encouraged the trip. As it turned out Carolyn and Ed became unexpectedly involved with spying on IRA terrorists who were negotiating the purchase of semtex explosives from Libyan representatives. While the operation was successful, it had been a subsequent leak from the British Embassy in Paris that had lead to members of the IRA kidnapping Ed in Canada, and ultimately Pat shooting and killing one of the IRA members.

Carolyn introduced Pat, outlined quickly what had happened after Ed and Pat had left the hotel, and gave all the details of the planned meeting tonight.

"You do make my life interesting, Miss Andrews," Edington commented dryly.

"Yes, sir. Sorry, sir."

Edington turned to Pat. "I must ask you this, Miss Weston. Are you sure you have the details correct?"

Pat's mouth was dry. She took a deep gulp. "Positif!" She spoke in French, stressing the accent.

Edington stood and rubbed his hands together. "Then let's move to my office and get things moving." He turned to Carolyn. "Perhaps some tea for our guests?"

"Consider it done," Carolyn replied.

"Just what the doctor ordered," Ed added, rubbing his hands together.

Pat refrained from commenting, but wondered how *they* had ever managed to build and run the British Empire.

Walking the length of the building on the main floor, the four entered the large reception area. As they entered the receptionist stood to recognize them. She was a little taken back by the group. "Good morning, Mr. Ambassador, Miss Andrews, and Mr. Crowe," the receptionist said quietly.

Ed walked over to her. "Good morning, Terri. It's nice to see you again."

Usually never at a loss for words, Terri spoke hesitantly. "Mr. Crowe, I am so sorry . . ." Ed interrupted and motioned to Pat.

"Terri this is Miss Weston. She's from Canada."

Pat nodded. "Hi, Terri."

Terri's face reddened. One hand went to cover her mouth and the other she extended to Pat. "Oh my God, I am so sorry, I . . ."

Pat looked at Ed, not understanding the conversation.

Ed raised his hand in a friendly manner. "We're both fine, Terri. We have to run but we'll drop by later."

Terri smiled, acknowledging his response. Ed and Pat turned and walked quickly to catch up as they headed to the ambassador's office. Once in the office they arranged themselves around his desk.

"Tea's ordered," Carolyn said.

Ambassador Edington tapped his desk to get everyone's attention. "A quick explanation is in order, Miss Weston." He was obviously concerned about his need to explain. "Unfortunately it was a leak from this embassy that led to the capture of Mr. Crowe by the IRA people in Toronto, and . . ." he left the rest unsaid.

Pat understood. "And me shooting one of the kidnappers."

Carolyn interrupted, wanting to clarify the matter. "And your *having* to shoot the kidnapper in order to saves lives: including your own and Mr. Crowe's."

Pat thought back momentarily to pulling the trigger and her reaction as the bullet entered the man's head, killing him instantly. "Thank you both for the explanation." She sat straighter in her seat. "It took a while for me to get over, but I now accept the situation for what it was. I'll speak to Terri later. Maybe I can help her somewhat?"

"More than generous, Miss Weston," Edington said, just as the door opened and a trolley of tea was wheeled in.

After they each helped themselves to tea, Ambassador Edington summed up. "We don't have lot of time to get a plan into action and dealing with the French police isn't easy. I think I need to phone the Interior Minister in order to get the speed and co-operation required. Agreed?"

It was unanimous. Ambassador Edington made the call. It took five minutes to get through to the Minister and another five minutes of explanation before Edington raised thumbs-up with a grin. The conversation had been in French, with Carolyn and Pat following it carefully. Ed enjoyed his tea. Edington hung up, pleased with the result.

"A unit of Gendarmes will enter the building in exactly," Edington looked at his watch, "fifty-four minutes. A small unit will be there in civvies in less than fifteen minutes. They will count the number entering the building to make sure the police are three to one in their favor." He took a deep breath. "I sure hope we've got this right."

"We do, sir," Pat assured him and smiled. "That's what the boss man said was going to happen, and he wanted to be there. If I'm wrong, then I'll owe you an apology."

Edington nodded and turned to Carolyn. "I think, Miss Andrews, you should get the three of you back to England 'toot sweet'. I'll look after things from this end."

Ed interrupted. "Can't we take a butchers, sir? It's on the way to the airport."

Carolyn leaned over to Pat and explained the 'London-English'. Pat shook her head in amazement, but committed to use that expression some time.

Edington laughed. "Haven't heard that one for a while. Makes a bloke homesick dunnit?" He turned to Carolyn. "Miss Andrews?"

"Who's the main contact, sir?"

"Inspector Martineau. Know him?"

"Yes, sir." She thought for a moment. "If we use the limousine, stay a block or two away. Should be okay, sir. Then straight to the airport."

Edington nodded, mulling over the idea.

"You do owe us one, sir." Pat offered.

"Yes, I do," he agreed. "But then straight to the airport. I'll arrange the limo and plane. Get going."

After shaking hands with Ambassador Edington, they left his office. Carolyn left for her room to pack. while Ed and Pat walked back to the reception area. Terri stood as they walked toward her. She offered a weak smile.

Pat took the lead. "Don't sweat it, Terri. It seems to be part of my job." Pat lowered her voice almost to a whisper. "In fact, if you can keep a secret?"

Terri crossed her heart. "Swear to God!"

Pat leaned closer to Terri. "I shot two men today."

Terri almost fell backwards. "Are you kidding me?" she gasped. She looked at Ed for help.

Ed nodded. "It's true. But mum's the word!"

Terri's eyes were like saucers. She wasn't sure if she should be pleased that she was part of a secret, or frightened of the not-much-taller-than-five-foot lady in front of her. She gulped, not sure of what to say next. Finally, she managed to speak. "Are they alive?"

Carolyn replied, as she joined them. "Both alive. One in intensive." She looked at Terri. "It'll be on the telly tonight, but no one will be charged. The two known criminals aren't talking and there are no leads. Officially it's a gang shooting. Drugs!" She handed Pat and Ed their bags.

Pat winked at Terri. "Bring in the usual suspects, eh? Gotta go." She tapped her purse.

Terri stood, mouth agape, and waved weakly as Pat walked to the front door followed by Ed and Carolyn.

The limousine was at curb at the front door. The three got in with their bags.

"I think you scared the crap out of her." Ed said.

Pat wrinkled her nose. "I think I scared the crap out myself!"

Carolyn slid back the window and gave the driver instructions. She turned to Ed and Pat. "We're going to see the sights of Paris for a while. Don't want to get there too early."

"And then we'll take a butchers," Pat said cleverly.

"Not you too," Carolyn sighed.

The driver went south to the River Seine and drove east through the Place le la Concorde, along the Tuileries Gardens and past The Louvre. He crossed the Seine at Notre Dame, slowing down for a perfect view. Once across the Seine, the tour was over. The limousine entered the shopping and residential districts heading south. Not wanting anything to go wrong, Ed and Pat put their guns in their respective bags.

The drive was slow. The driver wanted to arrive no earlier than had been agreed to. They were now in a less desirable residential area, and the limousine drew attention. The driver pulled over into an empty lot. Sliding the window open, he spoke to Carolyn. She nodded.

"We're two minutes away, and three minutes early," she updated Ed. "I told the driver to wait the full three minutes. Better late and miss it all than mess it up."

After what seemed to be a long three minutes, the limousine moved on. The driver took several back lanes, now empty of people. Turning left he drove half a block and pulled in behind a row of cars. The street was mostly made up of warehouses with an occasional shop, which were now closed. Along the street a variety of cars and scooters were parked. It was quiet and eerie. The sun was far into the west and the shadows allowed little light through. The driver pointed to one of the warehouse doors, identifying the address.

Then things changed. Almost without a sound a stream of cars and vans pulled up on the non-parking side of the street. Car doors opened and within thirty seconds what looked to be about fifty men, dressed in a variety of uniforms and headgear, stood in front of the entrance to the warehouse. Behind them standing in the center of the street, obviously in charge, was the only officer not wearing any form of headgear or carrying a glass shield.

Carolyn pointed him out. "Inspector Martineau."

Martineau raised one arm and held a whistle to his mouth. Almost immediately he dropped his arm and blew the whistle.

The door was battered open and shouting orders the officers ran into the building. In less then twenty seconds, they were all through the doorway. Martineau blew the whistle a second time and the rear doors to the six vans on the street opened. Two officers from each van, wearing headgear and holding a truncheon, jumped to the ground and stood by their doors and waited.

They didn't have to wait long. First a few men were escorted out, a policeman on each arm. Handcuffed, and some bleeding from around the head, they were helped, carried or thrown into the rear of the vans. As each van was fully loaded and the doors locked, the two officers checked in with Martineau and with his nod of approval they joined the driver in the front of the vehicle and the van left.

The orderly process continued. There was fighting and screaming, but it was just a matter of time. During a lull in the action Inspector Martineau walked over to the limousine. Carolyn lowered the window and spoke briefly to the Inspector who was obviously pleased with the results. He motioned to Ed and Pat with his head, spoke briefly to Carolyn, saluted her and left.

Carolyn turned to Ed. "He recognized you from television. He was not amused."

"Ouch!" Ed replied.

"On the other hand," Carolyn continued, "he is happy to have made such a good catch tonight. Apparently there are drugs and weapons on site."

They turned back to watch the few remaining stragglers emerge. One of the last to be dragged out kicking and screaming was the English skinhead. His shirt was almost torn off in the struggle.

"There's your English asshole!" Pat shouted, quickly opening the door and walking defiantly to the man. Ed went to follow her to bring her back, but Carolyn held him back.

"Let her have her say," Carolyn said.

They watched with interest as she stood in front of the skinhead, still being held on both sides and his hands handcuffed behind his back. Inspector Martineau stood close by.

They couldn't hear, but watched the action.

Pat was speaking to skinhead, waving a finger at him.

Skinhead laughed and shouted at Pat.

Pat slapped his face.

Skinhead laughed louder, being held back from moving toward her. He spat at her in defiance.

Waiting for the right moment, Pat adjusted her weight and kicked the skinhead in his groin as hard as she could.

Ed pulled a face in unintended sympathy.

Skinhead doubled up as best he could, still being held on both sides.

Pat moved in and kneed skinhead in the face.

Skinhead was pulled away, blood gushing from his nose.

Inspector Martineau waved Pat away, back to the limousine.

Pat walked back to the limousine with a slight limp. The driver didn't wait for orders; he pulled the limousine away from the curb and past the remaining police vehicles. Skinhead was being helped into a van as they drove by.

No one spoke for a couple for minutes as Pat gathered herself. Neither Ed nor Carolyn asked for an update. It was expected.

Pat started "I told him he was a foulmouthed limey asshole, and I was here to have a good butchers."

They nodded, holding back their smiles.

"He told me I didn't know what the eff I was talking about, and said I was an effing cow."

They nodded again.

"I slapped his face."

They nodded.

"The miserable sonovabitch spat at me."

Nods.

"I kicked him in his . . . his . . . groin area."

Nods of approval.

"He doubled over, grunting that he wished he had effing killed me when he could have, and said I was nothing but a watered down American."

Groans and looks of understanding.

"So I kneed him in his face."

Slight but very well intended applause.

"Now look," Pat said looking down, "I've got his blood all over my new shoes."

Carolyn chuckled. "Let me." She took a tissue from her purse and wiped the few drops of blood from Pat's shoe and carefully put in back into her purse.

"You're keeping it?" Pat groaned. "That's gross!"

"DNA," Carolyn said. "It's a new form of genetic identification."

Ed and Pat shrugged—whatever!

The limousine continued on its way to Orly Airport. The conversation was limited. Operation Remembrance was over. It was unclear to Ed if it had met its goals. They would find out tomorrow when they met with Lord Stonebridge at Stonebridge Manor.

Pat was deep in thought, twirling her 'wedding' ring on the ring finger of her left hand. She had never worn a real ring on that finger before, except the aluminum ring that she and Ed used as an engagement ring. She removed the ring and slipped it on the ring finger of her right hand. Suddenly something came to mind.

"So tell me," Pat asked, breaking the silence, "what does BNP mean; British Neanderthal Pig?"

Carolyn looked up with interest. "Why do you ask?"

"Because English asshole skinhead had that tattooed on the left of his chest. About three inches high, right where his heart is, or in his case where his heart is supposed to be!"

"The plot thickens," Ed commented.

"The plot curdles perhaps?" Carolyn added.

"I'm listening," Pat said, sitting forward and rubbing her hands together.

Carolyn thought for a moment to gather her response. "BNP, stands for British National Party," she began, "which sounds rather benign. In fact the party has very strong points of view most of which are certainly not standard fare in anything but a very small percentage of the British population. They are anti-immigration, anti-Semitic, almost certainly anti-anything except a 'white-only' Britain. Some of their members go back to the National Front, which was unabashedly pro-Nazi. In fact the current BNP is a combination of the National Front and the British Movement. The two parties combined a couple of years ago under the leadership of John Tyndall who founded the National front in 1982. The party ran about fifty candidates in last year's General Election. None were elected."

Pat listened intently. "Kind of a KKK?"

"Not in practice, perhaps in policy." Carolyn said. "They are quite open in their membership and have no concern in showing it. I suspect somewhere on your skinhead's body is a tattoo of '88', which represents HH—for Heil Hitler."

"That's a lot of information off the top of your head." Pat commented.

Carolyn nodded. "In my role as a Queen's government representative in foreign countries I need to be able to respond to questions about these sorts of people. Keep in mind it is a very open wound in Britain at this time."

They chatted further in generalities, and were happy to enter Orly Airport to see their private plane waiting for them. Storing their luggage they took their seats and were in the air in fifteen minutes.

As was his custom, Ed agreed to make coffee as soon as the plane reached cruising height. It didn't take long. Fifteen minutes later the three of them were enjoying a hot cup of coffee.

"So was Operation Remembrance a success?" Pat asked bluntly.

Carolyn chewed her lip and pondered that all-important question. "Pat, I've got to tell you I don't know. When I last spoke to London they were scrambling to figure it out. The television stations were having a hey-day. Retired army Generals were the catch of the day, and historians we've never heard of are now household names." She rubbed her forehead. "And I've got to let you know, Pat, it was just as popular on the Canadian channels. Even CNN had a few stories, and you know how narrow their focus can be."

Ed looked to the ceiling for help. None emerged. "I think the answer will lie in tomorrow's newspapers. They've had more time to reflect and work on the details. So" he said, lifting his cup, "let's enjoy a nice meal at the Inn tonight and tomorrow—what will be, will be."

"That would be que sera, sera." Pat muttered, lifting her cup. "I can see it now. My parents watching me on T.V., and I'm in Paris with my *husband* creating an international incident. Maybe we should have had a couple of our children handing out the questionnaires? Might as well find out you're grandparents on live T.V. while you're at it!"

Carolyn smiled at the thought. "Have faith in the process, people. We have all the resources of the British Secret Intelligence Service behind us."

Pat laughed. "That's all I need. MI6 phoning my mother telling her that her daughter's okay, and there's nothing to worry about!"

The light above the cabin door flashed on and the plane started its descent.

Carolyn agreed to stay at the Inn with Ed and Pat. They would face the circumstances of Operation Remembrance together. "Beside, I don't want to take the initial credit, or the blame, alone," Carolyn had quipped. All for one and one for all they had agreed.

There were only a few other residents at the Inn, which allowed the three of them to sit in a corner of the dining area by themselves. Nevertheless several of the other guests watched them and they were obviously the topic 'au jour'. The headwaiter asked if they wanted to watch the ten-o'clock news on BBC. They gratefully declined. He smiled an understanding smile.

"I feel like a rose between two thorns," Ed remarked to break the silence of the meal.

"More like a crow between two chicks," Pat quickly responded with a cheeky grin.

"The way you finished off your meal," Carolyn said, "how about piggy-in-the-middle?"

Ed grimaced. "Ouch. That hurts."

Carolyn continued. "You'll be interested to know that in Turkish it translates into rat-in-the-middle."

Pat laughed and clapped her hands. "I'll stick with piggy. A rat he ain't!"

Ed raised his hand. "I'll have you know that I had a tough day, and deserved a full meal. While in Paris on my honeymoon I had to watch my new 'wife' shoot two men, and then beat the poop out of a third man: a fellow Englishman no less."

Pat leaned into the table. "That was the part I enjoyed most!"

They went to their rooms laughing and feeling much better. As they left the dining area the remaining residents watched them curiously, turning on the television as soon as the three of them exited the room.

CHAPTER FIVE

THURSDAY,
AUGUST 15TH 1985.
7:30 AM

The three met early for breakfast. No one had slept well and the stress showed on their faces. Nibbling on cold toast didn't help, but the piping hot tea brought some color to their cheeks. The Inn Manager knew better than to offer them the daily newspapers, and as they left for Stonebridge Manor they kept their eyes away from their fellow residents' readings. Pat couldn't help but see one headline out of the corner of her eye, and groaned when she read it: CANADIANS ATTACK!! The headline was bold and large. She kept her thoughts to herself as they climbed into the limousine and headed to Stonebridge Manor.

The driver looked into the rear view mirror to speak to his passengers. "Newspapers anyone?" There was a definite smile hidden in his enquiring look.

"We'll pass," Carolyn replied. "Not much good news nowadays."

Ed kept his eyes on the countryside, quietly humming.

"What are you humming?" Pat asked, kicking his foot.

"O Canada," he answered. "What does it sound like?"

"Like a pig in heat," she replied.

He changed tunes.

"And what is that supposed to be?" Pat asked.

"There'll always be an England," Ed grinned back.

Before Pat could make a further comment, Carolyn raised her hand. "Hey, stop acting like an old married couple you two. It's going to be a tough enough day without you getting on each other's nerves . . . and mine too for that matter."

Her reaction surprised both Ed and Pat, and their looks showed it.

Carolyn put her hand to her forehead and rubbed it. "Okay, I'm sorry," she said, taking a deep breath. "Not a good night's sleep."

Pat leaned over and took Carolyn's hand. "Cheer up, Carolyn. At least we got our point across."

Carolyn tried a grin. "Yeah, we did that. And no one died."

Ed sat forward. "Can we be sure of that?"

Carolyn nodded. "For sure, for sure. If anyone had died, I'd have been phoned. Day or night, I'd have been contacted."

"I didn't shoot to kill," Pat said firmly. "If I'd wanted them dead, they'd be dead."

Ed grimaced at her comments. "I don't mean to question you, Pat, but Jesus you were lying on the floor."

Pat nodded. "Exactly!"

"Of course," Carolyn exclaimed. "You were in the prone position! Damn, that's good news. Not a shoot-out, but a well managed defensive maneuver."

Pat extended her comment. "Body spread comfortably, leaning slightly to my left side. Left elbow on the ground and my right wrist resting comfortably in my left hand."

Ed's mouth dropped open. The fact that Pat had shot the men the way she had, seemed to change everything. He didn't understand the significance, but he wasn't about to argue the point. He turned to Carolyn. "Damn?"

Carolyn shrugged flippantly. "I'm allowed a damn once in a while."

Pat nodded. "Damn right you are."

The limousine pulled into Stonebridge Manor through the opening gates.

"Speaking of damnation," Ed muttered.

Lord and Lady Stonebridge's maid met them at the door with a slight bow.

"Lord Stonebridge is expecting you, miss," she said to Carolyn. "He asked that you go right up. He's on the phone, and the General is with him."

"Do you know who he's speaking with, Miriam?" Carolyn asked, trying to maintain a smile.

"I believe it is Prime Minister Thatcher," the maid answered, almost whispering.

"Of course, just as I suspected," Carolyn said, her smile disappearing as she headed up the stairs with Pat and Ed in tow.

Carolyn knocked quietly on Lord Stonebridge's door and entered without waiting for a response. Lord Stonebridge and Mr. Cooper were huddled around the speakerphone on Lord Stonebridge's large and messy desk. The mess was resulting from copies of each of the British daily newspapers. The sight put a chill through Ed's spine, but like Pat and Carolyn, he smiled as best he could.

Lord Stonebridge waved them over as he spoke. "Prime Minister, our world travelers have arrived." He motioned them to pull up chairs, which they did as silently as they could. Lord Stonebridge continued. "Go ahead, Prime Minister."

There was a brief but confident pause. Mrs. Thatcher spoke in her usual direct fashion. "So what have you to say for yourself, Miss Weston?"

Pat gulped and leaned toward the desk. Her voice was just audible. "Well I, er, I mean we . . ." She took a breath to settle her spinning head.

"Brilliant! That's what I think," Mrs. Thatcher said forcefully. "Just brilliant. Isn't that so, Lord Stonebridge?"

Now smiling, Lord Stonebridge nodded. "Better than we ever expected, Prime Minister. A wonderful success."

Pat fell back into her chair, holding her hand to her mouth to stop from crying aloud. Tears of happiness ran briefly down her face. She wiped them away bravely, and then leaned forward again to speak. "Thank you, Prime Minister. I hadn't considered the word brilliant, but who am I to argue?" She was beaming now and held her hands clasped together in excitement.

Carolyn leaned back in her chair and closed her eyes to savor the moment.

Ed was shaking hands with Mr. Cooper who had stood and leaned over to congratulate him.

Lord Stonebridge gently raised his hands to gather everyone's attentions. "You have a very happy team, Prime Minister. Are there other questions or comments? I understand you have to enter the house for Question Period."

Mrs. Thatcher spoke frankly. "This will, of course, be my only opportunity to thank you all for your wonderful work. Operation Remembrance was a huge success, and alas I am not permitted to admit that it ever existed. Thank you all." There was a slight pause. "One question perhaps? Miss Weston: was it accurate that your two uncles fought in the war as described by Mr. Crowe to the BBC?"

Pat sat up straighter in her chair. "Absolutely, Prime Minister." She smiled. "A lady cannot tell a lie now, can she?"

Mrs. Thatcher replied and her smile was almost visible to everyone in the room. "Absolutely correct, Miss Weston. A lady should never tell a lie."

The phone went quiet and Lord Stonebridge pressed a button on the phone. He looked about the room, clearly pleased with the results of the operation and the conversation with the prime minister. He rubbed his hands together. "I suggest we celebrate this with a nice cup of tea," he said. He walked around his desk to shake hands with Pat and Ed, while Carolyn ordered tea.

When they had settled down from sharing the positive feed-back, Lord Stonebridge motioned for them to sit. "Perhaps it would be helpful if someone related to the General and me the actual order of events that led to such a successful operation?"

Mr. Cooper expanded. "Please keep in mind that there can be no actual written report." He looked over his glasses. "Regrettably, I might add. I suspect we could learn something from this operation to apply to future endeavors."

Carolyn spoke first. "Before Mr. Crowe and Miss Weston begin, perhaps I should arrange for their flights home tonight, and I would suggest we travel via Ed's mother, who must be wondering what is happening. I will phone Mrs. Crowe."

Receiving approval, Carolyn left the room.

"Before we start," Pat said, "I should return this." She took the wedding band off her right hand and passed it to Lord Stonebridge. He put it carefully into his desk, and Pat began retelling the events of Operation Remembrance.

Carolyn returned just as Pat was explaining the shooting of the two men in the garage. Pat smiled at Carolyn as she sat down, and continued speaking.

"So my goal was to put them out of service, without killing either of them. As I said, if they had found our guns, and Ed's was going to be a give-away, we'd be goners." She paused. "So I shot them."

Carolyn took the opportunity to expand on the details. "If I may? It's not very often an opportunity arises when an operative gets to shoot their guns the way we are taught on the shooting range, but Miss Weston took full advantage of being in the prone position to ensure her shots were as effective as possible and with as little risk of death as possible."

Lord Stonebridge nodded slightly. "Almost like it was planned."

Pat shook her head with a mild smile. "No, sir. Not planned as such. Luckily Mr. Crowe was standing over me and I knew where his gun was strapped to his leg."

"Well I think it was bloody marvelous work," the General said, making his point loud and clear. "As the saying goes, I'd rather be lucky than good."

"I totally agree," Lord Stonebridge said, clasping his hands together. "Ah, tea is served." The door opened and the maid wheeled in a trolley of tea and sandwiches. "Let's top up," he continued, "and then, Miss Weston and Mr. Crowe can complete the details of this very interesting operation."

Carolyn gave Pat the tiniest of winks, and they helped themselves to tea.

As they drank their tea, Ed continued on the story of the drive to the Eiffel Tower, the meeting with Carolyn and the plans they organized for the meeting of the English skinhead and his associates.

Carolyn explained the connection with the police and the involvement of Ambassador Edington. She stopped and turned to Pat when she got to the Pat and skinhead altercation.

Lord Stonebridge settled in his seat. "I'm looking forward to this episode." He offered an official look.

"Me too," the General added.

Pat squirmed in her chair. "It wasn't *that* exciting," she said coolly. "I just had a few words with him."

"Pray tell," Lord Stonebridge said, now looking over his glasses at her.

Pat licked her lips. "When I approached him I told him he was less than an English gentleman."

Ed interrupted. "I think the expression was a, 'foulmouthed limey asshole', to be precise."

Pat rolled her eyes knowing she wasn't going to get away easy. "Whatever! Anyway he told me I didn't know what I was talking about and I was an effing cow." She waited for a response but got none. "So I slapped his face! Big deal."

"Well done," the General said.

Pat now felt bolder. "Then the SOB spat at me. That's disgusting."

Lord Stonebridge nodded in agreement.

Pat continued carefully. "So I kicked him in . . . in . . . in his lower-front region."

"That would be his groin area," Ed added nonchalantly.

"As he doubled over," Pat continued, "he said he wished he had killed me when he could of, and then he *really* insulted me!"

Lord Stonebridge took off his glasses and leaned forward. "Really? What could he have said that was more insulting than wanting to kill you?"

Pat raised her head high. "He said I was nothing but a watered-down American." She took a deep breath. "So I kneed him in the face and gave him a bloody nose. Cheeky bastard!"

"Cheeky indeed," Lord Stonebridge said. "Well done, Miss Weston."

"Thank you, sir," she replied with a grin. "It's the lumberjack in me."

"I don't know about lumberjack, Miss Weston," Lord Stonebridge said, "but you're a smart gutsy person and you can work with us anytime you like. My verbal report to your superiors will be appropriately positive. Incidentally your parents have been spoken to, and they are aware of at least some of the facts. And your superior is very happy with the results, as he should be."

Pat wanted to stand up and punch the air with her fist. But in keeping with the circumstances she nodded her thanks with a smile.

Carolyn completed the details, which brought them to the present time. "I would only add," Carolyn summed-up, "that flights have been arranged, and we are expected at Mrs. Crowe's this afternoon for tea." She turned to Ed. "Roy Johnson has also been invited by your mother."

Ed frowned. "Bloody hell. We had better get our stories perfect with him around. He doesn't miss a thing."

Carolyn gave a knowing nod.

"Which reminds me," Lord Stonebridge said, extending his hand to Pat. "You had better leave the Marriage Certificate with me." He grinned. "Unless you have a reason to keep it that is?"

Pat handed it to him from her purse. "Just used it for note paper, Lord Stonebridge. Not worth the paper it's printed on, eh?"

"Charming I'm sure," Ed muttered as they all stood to shake hands to end the meeting.

Carolyn, Pat and Ed walked downstairs, but did not get to the front door before Lady Stonebridge called them back. "Carolyn, dear, why don't you introduce me to the young married couple?" Lady Stonebridge turned and walked into the large living room followed by Carolyn, Ed and Pat, none of whom wanted to lead the way. Carolyn was pushed ahead.

"Mother this is Miss Weston," Carolyn said as an introduction, stressing the word 'Miss', "and, of course you know Mr. Crowe."

Lady Stonebridge shook hands with Pat and motioned for everyone to take a seat. "You're prettier than you show on television, Miss Weston. And Mr. Crowe, it's nice to see you again."

Pat and Ed nodded their thanks.

"You know, Carolyn, my dear," Lady Stonebridge began, speaking to Carolyn but making it clear the message was for all to hear, "I often wonder what you and your father get up to in the strange worlds in which you choose to live and work. You have me worried from time to time and I often wish you had chosen a more, shall I say, normal career." She looked at each of them. "However, today I want to say how proud I am of what I saw on television these past couple of days, and each of your respective parts in it. I neither know, nor care to know, why it occurred, but for me it was a fresh and honest interpretation of events from that terrible war. You are all to be proud of yourselves and the way you represented your country," she turned to Ed, "or countries as the case may be."

Lady Stonebridge stood. The message was completed and no response was required. Thanking her for her hospitality, they left her standing erect and proud. Carolyn closed the door behind them, still a little stunned at the experience. She walked to the front door. Outside was the family Jaguar.

Carolyn pointed to the car. "Your luggage is in the boot. I'm the driver. Let's go see Ed's mother."

Ed offered to sit in the rear of the Jag to allow Pat the opportunity to get a better view of the countryside and the part on London they would drive through. In reality he did not want, in any way, to get between his two friends. Neither did he want to be asked any awkward questions as they headed to his mother's house. With Roy at his mother's house, there would be plenty of questions the three of them would need to address.

Carolyn kept to the less busy roads as they drove through the Chiltern Hills and pointed out the villages and towns to Pat as they passed through them, adding historical facts and local lore. Pat was engrossed in the details and asked numerous questions. Sitting in the rear leather-bound seat, Ed enjoyed the commentary and the exchange of information. Being in the same car with both the one person he loved and hoped to marry and his lover and close friend from Canada, he wasn't sure if he should feel guilt or happiness. He thoughtfully chose happiness and settled back in comfort.

As they entered the greater London area, Ed took over as tour guide. There were less interesting stories to tell on the outskirts, and passing Wembley Stadium somehow seemed the most interesting. He had to acknowledge that most of the good stuff was downtown London and they wouldn't be seeing any of that today. He sat back as Carolyn pulled onto his mother's street.

"Oh, oh," Carolyn said, "looks like we've got a welcoming committee."

Standing at her front door, Mrs. Crowe waved as the car pulled up. Her neighbors, mostly women, each holding a small Union Jack, surrounded her. One had managed to find a small Maple Leaf flag, and the Polish lady that lived down the street, whose name Ed could never pronounce, held both a Union Jack and a Polish flag. The cheering was muted, but very real. Several ladies gave Ed a hug, telling him what a grand job he and his wife had done. Mrs. Haylings organized 'three cheers', then everyone headed back into their homes. The Polish lady went out of her way to kiss Pat on both cheeks, and then, crying silently, she walked home.

Ed introduced his mother to Pat in the hallway, with the full 'Miss Pat Weston'. Mrs. Crowe gave her a hug and ushered everyone into the living room. Roy was standing by the table where there was a spread of tea and fancy sandwiches. "Alas, no crumpets," he said with a grin. He shook Ed's hand and gave Carolyn a big, long hug.

Before anyone could introduce them, Roy extended his had to Pat. "You must be the lady not married to my mate Eddie? I'm Roy."

Pat shook his hand. "That's me."

Roy poured Pat her tea and motioned her to sit down. "If you don't mind my saying so, you are very pretty. Much prettier in real life than on the telly."

Pat remained standing. He was at least a foot taller than she was and she didn't want to add to the distance. "I bet you say that to all the ladies," she smiled. "Besides you're not such a bad looking bloke yourself. A bit tall for me perhaps."

Roy smiled and winked. He looked down to meet her eyes, exaggerating the distance. "Now I bet you say that to all men you meet. Even the shorter ones."

Ed and Mrs. Crowe stood to one side, silently listening. Carolyn smiled knowingly; she was enjoying this.

Pat stood as tall as she could. She returned the wink. "Where I come from, we measure a person from the chin up, not from the chin down."

Roy clapped his hands. "Lloyd George! Excellent!" He bowed slightly. "Pat, I think this is the beginning of a beautiful friendship!"

"Humphrey Bogart, Casablanca, 1942. Three Oscars." Pat said.

"Directed by Michael Curtiz," Roy added.

"Hairstylist: Helen Hunt," Pat quickly responded.

"Bang on," Roy said.

Pat smiled. "I just made that up."

"I know you did," Roy said, "but I would never want to embarrass you by mentioning that fact, especially since I may ask you out some time in the future."

Pat turned to Carolyn, motioning her head to Roy. "Is he for real?"

Carolyn nodded. "Absolutely. One-hundred percent."

Mrs. Crowe summoned everyone to the table and offered the sandwiches around.

"Fancy sandwiches," Ed commented, taking several.

"Not often we get television personalities, is it now?" Mrs. Crowe commented, pouring tea. "I think you did a wonderful job, Pat. I don't understand a word of French, but I could see on the telly how much your comments were striking a blow. And oh those nasty skinheads at the end. Don't need that nasty type around do we?"

Pat nodded her thanks. "No we don't. Not nice people at all."

"So tell us more, Edwin," Mrs. Crowe said, turning to Ed. "We all know you're not married, but that's about all we do know. Why Paris? Why now?"

Ed related the story the three had agreed on, keeping as much to the truth as he could. The fact that Pat's uncles had fought in the war helped, and Pat expanded on those details. Whether Mrs. Crowe believed it all was not easy to tell. She accepted the facts as they were presented, and totally enjoyed hearing of the reactions from the passers-by to Pat's details of Vichy France.

When Ed and Pat finished the story, Mrs. Crowe turned to Ed. "I'm glad, Edwin, you finally found out the truth about the French during the war." She turned to Pat. "He never listened to me when

I tried telling him. Too much stuff on the telly about the French freedom fighters. Too few of them and too many Vichy types."

"So what's the honeymoon part got to do with it," Roy asked.

Pat had agreed to expand the truth on this matter. "Well, that was a bit of what you call a porkie. You see I work for the federal government—Export Canada, and I was in Paris for work purposes. When Ed agreed to join me for the couple of days in Paris to help in the publicity, I could hardly say I was on my employer's time—so we lied." She turned to Mrs. Crowe. "I'm sorry you had to see that on television, Mrs. Crowe. We never expected it to be picked up on television, let alone the BBC."

Mrs. Crowe nodded knowingly. "We all have to tell a porkie once in a while, Pat."

"Yes indeed we do," Roy agreed, not believing a word of the explanation. "And how did Carolyn fit into the picture, pray tell?"

It was Ed's turn. "Well, by coincidence Carolyn was working at the British Embassy in Paris. We really felt we had to get out of Paris after starting such an uproar, so we turned to Carolyn to help us get to England."

"And tonight we return to Canada." Pat added with enthusiasm.

"Coincidence is a good thing." Roy said with a sly look at Ed. "What time is your flight?"

Carolyn answered. "Pat flies to Ottawa at four-thirty and Ed catches the ten-thirty to Toronto." She stood. "Which reminds me— we had better get Pat to Heathrow rather soon."

Roy stood and bowed graciously to Pat. "Perhaps you would allow me the pleasure of driving you to the airport? And I promise you I won't ask any questions that you'll have to answer with a porkie."

Pat beamed at the offer. "How could I turn down such a generous offer? Thank you, Roy."

After saying their farewells and switching Pat's bag to his car, Roy and Pat left for Heathrow. Ed waved them off at the curb, while his mum and Carolyn cleared the dishes. When everything was put away and after catching up on Carolyn's parents, Mrs. Crowe announced she had to go out.

"Where to, Mum?" Ed asked, knowing the answer.

"There and back again," she answered, picking up her shopping bag. Saying good-bye to them both with big hugs, she left briskly for her trip.

Sitting across from each other at the table, Ed took Carolyn's hands in his. "Can we go upstairs and make love?" he asked.

Carolyn shook her head. "Not here, Ed. Not in your mother's house. It wouldn't be right."

There was no sense arguing, he knew that. "I do love you so much Carolyn."

She winked. "Yes, I know you do. And I have a surprise for you." She raised his hands and kissed them. "I have booked a room at an airport hotel. Perhaps we should head there now? I'm looking forward to you undressing me."

Ed gulped at the thought. "Lead on, Miss Andrews."

Carolyn shivered. "I love it when you call me that."

They wasted no time in closing up the house. Ten minutes later they were on the way to Heathrow in the comfort of Carolyn's Jag. Carolyn turned on the radio to catch the 3 o'clock news.

The last item of the news caught their attention. A blue Vauxhall car had been found abandoned and left running at Heathrow airport. Ed's heart sank when the license plate number was announced. It was Roy's car. Before he could speak, a ringing came from the back seat. It was coming from Carolyn's purse. She slammed on the brakes and pulled over to the side of the road.

"My mobile!" She grabbed her purse and pulled out the phone. "Crowe's nest!" she answered. She was using Ed's regular answer at his apartment in Oakville, but he knew it was a password. His stomach grew tighter.

Carolyn answered "Yes" several times, mostly listening with her eyes closed and her head shaking. When she spoke, she spoke with authority. "Phone me again in forty-five minutes. I'll be based out of a hotel by the airport. I'll give you the name and room number then." She pressed a button on the mobile to hang up.

She pulled the car back into traffic, driving fast but carefully. She spoke slowly. "They've been kidnapped. Not sure by who, but a van load of skinheads was seen driving away from the area. Pat's luggage was still in the boot, so they won't have her gun. Bells began to ring when Pat didn't check-in for the flight. She was on the 'Call this number' list with no check-in. The number was MI6. Then they found the car. The General is at your mother's house to get her somewhere safe. My father has phoned Pat's boss."

"Shit, shit, shit," was all Ed could muster.

"Do two things please, Ed. Reach under my seat. There's a gun attached to the underside of the seat. Bring it out and have a look at it. Be careful, it's loaded. Secondly, use the rear view mirror to keep an eye behind us to see if we're being followed. If we are, get the license plate number and write it down." She looked at him. "You okay?"

"I'm okay now." He adjusted the rear view mirror and got the gun.

"We'll get them, Ed. I promise you that. The police at the highest level are involved. Pat's turned out to be a bit of a national hero. Her photo will be all over the television news. Thank God for the BBC."

Ed kept his eyes on the mirror. "Never thought I'd agree with that."

Little was said as they made their way west toward Heathrow airport. Ed could see no car following them. Carolyn drove slowly enough for them to be easily followed.

"I feel terrible that we let Pat go with Roy," Ed finally admitted.

"Don't get me wrong on this, Ed," Carolyn replied, "but if we had gone together, then the three of us would be in trouble."

"And?"

"And we can do things the police can't."

"Such as?"

"Such as carry that gun and use it if we see fit."

"That's not legal is it?"

"No."

He thought for a moment. "Yeah, okay."

"We can also break down doors without a search warrant. We can beat the truth out of anybody we need to. We know who we're dealing with. We can act accordingly."

"But that's still breaking the law."

"So what's your point?"

He shook his head. "No point!"

"We don't have to do those things, Ed. I hope it doesn't come to that. But if it does, we'll do whatever it takes."

"All that on our own authority?"

"No."

"Your father's?"

"Higher."

He rubbed his eyes. "Oh God!"

Carolyn reached over and touched his hand. "Not that high."

The man shouted as he threw water on Pat's face. "Not so fucking brave now, are you bitch?" He slapped her face, increasing the flow of blood from her now swollen lip. He was huge, and his weight hit her full force

Pat looked up at him. She wanted to speak, but the pain was too much. If only they would leave her alone. She licked the water that ran to her mouth. Her head rolled forward and she passed out again. He hit her again, just because he could.

Ed tipped the bellboy, and thanked him. Carolyn was switching channels, trying to find the news. Their bags were side by side. The flowers Carolyn had ordered were on the table by the side of the bed.

"Not what I had planned," Carolyn muttered, taking her mobile out of her purse and looking at her watch. "Three minutes."

Exactly on time the mobile rang. Carolyn let it ring twice and answered it. "Crowe's nest."

Ed watched as she listened intently on the phone. She took no notes. He was amazed at her manner. He wanted to swear and curse, throw something at the wall. She looked at him as she nodded her understanding. She gave the hotel name, the room number, and hung up.

Carolyn picked up the remote and changed channels to BBC. "Your mum is on the way to Stonebridge Manor for a visit. In less than ten minutes there will be a special broadcast about the kidnapping," she announced. "It will be on most channels. A reward is being offered, and a special telephone number has been set aside for calls."

"Surely they don't expect any real calls?"

She shrugged. "They expect one from the kidnappers. They want it easy for them to get in contact."

"How much is the reward?"

"Ten thousand pounds."

Ed gulped. "Christ! That's a lot of money."

"Maybe enough to squeal on your friends for. That's a possibility."

"What do we do?"

"Sit and wait. Order some food. We'll have guests in less than an hour."

"Police?"

"Scotland Yard. The SCD—Specialist Crime Directorate."

"Is that good?"

"It's their best and brightest."

"That feels good."

As best she could, Carolyn smiled. "By the way, my father is like a raging bull. And to make matters worse my mother is ready to divorce him if he doesn't get Pat back; and soon."

Ed rolled his eyes. "Hopefully she'll calm down before my mum gets there."

"Don't worry about that, she'll be like nothing is happening. She has a way of controlling her anger very well."

"Runs in the family does it?" Ed asked, raising his eyebrows.

She nodded. "I'm sick inside, but I know its best not to show it."

Ed walked to her and gave her a hug. "Let's do what should always be done in an emergency."

Carolyn frowned. "I hope you're not thinking . . ."

Ed interrupted, picking up the phone. "I'll order some tea."

Hanging her head in embarrassment for thinking what she did, she muttered to herself something about 'bloody tea'. The television screen broke away from the program it was running, announcing a Special Bulletin. Carolyn turned up the volume, and they sat to watch.

The screen opened to a podium and a police officer standing behind it. At the bottom of the screen, his name was shown: Sir Robert Newman, Commissioner, Metropolitan Police. He was in full uniform. He waited for a second for the people in the room to stop talking.

> *"Good evening ladies and Gentlemen. My name is Robert Newman and I am the Commissioner of the Metropolitan Police, sometimes known as Scotland Yard.*
>
> *I am speaking to you tonight to ask for your assistance in finding a very brave young lady and her friend. You may remember her from the many photos and television news broadcasts about her and her husband's public announcements in Paris yesterday. A photo of her is on your television screen at this time. She is a Canadian guest in Britain and she was kidnapped, along with a family friend, less than two hours ago from the parking area at London's Heathrow Airport. The whereabouts of her husband is unknown at this time."*

Ed gasped at the comment as a photo of him filled the screen

*"While we have some information about the kidnapping,
I am personally asking for everyone's assistance in finding
her and her friend. Her name is Pat Weston. Her friend's
name is being held confidential at this time. However I
can tell you he needs daily medication for diabetes. If he
does not receive his daily medication by early tomorrow
morning he will slip into a diabetic coma. The person, or
persons, holding him captive will be held accountable to
the full extent of the law.*

*If you have any information on the location of Pat
Weston or her friend, then I would ask you to phone the
Metropolitan Police at the number now on your television
screen.*

*A reward of ten thousand pounds is being offered to
anyone providing information to the safe release of these
two people.*

Thank you and good evening"

Ed turned to Carolyn with a genuine look of amazement. "Me lost? Diabetes?"

Carolyn shrugged. "Method in their madness. If someone phones to say they have you too, then that's a crank call right? If, on the other hand, someone phones claiming to have them and they start asking questions about what kind of medication is needed." She paused. "Well maybe, just maybe."

In a dingy room in a dilapidated house in the Kilburn area of London a television was switched off. Four men were in the room, standing and sitting around a kitchen table that hadn't been cleaned for weeks. Empty cans of beer were strewn around the room and on the table.

"What the fuck is going on?" the man shouted, turning back from switching off the television. "Ten thousand fucking notes is more than we were going to demand in the first fucking place. And what the shit is this bollocks about medication?"

The remaining three men said nothing.

Pacing the floor, he continued. "I don't believe this medication shit. It's a fucking trick I say!"

A man with a tattoo of a swastika on the back oh his neck spoke up. "He's a goner if it's real, Mike. My aunt in Watford . . ."

"Fuck your aunt in fucking Watford." Mike shouted. "Who gives a fuck about your aunt?"

"Maybe his fucking uncle?" A man sitting at the table made the comment with a grin. He was older than the others, balding and massive in size. He crushed an empty beer can and threw it on the floor. "I say we kill them now and toss 'em in the canal."

"Fuck you, arsehole," the youngest man shouted, tipping the table as he stood. "I ain't killing no-one." He waved a piece of paper. "Let's make the call, get the fucking money and dump 'em—alive."

Mike raised his hand to get silence and spoke with authority. "Okay, cool it. Tiny, we ain't about to kill 'em unless we have to. They're white for Christ's sake." He turned to the younger man. "Control yourself, Billy. And have some respect for your fucking elders!"

Billy nodded his understanding and put the table back in its place. Acknowledging his role, he got four more beers from the fridge. He flipped opened Tiny's beer and handed it to him.

"Okay, that's more like it," Mike said, opening his beer. "Now let's discuss what we do to get our hands on the money like fucking business men."

They banged their hands on the table and laughed.

In the next room, Pat pulled at the ropes that held her hands behind her. They didn't give. The ropes were attached to the chair she sat in. Her head hurt and her face was swollen. Worst of all she needed to pee. But she wasn't about to give the bastards that held her the pleasure of seeing her pee her pants. She turned her head toward Roy who was tied and gagged on the floor behind her. She had heard him come-to.

She whispered over her shoulder. "Roy, you okay?"

Roy grunted through the smelly rag tied around his head and through his mouth.

Relieved, she tried to smile. "Kick the floor once for 'yes', and twice for 'no', okay?"

He kicked the floor once.

"Good man," she whispered. "I bet you regret offering me a ride . . ."

He kicked the floor twice.

"I owe you a beer," she whispered.

He kicked the floor three times.

She thought about the message for a second. "Okay, three beers."

He kicked the floor once.

"Deal." She replied. "Listen Roy, when these guys return pretend you're still unconscious, okay?"

He didn't respond.

"That's an order, Roy."

He kicked the floor once.

They heard movement from the next room. Roy closed his eyes and relaxed. Pat shook her head to clear her thoughts.

The tea arrived at the same time as the two police officers. Ed poured, as Carolyn gave the official report of what had happened. She managed to provide enough data without delving into the details of the involvement of the prime minister and the Canadian government. Ed smiled inwardly and made a mental note to ask her if the providing of filtered information was an Oxford University course. If it was, she must have passed with honors. The two officers had presented themselves as Detective Sergeant McMahon and Detective Constable

Nash They wasted no time with informalities, taking detailed notes as Carolyn outlined the details.

McMahon turned to Ed. "And you're the young lady's husband?"

"No," Ed answered.

"Yes," Carolyn replied at the same time.

The detective closed his notepad. "What we have here," he said calmly, "is a failure to communicate." He adjusted himself in the chair and crossed his legs. "Now D.C. Nash and I are currently working on a double murder of a young couple in East London. They did not have a very good life these young people, but had a terrible death. Now if we're here to work on a kidnapping that is only hours old, either we've been demoted unceremoniously, or someone has pulled strings." He offered a quick smile. "Now it isn't likely that we've been demoted, since we are the most successful partnership in the SCD. So perhaps, nice people, you could eliminate the BS and give us the straight goods?"

Detective Constable Nash spoke for the first time, adding with a phony American accent. "Just the facts ma'am, just the facts."

Ed held off responding as Carolyn lifted her hand to get attention. She thought carefully before she spoke.

"It's not our intention, gentlemen, to make things difficult for you; in fact the opposite is the case. There are some details that we are simply not at liberty to divulge. I will assure you however, that we will not hold back anything that will help in finding Miss Weston and Mr. Johnston. In the matter of your specific question, Mr. Crowe and Miss Weston are not married and were not on their honeymoon in Paris."

McMahon took a deep breath. "And you are, miss? And how are you involved in this chain of events?"

"I am Carolyn Andrews. I work for The Commonwealth and Foreign Office and was at the British Embassy in Paris when the world was watching the events of yesterday."

D.C. Nash turned to Ed. "And why would you turn to the British Embassy in Paris, when both yourself and Miss Weston are Canadian?"

Carolyn responded before Ed could speak. "I am a personal friend of both Miss Weston and Mr. Crowe, gentlemen. Miss Weston works for Export Canada and we have had dealings when promoting trade between the two countries."

"And Mr. Crowe?" Nash continued.

"He is a close friend of my family and has been for some time," Carolyn answered.

Nash looked at his notebook. "I see Mr. Crowe's mother lives in Kensal Rise. Is that where your parents live, Miss Andrews?"

Carolyn smiled. "No."

McMahon flipped open his notebook. "This room was booked earlier today for one night, is that correct? And for what purpose was it rented?"

Carolyn was ready. "After I drove Mr. Crowe to the airport, I was to stay here tonight and head back to Paris in the morning," she lied.

McMahon nodded slowly. "Good answer, Miss Andrews, very good. Now one final question for you, Miss Andrews: are you carrying a gun?"

She coughed to give her time to think. The gun from her car was tucked into the back of Ed's belt. She wanted her response to be as accurate as possible. The detectives were obviously aware something was far from normal. "No, Detective, I am not."

He turned to Ed. "And your gun, Mr. Crowe. Where is it?"

Ed blinked, and repeated the question in his head. He hoped his relief didn't show. "My gun is safely stored in its regular location, Detective Sergeant McMahon."

McMahon picked up his cup of tea and toasted them. "I'm glad we know where we all stand. Now let's work together to get your friends back safe and sound."

Tiny led the four men into the room. He kicked Roy's legs as he passed him, not bothering to see if he responded in any way. He didn't. Tiny was more interested in Pat. He walked to her and with his huge frame only inches from her he swung his arm to hit her. His arm stopped dead in its tracks as Billy grabbed it and shoved Tiny backwards. Steadying himself, Tiny turned on Billy ready to fight. Billy was ready. His arm was aimed at Tiny and the knife in his hand was large enough to do serious damage.

Billy sneered, spitting with anger as he waved the knife. "Leave her the fuck alone, fat man. She's a lady and you're just a fat pig."

Tiny knew better than to attack. Billy had used the knife before. Instead he turned to Mike. "Who d'think he is? Some knight in shining fucking armor?"

Mike laughed at the scene. "Put it away, Billy," he said, standing between the two men. He turned to Tiny. "And you keep your hands to yourself. This little lady," he continued, "is worth a lot of money to us." He walked to Roy and shoved him with his feet. There was no response. "How hard did you hit this bastard," he demanded of the fourth man.

The man shrugged. "Just coshed him didn't I?"

Mike turned back to Pat. "Who is this bloke? He's not the one on the news with you from Paris."

Pat licked her lips. "He's my husband's best friend. He was driving me to the airport."

Mike paced the room several times. The three other men watched. Mike was the boss. They didn't interrupt his thinking. He did all of their thinking, and they were happy with that. They had plenty of money, beer, and drugs. They wanted nothing more—except Tiny who wanted to beat on all women.

"So what do you know about him?" Mike demanded.

Pat closed her eyes to think. What was going on she wondered. Mike looked worried, and it was obvious it wasn't about her. Her mind raced. What is he looking for?

"He's not a cop, if that's what you're thinking."

Mike shook his head in disgust. "That's fucking obvious for Christ's sake. What else?"

Pat shook her head. "Look I need to go to the washroom.'

"What!" Mike shouted.

"The toilet," Billy said. "She needs to go to the bog."

Mikes eyes rolled. "Too bad. Tell me more about your fucking friend and then Billy here will escort you to the fucking washroom, toilet, bog, or whatever else you want to call it."

Pat screamed back at him. "I barely know the guy. He's a printing salesman for crying out load." She started crying and an idea exploded in her head. "He's been unconscious for a long time. Is he okay? He had to take a pill earlier. Christ, I'm feeling sick myself."

"Just like my fucking aunt in Watford," the fourth man said. "I told ya, that diabetes shit is bad."

Mike turned on him. "Shut your face, Terry. And you," he said turning to Billy, "gag that bitch."

Billy walked to Pat and pulled out a hanky from his pocket. He twirled it to make a gag. "It's clean lady. My ol' lady washed it yesterday. I haven't used it, honest."

"Who gives a toss if it's clean you turd," Tiny shouted. "Just gag her or I'll do it."

Pat opened her mouth and Billy tied the hanky at the back of her head. He tied it hard enough for everyone to see he did it properly. He didn't want anyone else touching Pat. She was a lady. His lady.

Mike nodded to the door. "Let's go make the call."

Tiny checked the gag as he walked passed Pat. Billy stood by her, making it clear he was Pat's protector. He wiped away Tiny's touch from her face. "I'll be back to let you go to the toilet," he said quietly. "Soon."

Pat smiled at him through the gag and thanked him with her eyes.

McMahon and Nash left the hotel room, agreeing to contact Carolyn and Ed as soon as they heard anything of interest. The four had concluded that if the ransom money is to be dropped then Ed, the husband, would be the carrier. Ed ordered more tea. After ordering he sat across the table from Carolyn, reached for her hand and held it in his.

"Tea's on its way, Miss Andrews," he smiled.

"We nearly lied about the gun." She squeezed his hand.

Ed shook his head. "You can't *nearly* lie, Miss Andrews."

"Then you came awfully close to nearly telling the truth."

He shrugged. "Somehow I think they knew we have a gun. He asked the question very carefully. Bye the way, I do love you, Miss Andrews."

She closed her eyes and smiled. "Yes, I know you do. Thank you for saying so. It makes me feel good."

He lifted her hand and kissed it. "I have an idea."

"I just bet you do," she laughed.

"Let's have another cup of tea, and then call it a night." He looked at his watch. "It's ten o'clock now. Maybe the call will happen during the night."

"And where will we sleep?"

"On the bed . . ."

"Really?" she interrupted.

". . . fully clothed, except for our shoes—and the gun."

"And ready to go!" she added, regretting her comment.

"At the drop of a hat."

"Sounds good."

"Just one request."

"Oh, oh. What is it?"

"You let me put my arms around you."

"No 'how's yer father' now."

"Just my arms around you."

She leaned over and kissed his cheek. "That would be lovely, Ed."

The tea arrived. Ed played mother.

Billy re-tied Pat's hands behind her back—tight, but not too tight. She was relieved and thankful for the washroom break. It also allowed her a precious few minutes with her gag removed. With Roy still bound and gagged on the floor behind her, she couldn't afford to waste any time.

"Billy," she asked quietly, "is my friend diabetic? If he is, that could be dangerous."

"I dunno." He stepped back from her, hanging his head slightly.

"How old are you, Billy," Pat asked.

"Old enough."

She nodded. "Okay, Billy. Can I call you Billy, or is it William?"

He grinned a little. "Only me mum calls me William. Friends think its sissy-like."

"Okay Billy it is. You can call me Pat. Okay?"

He nodded and shuffled his feet. "Yeah, okay—Pat."

Pat continued, keeping her voice low. "Look, Billy, I know you have to go back with your friends, but I want to thank you for treating me like a lady and escorting me to the washroom. Okay?"

"Yeah," he grinned. "Sorry 'bout what Tiny did to ya face. Won't happen again, promise."

"Thank you, Billy. You're a gentleman."

He blushed and pulled out his hanky to put back the gag.

"Just one thing, Billy," Pat said, motioning with her head to Roy behind her. "If my friend Roy is diabetic, he needs medications. If he doesn't get them he'll have a fit, and he could die."

Billy gulped. "Christ!" he muttered, and put the gag back on Pat. "Gotta go." He left the room, closing the door behind him.

Pat waited for a minute. No sound from outside.

Roy kicked the floor once—an okay signal.

Pat grunted an 'Okay' as best she could.

The phone rang, and within seconds Carolyn picked it up. She shook her head to wake up. Ed quickly jumped from the bed, tucked the gun into the back of his belt and slipped on his jacket.

"They'll be up in two minutes," Carolyn said.

They straightened the bed covers and pillows. Carolyn went into the bathroom to freshen up. Ed combed his hair with his fingers and stepped into his shoes. He looked at his watch. It was two-thirty in the morning—three and a half hours rest, little actual sleep. When the knock on the door happened they were both ready and fully awake. As if planned, Carolyn walked to the door and Ed dialed Room Service to order tea.

McMahon and Nash entered the room wearing the same clothes they had been wearing hours ago. If they were tired, they didn't show it. McMahon acknowledged the order of tea with a smile and a nod.

"We got the call," Nash said looking at his notepad. "Fifteen minutes ago. Not long-distance, so somewhere in London. Not enough time to trace."

McMahon sat at the table. "We're reasonably sure it's for real. London accents. Want to move quickly. We assume because of the medical issue." He shrugged. "Who knows?"

Carolyn jumped in. "Did they say . . . ?"

"They said they were both fine." Nash answered, interrupting.

"Anything else?" Ed asked.

Nash nodded. "They, or should I say he, was more than interested in the ten grand. It's got to be a lot of play money for them. We think that may have helped the situation."

"Now what? Carolyn asked.

McMahon answered. "They phone us back at five this morning and tell us where to deliver the money. We're to ask no questions, just get the address. So for now, the four of us head to Scotland Yard and wait. They'll be assuming that's where the money is, so that's our base." He grinned. "But first, that cup of tea."

Mike and Billy entered the room, switching on the light. Roy tried to sit up, mumbling through the tape over his mouth as best he could. He looked up at the men entering the room, begging them with his eyes to remove the tape. Mike motioned to Billy, who swiftly cut the tape and ripped it off, skin and whiskers included. Roy opened and closed his mouth to get comfortable.

"What the sodding hell are you doing?" Roy demanded. "And who the hell are you?"

"None of you fucking business," Mike replied. "Just shut your mouth and listen. You too." He stood in front of Pat, pointing at her.

Roy motioned to speak, but backed off as Billy held the knife in front of him.

Testing to make sure Billy had Pat's gag tight enough, Mike moved behind her and untied it. He let it slip. It rested on the swell of her breasts.

"Thanks," she said, ignoring the gag's location.

Mike crossed his arms, taking on a superior role. He spoke as if he was doing everyone a personal favor. "You're out of here soon; just as soon as we get the money and make our escape. Do as you're told and you'll be fine. Lip off, and Billy here will mark you for life." He pointed to Pat. "And that includes you lady, don't it, Billy?"

Billy nodded.

"How long?" Roy asked, coughing as he spoke.

"What the fuck do you care?" Mike responded, walking to Roy. "In a rush are we?"

"Nah," Roy responded indignantly, "I've got all the time in the world, dun I?"

Grabbing Billy's knife, Mike shoved it within inches of Roy's face. "Do'ya now? Well that's just fucking brilliant, init?"

Pat closed her eyes, waiting for Roy to reply.

Roy closed his eyes and spoke slowly. "Well maybe not all the time."

"Oh fuck," Billy groaned.

"Shut the fuck up, Billy," Mike demanded. He looked down to Roy, gesturing with the knife. He was visibly nervous. He spoke slowly to control his emotions and retain his superiority. "What are you talking about mister?"

Roy licked his lips. "I'm on medications. I need them by nine a.m."

"Oh holy fuck," Billy groaned, turning his back to the room.

"Jesus Christ!" Pat muttered.

Mike turned on her and smacked Pat's face as hard as he could muster.

Billy went wild, reaching for Mike with his hands and stopping only when he faced the blade of his own knife and a furious leader.

"Shut the fuck up, Billy," Mike screamed, bringing the action to a quick end. He motioned toward Pat. "Look after your girlfriend, Billy. She'll be gone soon."

Gingerly Billy removed the gag from Pat's chest and wiped the blood dripping from her lip. He mouthed 'sorry'. Pat nodded her thanks.

Mike closed his eyes to think. He paced the floor, returning to face Roy.

"And what happens if you don't get these medications?"

"They're in the glove compartment of my car," Roy said casually. "Just bring them to me, no big deal."

Mike's face grew red, his anger showing through. "We didn't take your bloody car! What happens?"

Roy pulled a face and swallowed. "I'll go into a coma."

"And then what for Christ's sake?"

As best he could, Roy shrugged. "If I don't get an injection in a few hours, my insulin levels reverse inconsistently and . . ."

"And what?" Mike shouted.

"I die."

"Billy," Mike shouted, "let's go. We've got to work something out."

The two men left the room, leaving the lights on.

Pat waited several minutes, turned her head to Roy and whispered. "Insulin levels inconsistently?"

"Best I could do." Roy whispered back.

"Let us pray for ignorance."

"Our Father . . ."

"Yeah right."

CHAPTER SIX

FRIDAY, AUGUST 16TH 1985

At exactly five o'clock the phone in the SDC war room rang. McMahon let it ring three times. Also in the room were DC Nash, Carolyn and Ed. Each wore a headphone attached to the phone set. In the next room a specially trained police officer sat at a computer, ready to search for the number of the incoming call on a computer attached to British Telecom. McMahon leaned into the speaker phone and spoke slowly.

"Detective Sergeant McMahon speaking, who is speaking please?"

Mike wasted no time. "You got the money?"

"Yes we do. How are . . ."

"Shut up and listen. Take the money to Hampstead Heath railway station and be there in twenty minutes. Walk up to the ponds. Just one person and the money. No cops. Understood?"

Nash quickly removed his headphone and quietly left the room.

McMahon continued. "We understand. The money will be there. For your information it will be the lady's husband who will be delivering the money."

"Very romantic. Now goodbye."

"Whoa, hang on there. We need to know these people are okay, and how do we recover them?"

"We'll phone you when we get the money. They're safe."

McMahon took a risk. "Then let me hear them speak. They must be with you. No proof, no money."

Mike beat his hand against the table. His nerves were showing and he knew it. With his mobile gripped in his hand, he ran into the next room.

He shoved the mobile in front of Roy's face. "Say something!"

"Good morning." Roy said.

Mike moved over to Pat and held the phone in front of her.

She grinned at Mike. "Piss off."

"Twenty minutes." Mike clicked the phone off.

"Well that was Pat for sure," Ed said.

"And Roy," Carolyn added.

McMahon walked for the door. "Let's go."

The officer working the computer turned to the three of them. "Mobile, sir. Can only tell you it was a Kilburn sub-station number, but they could have phoned from anywhere."

McMahon punched the air. "Good. We're closing in!"

DC Nash watched from a park bench. He could see the Hampstead Heath railway station to his right and the ponds behind the trees to his left. He sat comfortably, feeding the pigeons that danced around him pecking at the breadcrumbs he threw every so often. The microphone was attached to his chest, and the earphone ran through his hair into his left ear. He hated pigeons, considered them no better than mice with wings. Feeding birds was a perfect blind for surveillance. It allowed him to look around and watch the world, even chat to people walking by.

"Here birdie, birdies," he called, throwing a few more breadcrumbs.

The taxi dropped Ed off outside of the train station and took off right away. He carried the briefcase with ten thousand pounds packed neatly in small bundles. The bills were real and not in numerical order. The goal was to recover the people, not the money. That would come later.

Ed looked around, taking in the view. It had been eighteen minutes of hair-raising driving, and a promise of a large tip, to get him to the station on time. He turned to his right and walked toward the ponds. He had made this walk many times, mostly when the annual fair with its rides and games took over the lower end of the Heath. No toffee apples today he realized. No sneaking a kiss on the Haunted House ride. Strictly business today, and serious business at that. He walked slowly holding the briefcase tightly and his head high. He wanted to see everything around him.

Nash watched from across the street. There was little traffic this early and the sun was barely into the sky. He opened his thermos and poured himself some tea. As he took a drink, he spoke quietly.

"Crowe's arrived." He smiled as he thought about the remark. Feeding the pigeons and a Crowe arrives on the scene. The humor wasn't missed at the other end.

"Don't feed him." McMahon said blandly.

Nash threw some more breadcrumbs. "Here birdie, birdies," he said, talking to the birds. "Walking up to the ponds. No one in sight."

Ed stopped. Maybe he was too early. He looked around. A few people were walking quickly to the train station, and an old man was feeding birds at five-thirty in the morning. Bloody idiot, he thought. He continued walking. Twenty yards ahead he met a short heavy man dressed in working clothes and an Andy Capp hat searching his pockets for a match to light the cigarette drooping from his mouth.

"Got a light, mate?" the man asked, smiling.

"Sorry don't smoke." Ed moved to walk on.

"Okay, just give me the fucking money." The smile was now gone, replaced with a smirk and a row of rotten teeth.

Ed gripped the briefcase tighter. "Where's my wife?"

Tiny held out his hand. "Just gimme the fucking money or you'll never see her again."

Ed followed instructions. Make the man nervous. Get him to say something—anything.

"Just tell me where she is. I don't care about the money. What about my friend? Are they okay?"

Tiny looked around, expecting a police car to pull up at any time. "They're just fucking fine. They ain't far from here, but you won't see 'em again if you don't smarten up." He held his hand out further.

Ed put the briefcase on the ground between them and stepped back.

Tiny was now feeling comfortable. He was a winner. He picked up the briefcase, keeping his eyes on Ed. "Okay, now give me your wallet." He grinned. "Just for me."

Ed shook his head. "Not part of the deal."

Tiny grinned and made a huge mistake. "Just give me your wallet, and I'll make sure she don't suffer no more."

Ed reached back for his wallet.

"Jesus Christ!" Nash shouted. "Crowe's just shot the fat bastard. Send in a car and an ambulance—rush!" He ran across the street, scattering the pigeons as he ran.

Tiny rolled in the dust grabbing his left leg, screaming at the top of his voice. "You shot me for fuck's sake. You shot me!"

Ed walked closer to him, training the gun to his head. "Now where are they?"

Nash stopped six feet away from Ed, raising his hand as a warning. Ed nodded to him and turned to Tiny. "If you don't tell me where they are, I'm going to blow your balls into the middle of next week." He lowered the gun to Tiny's groin.

Tiny looked at Nash hoping for help, still trying to stop the blood from the bullet wound in his leg. "He can't do that! This is England for fuck's sake."

Nash shrugged. "He's Canadian."

Ed lowered the gun, inches from Tiny's groin. "One, two . . ."

"Okay, okay, I'll tell ya." He burst into tears of pain as he spoke.

Nash relayed the address quickly into the microphone. "Eight Kimberly Rd, in Kilburn. I'll go with the fat man to hospital; Crowe to the address. Out!"

The sounds of the police car was immediate, it had been sitting just a few blocks away ready to assist. The sound of the ambulance was further in the distance. Nash handcuffed Tiny, allowing him room to keep pressure on his wound. He turned to Ed.

"You said you had no gun, cowboy!" He gritted through his teeth.

Ed nodded. "Look I'm sorry, but I said my gun was stowed away. It is." He slipped the gun back into the holster and walked to the waiting police car. "I'll return this to its owner—immediately."

Tiny took his best revenge. He shouted at Ed. "Don't blame me if young Billy knifes your fucking old lady!" He grimaced outwardly, but grinned inside.

Ed's heart sank at the comment. He slipped quickly into the rear of the police car, which sped off immediately. He gave the driver the address. "Emergency. Please rush. It's off Willesden Lane," he added.

The driver nodded. "Just down the street from the State cinema. Used to live just 'round the corner."

"Kensal Rise myself," Ed offered, trying to control his emotions.

"Nice to meet ya' I'm sure," the driver said over his shoulder. "Hang onto your hat." He flipped on the siren and warning lights, and stepped on the accelerator.

The car all but flew through the streets of London heading west to Kilburn through Kentish Town and Swiss Cottage. Crossing Kilburn High Rd from Quex Rd into Willesden lane, Ed was now in an area he had played in as a child and where he had shopped with his mother. Thinking back allowed him, temporarily at least, to stop thinking about the danger Pat and Roy were in. His mind cleared of the past quickly as the driver turned left onto Kimberly Rd, and past the two police cars that had blocked all other traffic. The fact that Kimberly

Rd was a 'Dead End' road, with a sign to remind him, didn't help. As the car drew to a stop he jumped out, reaching back to ensure the gun was safely tucked in his belt.

Police, some carrying what looked like semi-automatic weapons strapped to their shoulders, surrounded the house. The weapons surprised Ed. He had never seen a Bobby carry a gun before. It struck him as a strange sign of progress. An ambulance sat parked up the street. In the alcove by the front door were DS McMahon and Carolyn. Neither carried a gun that could be seen. Ed walked up to them, not needing to ask a question.

McMahon spoke clearly and concisely. "At least one man in the back room with the hostages. We're assuming it's the 'Billy' your man mentioned. Back door is barred. We tried to break in . . ." He shook his head. "When we got close, he threatened to hurt someone. He sounds young and very scared."

"He threatened Pat, right?" Ed asked.

Carolyn shook her head. "He said he'd carve-up the bloke with the mouth! His words."

Ed closed his eyes. "That's Roy then!"

McMahon continued. "The rest of the house is empty. Obviously more than just the two of them were holed up. We have to assume the remaining number left to meet up with your fat man—and the money."

"What's the plan?" Ed asked.

"No choice," McMahon answered. "The longer we wait the more dangerous he gets. You go in and get your wife and friend out. Take the money with you."

Ed gasped. "I didn't bring the bloody money."

McMahon waved to a constable. "We have more. Don't worry, it's real."

The constable walked over with a briefcase and set it on the step.

"Here's the plan," McMahon said, sliding the briefcase to Ed with his foot.

Roy was now sitting up leaning against the wall. His eyes were half closed, his head hung to one side, and he gurgled every thirty seconds.

Billy walked nervously up and down the small room, shaking his head at every gurgle. "What am I supposed to do with him?" he asked Pat with fear in his voice. "I don't want him dead for Christ's sake. Can't he just get up and walk out of here?"

The thought crossed Roy's mind, but he decided to stay with the plan—he gurgled again.

"Billy," Pat said firmly, "listen to me. When they come back, and they will come back, let them take Roy. Billy, do the right thing now. Do what your mother would want you to do, Billy." She paused. She spoke softly now. "Billy, he's my friend. He's a good man, honest. Okay he spouted off a few times. He's just like that. He lips-off to everyone, Billy. Please, Billy, do the right thing from now on."

A knock on the door turned the room silent. Roy forgot to gurgle.

Ed counted to five. "Billy. My name is Ed Crowe. You have my wife and friend in there. Let me come in please. I have the money, Billy."

"Fuck the money" Billy shouted to the door.

Roy gurgled, louder this time.

Pat looked at Billy, begging with her eyes. "Let me, Billy. Please?"

Billy raised his hand holding the knife, and nodded to Pat.

"Ed," Pat called out. "Come in slowly. Not too many of you and no funny business. Your only goal is to take out Roy." She raised her voice. "Do you understand, Ed?"

"Understood," Ed said, and slowly opened the door.

The scene was not good. Pat was tied to a chair with her back to him, some six feet away. Roy was to his left, tongue hanging out and gurgling. On the other side of Pat, with his knife pointing at her was a very nervous Billy.

Ed moved slowly to his right, keeping his hands raised. Behind him, Carolyn and DS McMahon didn't waste any time. They half carried and half dragged Roy out of the room. Ed carefully closed the door behind them and lowered his arms to his side. "He'll live now," he said, motioning to the door. "Well done, Billy."

"Yeah right," Billy said, relaxing for a moment, closing his eyes.

When he opened them he was looking directly into the barrel of Ed's gun. He immediately raised his knife and moved closer to Pat, threatening.

Ed kept his look on Billy's eyes. "I've already shot one of your friends today, Billy. Don't think for a second I won't shoot you."

"Hey, hey," Pat shouted. "Cool it you two." She turned her head to speak to Ed. "Put the gun down, Ed. Lower it okay?"

"Not a chance, Pat. The fat man warned me about young Billy here."

Billy grinned. "You shot Tiny! I hope the fuck you killed him. Fat good-for-nothing slob."

For the first time Ed noticed the swell of Pat's face and the dried blood on her chin. He raised his gun, aiming it at Billy's heart. "You sonovabitch. You miserable . . ."

"Mister," Pat shouted, now using Ed's code name. "Put down the god-damned gun. Billy here has been my protector. The fat bastard you shot did this to me."

Ed lowered the gun. Pat had no reason to lie. He put on the safety and slipped the gun into the front of his belt. He moved forward to untie Pat. Billy made to gesture for him to stop.

Pat interrupted. "Ed—Mister, please go outside and come back in five minutes."

Ed couldn't believe his ears. "What? Are you frigging crazy? No way am I . . ."

Pat spoke calmly. "Five minutes, Mister. Then come back in slowly. And calm down out there."

Raising his hands in disbelief, Ed left the room.

"Now what, lady?" Billy asked. "I can't just give up. I'll be finished—a no-hoper. I can't just give myself up."

"Please call me Pat." She waited for him to smile. "Billy, we don't have a lot of time. Listen to me and do as I ask, please."

Billy shrugged acceptance.

"Now close the knife Billy, and step closer."

He did as he was told.

"Now, Billy. I want you to undo the two top buttons of my blouse and tuck the knife into in my bra."

Billy stepped back, almost falling over. "Are you crazy? Shit, your old man will kill me for sure."

"He's not my husband, Billy. He's a very good friend and we work together sometimes. Now please do as I say."

"Two minutes," Ed shouted through the door.

"Do it Billy. Now!"

Billy fumbled with her buttons, his hands shaking. He drew her blouse open and laid the knife on her breasts.

"Tuck it in, Billy."

Closing his eyes, he tucked the knife in, feeling the warmth of her breasts. "Oh God," he groaned. "I'm sorry, Pat, I didn't mean to . . ."

"Do the buttons up, Billy."

He did as he was told and stepped back.

"Now, Billy, put your hands on the top of your head. Not behind your head, on top. And intertwine you fingers. Remember, do as I say."

He did as he was told. "Okay."

"Okay what?"

"Okay, Pat." He smiled briefly.

"One final question, Billy. Just between you and me. How did you guys know we were in London?"

Billy thought before he replied. "Your friend's mother let the neighbors know you were going to visit. Her neighbor's son is Mike's best friend and told him, but he didn't know what Mike and us did then."

"You can come in now" Pat called out.

Ed entered the room followed by DS McMahon, DC Nash, and Carolyn.

Carolyn and Ed untied Pat, while the police officers patted down Billy.

"Okay, where's the knife?" McMahon demanded.

"He threw it away." Pat stood up adjusting her clothes.

"Like shit he did," McMahon grunted, looking around the room.

Carolyn looked up from Pat's chest with a questioning stare.

"I have to powder my nose," Pat said, and left the room. She returned less than a minute later. The knife was gone. "That's better," she said. She walked over to Ed. "The gun please."

Ed gave her the gun. She walked over to Billy, standing two feet from him. "Close you eyes, Billy." She spoke calmly, aiming the gun at him.

McMahon and Nash couldn't believe what they were seeing. "What the hell are you doing?" Nash demanded to know.

"She's saving my life," Billy said, squeezing his eyes shut tight.

Pat pulled the trigger. The bullet ripped a three-inch wound in Billy's side. He knelt on one knee to help stop the bleeding. His hands didn't move from the top of his head.

Nash spoke into the microphone on his lapel. "We need a medic in here!"

McMahon shook his head. "Resisting arrest, right?"

Pat nodded, handing the gun back to Ed. She walked over to Billy, now on both knees to ease the pain. Pat knelt down by his side.

"Billy. I'm going to give this nice policeman my address in Canada. When you end up in a place where you feel comfortable to write, write me okay?"

"Yeah, I will, Pat," he managed through the pain. "Thanks for shooting me, yeah?"

"One question Billy. Where did Mike and Terry go?"

"Bradford," Billy answered. "They're heading to Bradford."

"Look after your mum, Billy." Pat left the room, followed by Carolyn and Ed. As they left two medics entered the room and quickly started working on Billy.

In what was intended to be the living room but looked more like a run-down bar, Roy stood in the corner giving an outline of the events to DC Nash. DS McMahon joined them as two officers walked Billy out of the house, now handcuffed and bandaged.

"Don't say anything without a lawyer present, Billy," Pat called after him.

"And whose side are you on?" asked an amazed McMahon.

Pat smiled up at him. "The side of justice, sir. May I ask . . . ?"

McMahon introduced himself and DC Nash who had wrapped up his note taking.

"You won't get much out of Billy," Roy said, walking over to Pat and shaking her hand. "Our Canadian friend here found out more about Billy and the rest of his associates than he'll ever tell you. She had him wrapped around her little finger." He looked at Pat. "And I do mean little."

"He's just a kid," Pat said, ignoring the remark. "Just a poor kid being led around by those other English assholes."

"Just a poor kid that regularly carries an illegal flick-knife," Nash added coldly. "Society's to blame I'm sure!"

"Well if you listen to Billy," Roy responded, "yes, society is to blame. His belief is that foreigners have overtaken Britain, certainly his part of London. Foreigners that don't speak English, don't want to learn English, and never will speak English. They've taken our jobs and our homes and to quote him, 'they don't give a shit about the Queen or the English way of life'"

McMahon raised his hands. "Not our job to sort out the world's problems, ladies and gentlemen. Let's finalize our reports and send you people home. And for God's sake," he said, turning to Carolyn, "put that gun away will you. Two shootings in one day is New York thank you very much, not London."

Roy leaned over to Ed. "Did you really shoot a bloke today?"

"Yeah," Ed responded, "but only in his leg."

"Only in his leg?" Roy groaned. "Wasn't he lucky!"

Nash added to the conversation. "He threatened to shoot him elsewhere actually."

Pat chuckled. "You didn't?"

Roy grimaced. "You mean in his . . . ?"

"Hey, it was just a threat," Ed replied quickly.

Roy shook his head. "What has Canada done to you, my boy? If only your mother knew."

Carolyn felt a need to comment. "It's the results that count, not the process. You're both free," she said, looking at Pat and Roy, "and it didn't cost the government a penny! Good day at the office I'd say."

"Oh my God," Roy exclaimed. "My friends are turning into a television program, and an American one at that!"

Pat jabbed Roy in his ribs. "Don't be rude now. No one died, did they?"

Roy chuckled at the thought. "How very Canadian. We shoot—but not to kill!"

"Now you've got it," Pat said with a wink. "We keep our *real* violence for hockey."

Roy checked his car over before he and Pat got in and did up their seat belts.

"Seems like I've been here before," Pat commented, looking around.

Roy nodded. "This won't be as interesting a drive," he quipped. He pulled the car out of the Police car park and headed toward Heathrow Airport.

"Appreciate your driving me," Pat said with a slight grin. "Maybe I'll catch the plane this time."

Roy looked at her from the corner of his eye. "I'll see you right into the security area this time, just to be sure."

"Make sure you're rid of me?"

"Make sure you're safe."

She looked out the rear window. "I assume the police escort right behind us is our safety net."

Roy grinned, looking in the rear view mirror. "He'll help, I'm sure." He paused. "So tell me something."

"Ask away."

"How come the police interviewed me and not you?"

She pretended to think. "Maybe they didn't want to bother me, what with my split lip and all."

Roy shook his head. "Don't play silly buggers."

Pat laughed. "Okay. Carolyn will answer all of their questions. It's the way it works."

"The way what works?"

Pat shook her head as an answer.

Roy could tell he wasn't going to get any further, and changed the discussion. "She's a nice lady; Carolyn."

"Yes she is." Pat turned to face him, eager to continue. "I understand you asked her to marry you the first day you met her?"

"Kind of."

"Kind of? How can you *kind of* ask someone to marry you?"

Roy kept his eyes on the road. "Well it really wasn't a marriage proposal. It was my way of inviting her into our circle of friends." He chuckled. "It had Eddie worried, but she knew what I meant."

"I see," Pat replied, turning to face the road ahead. Her lips took on a slightly sulky look.

"Hey, don't give me that look," Roy laughed. "You should be inviting me into your circle of friends. I'm the outsider here."

"Well I hope you're not expecting me to ask you to marry me, for God's sake?"

"That would be a first."

"I'm sure."

"Scared I might say yes?" He turned to see her response.

She held her hand to her face, feigning fear. "No, Roy, I don't think the word would be *scared*."

"Hmm," he mumbled, thinking. He kept his eyes on the road, turning south toward Heathrow. "So what would the word be?" he finally asked.

"Terrified, perhaps?"

"Ouch!"

"Can we change the subject, Roy?"

"Sure."

They drove in silence for several minutes. The signposts indicated they were only a few kilometers from Heathrow.

"Can we be friends, Roy?" Pat asked, putting her hand on his arm.

"I'd like that, Pat," Roy grinned. "I'd like that a lot."

She took a business card from her purse and slipped it into his pocket. "Please phone me sometime."

"I will," Roy confirmed. "And I'll know better than to ask you about things you can't tell me."

"Just a civil servant doing her job," she quipped.

The police escort stood thirty feet back as Roy and Pat stood at the security entrance at Heathrow. He smiled at the difference in their height. Pat had to look up to speak to Roy, and he had to look down to maintain eye contact.

Roy looked at Pat's business card, turning it over. "Do you always put your home phone number on the back?" he asked.

Pat gave a quick shrug. "I knew I was going to give you one."

"Organized little bugger aren't you?"

Pat waved a finger at him. "Enough of the *little*, if you don't mind. Little finger; little bugger. I don't call you Gulliver do I?"

"Nothing intended," Roy chuckled. "But I do think you'd make a terrific Munchkin lady."

Pat stood taller, now with her hands on her hips. "Listen Mr. Giraffe-man, enough of the lip, eh!"

Roy cringed. "Ouch. You sure can hurt a person's feelings."

She extended her right hand. "I've gotta go Roy." She spoke without humor.

Roy looked at her hand. "What am I supposed to do with that?"

"Shake hands," Pat snapped back. "Just like civilized people do. Pretend if you have to!"

"A gentleman doesn't shake hands with his lady friends."

Pat kept her hand extended. "Doesn't one? Pray tell what a gentleman doth do."

"'Tis better that I demonstrate than to explain through discourse." He took her right hand with his left hand and held it gently.

Pat kept eye contact. "That ain't shaking hands, mister."

Roy nodded. "You got that right."

"Are you flirting with me, Roy?"

"I do believe I am."

"Well, now listen . . ."

The police escort watched as Roy bent down and kissed Pat on her lips. As she responded in kind, Roy swooped her up and lifted her off the ground, bringing her to his own level. One of her shoes slipped off as she wiggled her feet. As the embrace continued Pat put her arms around Roy's head, holding his lips to hers.

As he lowered her on the floor, she slipped the shoe back on her foot. "And what was that all about?" she asked, realizing it was a meaningless question.

"A goodbye kiss," Roy replied. "And a very nice one if I might say so."

Pat wrinkled her nose. "Not bad."

"Did things look different from up here?"

"Don't be smart. I had my eyes closed."

"Ahh," Roy said. "Scared of heights are we?"

"With my eyes closed," Pat said, holding her head high, "I pretended I was kissing Paul Newman."

He chuckled. "You sure know how to keep a man in his place, Pat. The way you handled Billy and the way you are with me, I think you're a bit of a cross between Mother Teresa and Attila the Hun!"

"Mother Teresa," Pat gasped. "What did I do to deserve that?"

Roy laughed—loud enough to have people turn to look.

Pat smiled, extending her right hand. "Look Roy, I've got to go. My plane leaves soon."

Roy shook her hand, lifted it and kissed it. "I like you, Pat." He held onto her hand. "In fact I think I like you a great deal. You okay with that?"

"That's your choice, Roy. Nothing I can do about it"

"You could squeeze my hand to indicate, non-verbally, that you're at least somewhat interested in my interest."

Pat looked up at him, thought for a moment and without changing her facial expression, squeezed his hand. She squeezed it hard enough to get the message across. "You have to let go of my hand before I can leave, Roy."

"Yeah, I know." Reluctantly he let go of her hand.

Picking up her bag, Pat walked to the security gate. She waved back as she entered the 'Passengers Only' area.

Carolyn had her hand on the hotel room door handle. "Ready?" she asked.

Ed stood at the end of the bed. He looked at the bed, and then at Carolyn. He raised his eyebrows.

She shook her head.

He put his hands together in prayer.

She smiled, and shook her head.

He walked to her, took her hands in his and putting his hands around her, squeezed her gently. "I could be quick."

She looked up and kissed his lips. "No time, Ed."

He returned the kiss. "I love you so much, Miss Andrews. Next time, eh?" He let her go and reached for the door handle. "Let's get out of here."

"How quick is quick?" she asked.

Ten wonderful minutes later he exploded in her as she arched her back to take every inch of him that she could. They collapsed on the bed, naked, catching their breath in gulps of air. Ed pulled her into him, holding her as tightly as he could.

"You're very beautiful," he whispered.

Carolyn kissed his chin. "You're pretty good-looking yourself."

"May I ask you a question?" Ed asked.

"You may ask me any question—but one. And I will be as honest as I can."

He kissed her forehead. "Do you think the police escort down in the lobby is wondering what we're doing?"

"Don't be a smarty-pants," she said, gently pushing him away. "Let's get dressed and get out of here before I ask for more!"

Two hours into her flight, Pat sipped on a glass of red wine. She wasn't sure of her feelings for Roy. He was Ed's best friend; *but she had no long-term arrangement with Ed.* She enjoyed the flirting with Roy. It was not something she was used to; *but would these 'best mates' catch up and share stories?* The thought made her cringe, and she shook her head in disgust. She finished her wine in a quick gulp. *But it was fun, and he seems like a nice guy. What the Hell! You only go through life once.*

She set those thoughts to the back of her head, and started working on her report for her meeting with her boss tomorrow. Reports and analysis were her strong point. Men were not.

The police escort waited for the gates of Stonebridge Manor to close before he confirmed safe arrival on his radio and headed back to London.

Carolyn smiled over at Ed, who woke from a snooze as the car stopped in front of the Manor front door. Ed shook his head to wake fully, then leaned over and kissed Carolyn's cheek.

"I love you, Miss Andrews," he whispered.

"Yes, I know you do, Ed. But thank you for reminding me, and thank you for changing my life."

Ed looked quizzically.

"Just accept the statement, Ed." She smiled. "We'll talk about it when we have more personal time, and we're not rushed into a quickie."

The maid held open the front door as they entered the Manor.

She bowed her head slightly. "Lady Stonebridge requests your attendance please."

"Was that a request or a direction, Miriam?" Carolyn asked.

Miriam answered by opening the door to the living room. "Tea will be served in five minutes, Miss Andrews."

Lady Stonebridge was sitting in her regular chair, and beckoned them to sit. She looked tired, and lacked her usual air of control.

"Where and how is Miss Weston?" she asked, foregoing any formalities.

Carolyn looked casually at her watch. "She is on her way home to Canada, Mother. Likely there by now."

"Don't be flippant with me, Carolyn. How is she after this terrible ordeal?' She turned to Ed. "I hope you are satisfied with yourself, Mr. Crowe? I suspect you instigated her involvement?"

Ed gulped, taken back by the directness of the question. Carolyn spoke before he could collect his thoughts.

"Mother, please! I am not being flippant, just stating the facts. Pat, Miss Weston, is fine. She is a lot tougher than you might imagine. She was somewhat beaten, and has a sore face and a swollen lip."

"Somewhat!" Lady Stonebridge gasped. "You speak as if this is a daily occurrence."

Ed entered the fray. "She shot one of her abductors, Lady Stonebridge. Unofficially, that is."

Lady Stonebridge almost fainted, holding onto the arm of her chair to settle herself. "Is he . . . did she . . ?"

"He's alive," Ed said calmly. "If she wanted him dead, he'd be dead."

Lady Stonebridge rolled her eyes and struggled to control herself. The door opened and Miriam rolled in a trolley of tea.

Carolyn stood. "I'll be mother, Mother." She smiled nicely.

Carolyn put her mother's cup of tea on the table in front of her. Lady Stonebridge's hands were shaking too much for her to handle it fashionably. Lifting the cup she took a gentle sip, then replaced it carefully into the saucer.

Lady Stonebridge collected her composure. "Your father has not left his office all day."

Carolyn raised her eyebrows. "I cannot imagine why not, Mother."

"If I may, Lady Stonebridge?" Ed spoke carefully, and waited for a positive nod before he continued. "Miss Weston is in very fine shape, as is my friend who was with her. They were both shaken up, of course, but honestly they are doing fine."

"I take it the medical matter was a ruse then?"

Carolyn answered. "Yes, Mother. And if it makes you feel any better, Mr. Crowe shot another of the men involved. Unofficially of course. The man ended up a regular slubberdegullion."

Lady Stonebridge's jaw dropped. "That is intended to make me feel better is it, dear?"

Carolyn smiled. "I just wanted you to know that we won, Mother."

Lady Stonebridge picked up her cup and saucer, her hands now as steady as a rock. "Thank you, dear," she said sarcastically. "It is so important to know that I'm on the winning side."

"You're welcome, Mother," Carolyn nodded. "Mr. Crowe and I are due upstairs. I'll pass along your love to father should I?"

"Yes, why don't you do that, dear? Tell him he can come out now. But don't pass that along right away, Carolyn. He has a special guest waiting to see you both."

Now fully in control of the situation, Lady Stonebridge waved them out of the room.

Ed grabbed Carolyn's hand as they reached the stairs. "What the hell is a slubber . . . whatever?"

Carolyn smiled and gave a crafty wink. "It means a filthy, slobbering person. That's the way you left him wasn't it? And I think we can assume he was quite sevidical in his comments about you, don't you think?"

Ed kissed her hand and they took the stairs to Lord Stonebridge's office. "I give up! You're a word genius, Miss Andrews, a bloody genius. Who do you think the special guest is?"

"Probably the General. Let's go see."

Lady Stonebridge waited a few minutes, and then walked to a bookshelf to look for a dictionary.

The General, Mr. Cooper, was with Lord Stonebridge, but it was the other guest Lady Stonebridge was referring to. He stood as Ed and Carolyn entered the room. They both recognized him immediately from his uniform and his speech on television the day before. Lord Stonebridge introduced Sir Robert Newman, Commissioner of the Metropolitan Police: England's most senior policeman. His demeanor and serious look drained the pleasure from Ed and Carolyn's faces very quickly.

Lord Stonebridge took control of the situation. "The Commissioner has expressed some considerable concern about the use of firearms during the past twenty-four hours, and wanted the opportunity to speak to both of you about his very understandable anxiety." He turned to Newman. "That sums it up fully does it, sir?"

The Commissioner nodded, sitting straight in his chair.

Carolyn responded quickly. "There was really only one shooting that should raise concern, surely? Miss Weston shot the young man named Billy with his full understanding, and I might add with considerable insight into his assistance in aiding the police in their investigation."

Lord Stonebridge rubbed his chin. "She does have a point there, Commissioner."

The Commissioner thought through his response. "We can't go around shooting people on the grounds they are on our side, can we now? Imagine what the Sunday papers would say about that." He paused, raising his hands to check any response. "But setting that somewhat unusual situation aside, what of the first shooting? In public. On Hampstead Heath for good measure!"

Ed wondered if the Commissioner would have been happier if he had shoot the fat bugger in Kilburn High Road, but decided not to raise that question.

Ed spoke slowly "He had my wife and friend, and he had made it clear my wife had been hurt. I wanted to find out where they were as quickly as possible."

"But she is not your wife, Mr. Crowe."

"But he didn't know that, sir. To him, she was my wife. To him, my friend was in desperate need of medication. Besides," Ed shrugged, "I shot him on the outside of his leg; the good side, so to speak."

"The good side?" the Commissioner queried, obviously not happy with that explanation.

Carolyn interjected. "The major arteries are on the inside of one's legs, Commissioner. Shooting someone on the outside reduces the risk of serious damage."

The Commissioner closed his eyes, not quite believing what he had heard. He turned to Lord Stonebridge. "Is this what you teach your recruits, Lord Stonebridge? Shoot them here, not there, and everything will be dandy?"

Lord Stonebridge coughed to stifle a slight smile. "Not quite in those terms, but surely results must carry some consideration in the equation?"

The Commissioner shook his head. "I have a duty to uphold. I must charge Mr. Crowe with something. Carrying an unlawful firearm at the least." He stood and turned to Ed to make his point.

Carolyn gasped in disbelief.

The blood ran out of Ed's face and he felt faint to the point of having to cling on to the side of his chair to steady himself.

Mr. Cooper shook his head, not wanting to think of the ramifications for Ed and his future.

Lord Stonebridge rapped the table with his fist. He spoke with authority. "Sit down please, Commissioner. Let me tell you a story that involves Mr. Crowe."

The Commissioner sat in his chair, but made it clear he was not to be trifled with.

Lord Stonebridge continued. "You will, of course, Commissioner recall last year when one of your own officers was shot outside the Libyan Embassy?"

"Of course I do," he shot back. "I spoke at the young lady's funeral. What has that to do with anything today?"

Lord Stonebridge raised his hands to calm the situation. "Bear with me, Commissioner, bear with me. Now the Libyan soldier that shot the WPC died in Libya you will recall. I believe you saw the photo of him hanging?"

"That doesn't mean he was dead, Stonebridge. You know that. The photo was likely a fake, and he is still alive laughing at us!"

"Oh he's dead all right," Mr. Cooper said bluntly.

Lord Stonebridge nodded his agreement. "He is most certainly dead, Commissioner, but he was not hanged by the Libyan authorities. Indeed he did not die by hanging. He committed suicide in front of Mr. Crowe, knowing that the alternative was either to be returned to England for due process, or perhaps to be shot and killed by Mr. Crowe. His superiors were not protecting him. He was a failure both as a soldier and as a man. No doubt he took what he considered to be the easy way out." He turned to Ed. "You would have killed him. That was the case, was it not, Mr. Crowe?"

"Absolutely," Ed lied. "I was about to shoot him when he turned his bayonet on himself. I was tempted to shoot him after he fell to the floor, but that would have been cowardly."

The Commissioner shook his head, not sure if he should believe this most unlikely story. He chewed on his bottom lip, thinking. If it were true, then he could rest assured that the death of his officer had been avenged. Not full satisfaction by any means, but better than what he had to bear up to now.

"Perhaps," Lord Stonebridge continued, "I could ask our guests to leave the room and we could phone the old lady to clarify your understandable doubt?"

The Commissioner stood and reached across Lord Stonebridge's desk to shake hands. "Not needed. If Mrs. Thatcher broke the law by resolving the matter, I do not want you to further break the law to prove your point. The matter is resolved."

The Commissioner shook hands with Mr. Cooper and Carolyn, leaving Ed to last. "No more shooting, Mr. Crowe."

"No. Thank you, sir."

"Thank *you,* sir." The Commissioner turned sharply on his heels and left the room.

Lord Stonebridge pressed a button on his desk phone. "Could we get tea and biscuits for four please?"

Carolyn stood and moved to the door. "Ed and I are going to get some fresh air." She motioned for Ed to follow her, which he gladly did. They didn't speak until they were on the driveway. Carolyn took both his hands. She could feel his body still shaking.

"I love you, Ed Crowe." She kissed him briefly, standing on her toes to reach him.

"Out of sympathy?"

"Of course not, Ed. Don't be silly."

"I lied through my teeth up there. I had no intention of killing the man."

Carolyn smiled. "Exactly."

Ed looked down at her, trying to understand her meaning. She opened her eyes wide and shrugged. "If Lord Stonebridge can lie, surely you can. It's part of the job, Ed. The Commissioner doesn't give a hoot about you really. He was doing what he felt he had to do. Even he was flexible when he learned that his officer's killer is dead; really dead, that is. Sorry, it's the way it works." She smiled. "Besides, you did a good job of lying!"

Ed shook his head. "I think maybe I should go back to being a full-time travel agent in Canada, and forget this international spy stuff."

"You don't mean that do you, Ed?"

He thought about it. "No. If I did, I'd never see you again."

"Don't you dare say that," Carolyn said angrily. "That hurt. Your role with the department has nothing to do with my feelings for you."

Ed leaned down and kissed her forehead. "Glad to hear that, Miss Andrews. I do love you. Now let's go back, have a cup of tea, and see how things are going."

They turned to enter. Lady Stonebridge was standing at the open door. "Everything all right, my dear?" she asked Carolyn.

"Everything is fine, Mother. Ed and I were just agreeing on how much we like each other."

Lady Stonebridge smiled. "It's called love, my dear. Don't be afraid to say it." She stood to one side as Carolyn and Ed whisked by her and walked quickly up the stairs to Lord Stonebridge's office.

Ed and Carolyn helped themselves to tea and took their seats facing Lord Stonebridge's desk. Lord Stonebridge looked up. "So what do you have to say about all of that, Mr. Crowe?"

Ed maintained a straight face. "I don't like telling lies, sir."

Mister Cooper chuckled from behind his teacup. "No one does, Eddie. You make a mighty fine liar. Politics may be beckoning you very soon."

Lord Stonebridge nodded in agreement. "We all regret having to do these things, Mr. Crowe." He put his teacup down. "But you did do rather well." He shrugged. "Whatever. Let's see if plain old common sense can help us figure out how to get the remaining two bad guys."

Ed quickly and succinctly outlined what had happened at the Kilburn address, closing with Billy's statement that the goal for Mike and Terry was Bradford.

"Yorkshire is nice this time of year," Mr. Cooper said reflectively.

CHAPTER SEVEN

SATURDAY, AUGUST 17TH 1985. 9:30 AM

"No news from Bradford," Lord Stonebridge outlined to the group, now re-convened in his office after a much needed night's sleep. "The local police do not know our boys, and from what you've told us, Mr. Crowe, they did not have northern accents."

"Not according to my friend Roy Johnson, who had plenty of time to think about it. More London than north."

Lord Stonebridge shook his head, not happy with the lack of local information. "All we know is that there are considerable racial issues in Bradford and have been for some time."

Mr. Cooper offered a ray of hope. "Our plan can't take effect until Monday, perhaps we need to take a break and schedule a get together this time tomorrow? Perhaps . . ."

The door opened and Lord Stonebridge's secretary entered the room. "Important call from Canada, sir. Top priority. Line one."

Ed, Carolyn, and Mr. Cooper stood to leave the room, but the secretary motioned them to sit down. "It's Miss Weston: this operation." With those comments she closed the door and left.

Lord Stonebridge raised his eyes in interest. "This should be enlightening," he said and pressed two buttons on his phone. "You're on speakerphone, Miss Weston, and we're all here."

"Good morning, everyone," Pat started. "I trust *you* all had a good night's sleep. It seems our young friend Billy thinks the entire world runs on Greenwich Mean Time. I just got off the phone with him, and thought I should up-date you before I went back to bed."

"Good morning, Pat," Carolyn said with a smile. "We appreciate your phoning, and trust you can help us along. We seem to be getting nowhere."

"Well I'm here to help," Pat continued, "and I hope you don't have any plans for tonight. What I have to tell you is brief, but very important. Before you ask how comfortable I feel with the data, let me outline what Billy has just told me."

Lord Stonebridge took over. "Please proceed, Miss Weston. We are all at full attention, and the line is secure."

"He phoned from what he called a Borstal, from the warden's office. Sounded like prison to me, but that doesn't matter. They are planning a riot tonight in Bradford. The plan is simple, scarily so I might add. The idea is to have a young black man, whose name by the way is Damon, rape a young Muslim girl. The expected result will be a riot between the two racial groups, with nice-guy 'Mr. White-man' watching the fight from the sidelines. There is more, but that's the plan."

She waited for a response. There wasn't one.

"Are you still there?" she asked, raising her voice.

Lord Stonebridge replied hastily. "Yes we're here. I'm afraid you've caught us somewhat speechless. Perhaps you could convey to us the reason you feel the young man is telling the truth? The story seems incredible, and certainly potentially catastrophic."

"Of course, Lord Stonebridge, let me expand. Billy phoned me from the warden's office on the condition that both the warden and Billy's mother stand outside of the room. He wanted only me to know of the plan. Now I know that doesn't sound very good, but that was what he insisted on."

Ed interrupted. "He was helping someone who had helped him."

"I suppose so, Ed," Pat agreed. "That doesn't make me feel any better, but I think you've got it right." She paused. "Now I told him if he was lying to me, I'd come over there and . . . . well you know what I would have said."

"Make sure he would never have children?" Carolyn asked.

Pat groaned. "Quite a bit more specific than that; but yes. I also told him that if it turned out to be true, I would visit him the next time I was in England."

Lord Stonebridge raised his hand to change the subject. He leaned closer to the phone. "You've been involved in this operation from the beginning, Miss Weston. Do you have any thoughts on a plan of action?"

Pat replied enthusiastically. "I do have an outline of a plan, Lord Stonebridge, but it requires the use of a gun, and I know that isn't permitted in England."

Lord Stonebridge smiled, thinking of yesterday's discussions. "A timely comment, Miss Weston, but proceed with your thoughts."

Pat continued. "It may sound a bit unusual, my plan that is, but it is based in part to protect Billy from being identified as involved in any way. I'd hate to do something . . ."

Mr. Cooper interrupted. "Fully understood, Miss Weston, and we like the unusual. Why don't you proceed and we'll see how unusual it is."

In Ottawa, Pat took a deep breath and crossed he fingers. "Here we go then," she began.

Lord Stonebridge spoke first after they had listened intently to Pat's ideas. "I think *unusual* might be a bit of an understatement, Miss Weston. Perhaps a few questions first?"

"If it's too off-beat . . ." Pat started to say.

"Nothing of the sort, Pat," Ed said interrupting. "Unique thinking is what we need."

Carolyn chuckled. "I think it's a wonderful idea, Pat. And it'll be a new experience for me if we go ahead."

For twenty minutes they asked questions of Pat and of themselves. It was clearly understood that all avenues had to be considered, and the downsides balanced with the freshness of Pat's proposed plan.

Eventually Lord Stonebridge summed up. "By the looks on my associates' faces, I'd say we've got ourselves a plan!"

Pat pumped the air with her fist, but kept her enthusiasm to herself. "Thank you, sir. Please let me know how it goes."

"Not so fast, Pat," Carolyn said, walking toward the phone. "I think you had better be the one to speak to Roy Johnson. Officially we can't operate in the U.K."

"It'll be my pleasure," Pat replied.

"One final thought, Pat," Carolyn added. "We'll let you up-date your end in Ottawa. We can confirm later, but you should get the credit where credit is due."

The phone call ended with an agreement to move quickly and keep Pat up-dated.

"So have you ever worn one?" Lord Stonebridge asked Carolyn.

"Not even close," Carolyn answered.

"And you, Mr. Crowe," he continued, turning to Ed. "I assume you're not of that particular persuasion?"

"Not even close."

Mr. Cooper rolled his eyes. "Then God help us."

For reasons she couldn't quite explain to herself, Pat brushed her hair and checked her make-up before she phoned Roy Johnson. It was 10am London time.

"How's my favorite lady?" Roy asked, answering the phone.

"Hi, Roy, it's me, Pat. I'm phoning from Ottawa."

"Hey. Then how's my favorite lady from Canada?"

Pat forced a smile. "I'm fine, thanks."

"Couldn't wait to talk to me, eh?"

"Not quite, Roy. I'm phoning on business, so to speak."

"Oh. Okay, whatever. It's nice to hear your voice."

"So can I, or more accurately can we, ask you to do something, no questions asked?"

Roy raised his eyebrows in interest. "Absolutely, Pat, and nary a question from me."

"Good. Where's your driver's license?"

"In my wallet, at least I hope it is." He paused. "Yes, it's in my hand."

"Good. Now I'd like you to hide it somewhere in your apartment. Somewhere safe; where no-one else would look."

"Under my pillow?" he laughed.

Pat didn't respond.

"Okay, sorry. I'll put it in on the left hand side of the second drawer down, in the chest of drawers in my bedroom. Under my underwear."

Pat smiled. "Under your underwear. That should be easy for me to remember."

"It'll be in a silver cigarette holder."

"You smoke?"

"Not now."

"Glad to hear it. Now if anyone asks you where it is; it's in your wallet. Okay?"

"Got it."

"I didn't mean to be rude, Roy."

"You weren't. I was."

"Now when that person asks to see your driver's license . . ."

"I look in my wallet, and it's not there. I've either lost it or it's been stolen. And I'm damn perturbed since it's illegal to drive a car without carrying your license with you."

"Very good."

"So may I continue to drive?"

"Of course. You can trust me on that one."

"I do."

Pat spoke more slowly. "Look I've gotta go. I don't mean to be rude, but work must."

"Fine. Let me know what is happening when you can tell me sometime."

"Oh, that's a for sure. This call didn't happen, okay?"

"Absolutely," Roy said. "But can I ask you a totally un-related question?"

"Of course."

"I meant what I said about liking you. Next time you're in England, can we get together and catch up?"

"Yes, I'd like that."

"And next time I'm in Canada?"

Pat chuckled. "I'd like that too. Look I've got to go."

"One other thing, Pat. I thought it was my mother when you phoned."

"Yeah, right," she laughed.

"My mother. Honest."

"That is nice, Roy. I'll be in touch."

She hung up the phone, looked at her watch and headed to the shower. She wanted to be the first one in the office, and she wanted to type up her report in full before anyone else got there. Her boss was always in on a Saturday, and she wasn't above making sure he saw her in a good light.

As she showered she thought of Roy, and couldn't stop herself from smiling.

CHAPTER EIGHT

SATURDAY, AUGUST 17TH 1985. BRADFORD, YORKSHIRE. 8:30 PM

Carolyn walked carefully along Bridge Street and turned onto Sunbridge Road. As they had expected, the centre area of Bradford was busy on a Saturday night and tonight was no exception.

Several young men, boys really, made rude comments and gestures to her, but she said nothing and looked straight ahead. The gun strapped to her waist added some comfort, but not much. Of more comfort was the occasional comment from Ed in her earpiece. She limited her response to a quiet, 'Everything okay' into the microphone attached to the inside of her burka.

The burka covered her from her head to her feet and the slit for her eyes made her peripheral vision limited. She felt neither safe nor comfortable and hoped that if anything was going to happen that it would happen soon.

As planned she turned down a side alley. After walking fifteen feet she was out of the sound and view of the Saturday night activities. As warm as she was wearing the burka over her regular clothes, a shiver ran down her back and she touched the gun quickly for comfort.

Walking past the rear of a pub, she could hear the loud music and the conversations shouting above it to be heard. The song blaring through the night was Queen's, '*Bohemian Rhapsody*'. Very quietly she hummed along. It was one of her favorites.

The shove to her back was quick and hard. She ended on the ground of a parking lot confused but with her wits intact.

"What you want?" she shouted with a strong accent. "Leave me be."

Two men looked down at her, laughing and kicking at her legs. It was awkward to catch a full view, but she needed only to see that one was black and one white to know she had met her targets.

Ed covered his ears to make sure he heard every word as best he could. He turned up the volume, resisting the innate reaction to jump out of the car and rush to Carolyn's side. Two minutes. It had been agreed; two minutes before he could run to help her. Two minutes to ensure the trap was set. Mr. Cooper leaned over and squeezed Ed's arm gently. His message was clear—*Stay with the plan*. Ed nodded. Carolyn had a gun and she knew how to use it!

"Well look what the fuck we have here?" Mike said, keeping his foot on Carolyn's legs. "Just what you wanted? Right my friend?" He turned to Damon who was looking around nervously to make sure they were safe.

Damon sweated nervously. "What do I do, man? How do I fuck her here? It's too open."

Carolyn hand moved to her mouth under the robes. "No, no, no," she begged.

Mike leaned down to her, shoving the knife in his hand to her face. "Shut the fuck up you foreign cow." He laughed. "I think you're going to enjoy this."

"Oh, God, I don't know," Damon groaned.

Mike stepped harder on Carolyn and showed the knife to Damon. "We do what we planned. You grab her and throw her in the van." He grinned. "Then she's all yours. Just make sure you do it properly. She's likely a fucking virgin."

The two lowered their eyes to Carolyn and looked down the barrel of the hand gun. In an instant Carolyn was standing. "Now you shut the fuck up," she shouted at Mike, "and down on your knees, now! Both of you. Now!'

Damon dropped to his knees covering his face and groaning. Mike thought about running, but the sound of steps behind him changed his mind. He dropped to his knees and spoke slowly and carefully. "Go ahead and shoot me. Phone the police. What do I care? We haven't done anything wrong." He looked behind him and gasped at the sight.

Ed stood with his hands behind his back, smiling gently as only a priest could. "Good evening, son," he said to Mike in his best Irish accent. "Care to confess your sins?" He wore a priestly robe, feeling guilty only about the cross hanging at his chest and the 'dog collar' that was too tight for his liking.

Damon looked at Ed through his fingers and groaned further into his hands. "Holly shit," was all he could muster.

Mike couldn't believe what he was seeing. "What the hell's going on here?"

Ed responded by smiling and crossing himself with his left hand and pointing his gun at Mike with his right hand. "Put you hands behind your back and face your friend please." Ed spoke as nicely as he could, struggling not to reach out and hit Mike full force with his gun.

Mike did as he was told. He instinctively knew he was dealing with the authorities and the more left unsaid the better.

Ed pointed the gun at Damon. "Hands behind your head please, and move closer."

Damon moved closer, his face now three inches from Mike's.

Ed pointed the gun at Mike. "Now kiss him."

"Fuck you, arse-hole," Mike responded. "I ain't kissing no nigger!"

Before the words were out of his mouth, Damon's head drove hard into Mike's face. He hovered for a second then fell slowly sideways, out cold.

"No one calls me a nigger," Damon shouted, looking down at his 'so called' friend, "no one!"

Carolyn quickly tied Damon's hands behind his back. He gave no resistance. The evening had gone terribly wrong and he would accept whatever was forthcoming. Tears slid slowly down his face. He could never face his family, especially his mother, again. He hung his head in shame.

"Lie down and face the other way," Ed said, holding the gun at his side. Damon did as he was told, not caring what would happen next.

Quickly and silently Ed retrieved the keys to the van from Mike's pocket. Walking quickly to the van, he opened the rear door and slid something under the worn and filthy carpet. He returned the keys to Mike's pocket. For the third time that day he made sure there was only one bullet in his gun. Grabbing Mike's hands he put the gun in several positions to ensure Mick's fingerprints covered the gun and placing the gun in Mike's right hand, he aimed carefully and pressed Mike's finger. The bullet flew inches above Damon's head into the front tire of the nearest car. The sound of the gun and the exploding tire did the trick. Damon ducked crouching lower to the ground, now crying aloud.

"If you try to move, you're next," Ed said, leaving the gun in Mike's right hand and removing the latex gloves he had been wearing. Damon shook his head, now in total despair.

To one side Carolyn spoke softly into her microphone. "We're out of here in ten seconds."

In the distance the sound of police cars could be heard. Ed watched in disbelief as Carolyn stood over Mike and swiftly kicked him in his ribs. It wouldn't be enough to break any bones, Ed thought, but he would feel it when he gained consciousness.

Carolyn looked at Ed. "Not a word."

Ed crossed himself. "Confessions are sacred," he said.

Ed and Carolyn moved quickly down the alley in the opposite direction of the police cars now closing-in. They made an unlikely looking couple as they quickly walked through the lively streets of Bradford.

Turning onto Sunbridge Road, Carolyn slipped quickly into the back seat of Mr. Cooper's Vauxhall. Ed kept walking for two blocks and as Mr. Cooper's car pulled up along side him, he quickly got into the back seat. Carolyn, now in her regular clothes, grinned in fun as Ed took off his priest's robes.

"That was probably the shortest term as a father in history," Carolyn remarked.

"I've never felt so religious in my life," Ed said. "Maybe I should . . ."

"Forget it," Carolyn interrupted. "There are enough religious problems in the world without your getting involved."

They high-fived each other as Mr. Cooper turned the car south, heading back to London. He turned the radio to BBC for some comforting classical music.

They were well on the way to London when Ed turned to Carolyn breaking the silence. "You said the eff word, you know?"

Carolyn rolled her eyes. "And your point is?"

Ed shrugged, barely holding back a smile. "I guess I've never heard you swear like that. It quite surprised me. In fact I didn't know that Oxford graduates were allowed to swear."

Carolyn leaned to Ed, whispering in his ear. "You've heard me use that word before, smarty-pants."

Ed grinned. She had taken the bait. "Yes," he whispered, "but that was a request on your part."

Holding back her instinct to hit him, she turned and faced the road ahead. "Then I make a commitment not to use that word in front of you again, Mr. Crowe. Okay?"

Outsmarted, Ed said nothing. He hoped she would change her mind if the occasion arose. Reaching for her hand she pushed him away. He reached again. This time she took his hand and held it with both of hers on her lap.

Mr. Cooper drove in silence, recalling the time he and his wife were as young and as lovingly cheeky to each other. He couldn't help but smile.

"So did you need to use the new trainers?" Mr. Cooper asked Carolyn as the car turned into Stonebridge Manor.

"Not necessary," Carolyn replied, keeping her head high and her eyes straight ahead.

"New trainers?" Ed asked.

Mr. Cooper nodded. "First time we've used them. They're steel-toed. You'd feel it if someone kicked you wearing one of them!"

Ed looked down at Carolyn's feet, and then at Carolyn. She kept her eyes on the driveway ahead and showed no emotion. Ed nodded. "If you'd let me wear them, I'd have given one of them the boot," he said.

Carolyn smiled. "No sense getting personal, Mr. Crowe. It's just a job."

"Good point," he replied, reaching down and feeling the steel reinforced toe of her trainer, "if you'll excuse the play on words."

CHAPTER NINE

MONDAY, AUGUST 19TH, 1985 MAGISTRATE'S COURT. THE COURT HOUSE, LEEDS, YORKSHIRE

C hair of the Bench, Ruth Cole, peered over her reading glasses at the defendants standing in the dock to her left, and her two fellow Justices listened intently as she addressed the defendants independently. "Please stand, Mr. Marshall."

Damon stood quickly to his feet. "Yes, Missus," he said bowing his head out of respect.

His solicitor quickly stood, grabbed Damon by the sleeve, pulled him down and whispered in his ear.

"Yes, Madam," Damon said, louder this time to correct his error.

While she waited, Justice Cole looked about her court. In addition to the recording clerk, the court usher in his courtly gown, the police officer by the dock, the two defendants and their respective solicitors, only five other people were in the court. The cub reporter from the local newspaper, persistently searching for news worthy of the front page; two retired gentlemen were enjoying their daily lessons of the British justice system; a lady, apparently Mrs. Marshall, sat behind her son; and a lone young lady sat at the back of the court, outwardly disinterested in the proceedings.

"Now, Mr. Marshall," Justice Cole continued, "the circumstances you describe of the events of Saturday night are, one must surely agree, unusual to say the least?"

His solicitor nodded. Damon coughed to clear his nervousness. "Yes, Madam. Very unusual."

"Let me see if I can summarize the events as you described them." She didn't wait for any form of approval. "As you tell it, you and the co-defendant Mr. Pierce were walking through downtown Bradford on Saturday night when you were accosted by a lady dressed in Muslim clothing, a burka to be precise, to the point where she pulled a gun on you. Then she forced you both to get on your knees. Have I got it right so far, Mr. Marshall?"

Damon smiled nervously. "Yes, Madam."

Justice Cole continued. "And them, lo and behold, an Irish priest appeared and assisted this Muslim lady in her activities." She looked at Damon for agreement. He nodded quickly, but Mike rolled his eyes not missing the sarcasm. She continued. "You then head-butted Mr. Pierce . . ."

"He called me a nigger!" Damon shouted. His solicitor glared at him, motioning him to calm down. Damon took a deep breath. He spoke calmly. "He called me a nigger, Madam."

Justice Cole continued. "Yes, I recall your evidence, Mr. Marshall. Then you said that after the Irish priest warned you and had you lie on the ground, a shot was fired from a hand gun, the said gun being found at the scene." She paused. "Is that correct?"

Damon nodded. "Yes, Madam. That is how it happened."

Justice Cole spoke briefly with the two other Justices at the bench, removed her glasses and addressed Damon with an aura of authority and advice. "Now, Mr. Marshall, earlier on this morning you promised to tell the truth, in fact the whole truth, correct?"

Damon looked nervously at his solicitor, who could only shrug. Damon pointed to Mike, and replied casually. "He told me I could screw her."

The courtroom exploded. Mike shouted denials; the cub reporter started writing as fast as he could; Mrs. Marshall wailed aloud, and the two retired gentlemen sat up, enjoying the moment. Meanwhile the two solicitors argued with each other on legal matters in whispers. Only the lady in the back of the court sat motionless, but she smiled enjoying the results thus far.

Justice Cole exchanged glances with the two other justices beside her and after allowing time for things to settle down she called for order. Her request didn't stop either Mike from protesting his innocence or Mrs. Marshall from crying in despair. The solicitors continued their well controlled argument, neither one giving and inch. The cub reporter sat, pen in hand, anxiously awaiting the next action to be taken.

"Order please," Justice Cole demanded, speaking louder now and leaning forward in her seat. "Order or I'll fine the lot of you." Almost immediately everyone sat down, and only the cub reporter moved as he captured the moment. "The court will take a thirty minute recess," she continued, "and I expect the defendants and their respective counsel to return with a clearer understanding of the matters before the court and the risks involved in perjuring themselves." She waited for the solicitors to nod their understanding then lifted her head to address the lady in the back row. "Do you have any personal interest in this matter, may I ask?"

Carolyn stood. "No, your Worship," she lied, "none whatsoever."

Justice Cole acknowledged the response and left the courtroom with the two other justices.

The cub reported left the courtroom running, heading to the closest public phone.

Mike thought for a second then turned to see the lady in the back row, but she had left. He was distracted by his solicitor who ushered him to one side of the courtroom.

The three justices returned in forty minutes. The court room was silent with everyone anxious to hear their opinion. It was obvious something was different in their attitude as they sat up straight in their chairs not looking directly at either of the defendants. Finally Justice Cole broke the silence.

"Mr. Pierce, please stand up."

He stood up and was joined by his counsel. "Yes, Ma'am." He spoke without fear, with a level of confidence not shared by his counsel.

"Mr. Pierce, do you know who Mr. Roy Johnson is?"

His confidence cracked, but he maintained his posture. "No, Ma'am. I've never heard of him."

She looked down at her desk and then back to Mike. "Can you tell me, Mr. Pierce, why a driver's license issued to Mr. Roy Johnson was found by the police in the back of your van?" She held up her hand to stop him from replying. "You may want to confer with your counsel before responding. In fact I would strongly recommend that you do so."

Mike turned to his counsel. They sat and held a three minute hushed discussion. Not a person moved in the court. Even the cub reporter held his breath and his pen didn't move.

Mike stood. "My counsel recommends that I request of the court sufficient time to respond to the court's question, Ma'am."

"A good decision, Mr. Pierce." She rapped her gavel. "Mr. Pierce, you are to be remanded in custody pending this and further criminal actions to be considered."

Mike sat, now closing his eyes, fully understanding the trouble he was now facing.

Justice Cole continued. "Please stand, Mr. Marshall."

Damon stood, almost unable to keep his eyes from Mike. He swallowed and faced the justices.

Justice Cole turned to him. "Mr. Marshall. You are placed on Bail of two hundred pounds on the condition that you and counsel speak further with the police regarding the events surrounding this hearing. Do you understand, Mr. Marshall?"

"Yes, Madam," Damon answered, happy with the results and aware of his mother's tears of joy behind him.

CHAPTER TEN

FRIDAY, AUGUST 30ᵀᴴ, 1985, OTTAWA 11:30AM

"Nice flat," Roy said, looking around and dropping his suitcase on the floor.

"It's called an apartment," Pat corrected him.

"Nice apartment."

Pat nodded, almost smiling. "Thanks."

"I really appreciate your inviting me over to visit you and to see Ottawa," Roy continued, trying to get Pat to say more than a few words. She hadn't seemed very excited about meeting him at the airport and barely held together a conversation on the drive from the airport.

"I don't want to be picky, Roy, but I didn't as much invite you as agree you could come and visit."

Roy nodded. "Very true, very true. Am I really not welcome then?" He wanted to get to the bottom of her concern.

Pat shrugged her shoulders in response. "I just hope you don't think . . . you know."

"Ahh!" Roy grinned. "You mean I may be thinking this is some kind of dirty weekend?"

"If you want to be that blunt; yes."

"Oh, that's not bluntness, Pat, that's just honesty. No I wasn't thinking that I was in for a dirty weekend. I was hoping we could get to know each other better, and I don't mean in the biblical sense. I was hoping you'd enjoy showing me Ottawa which, from what I've read, is a really interesting city."

Pat shook her head, now regretting her welcome—or lack thereof. "Okay, look I'm sorry. Let's try again." She walked across the room and stood in front of him. "Give me a Heathrow hug," she said. He responded with a wide grin and picked her up gently and held her for a few moments before placing her back on her feet. She smiled up at him. "I'm not used to having guys spend the weekend at my place, nor blokes for that matter. I need to get the record straight, that's all."

"Fully understood, Pat," Roy said, shaking her hand in understanding. "This is not to say, by the way, that I regularly fly thousands of miles to see a young lady. A young lady, incidentally, that I like. And if you don't mind my repeating myself, I like you a great deal."

"Yeah, yeah," Pat responded gesturing with her hand. "Ed tells me that you have girlfriends all around the world. A girl in every port so to speak."

"Did he now? And what else did my friend Eddie tell you about me?"

Pat smiled, now enjoying the upper hand. "Oh, it was a long time ago. It was just him telling me more about himself, his friends and family. He has a great deal of respect for you."

"And I for him," Roy added. "I didn't tell him I was visiting you, so unless you told him . . ?"

Pat shook her head. "No. We haven't chatted for a while."

"Good," Roy said. "Now what?"

Pat pointed to the guest bedroom. "That's your room. Please unpack. You're here until Tuesday, and I want you to feel at home. I'm going downstairs to Tims to pick up a couple of coffees, and we'll meet on the balcony in ten minutes. Okay?"

"Deal. Just milk please."

Pat walked to the door and turned. "I think you're an okay bloke, Roy." She left before he could respond.

"Good coffee," Roy commented. They were on the balcony, now relaxed and feeling more comfortable having crossed the first bridge of their new friendship. "Nice view, nice company, nice everything," he added.

"Nice chatting-up," Pat said, smiling.

"Oh, I'm not chatting you up, Pat. I'm way beyond that. I like you, it's that simple." He turned to face her to make his point.

Pat let it pass. "Tell me about yourself, Roy. Let's see if it fits with what Ed told me."

"Oh, I'm sure it will."

Pat looked at her watch. "You've got twenty five minutes, and then we go on our first tour of the city."

Roy began. "Well I was born very young . . ."

"Oh God . . ."

"But I grew up quickly. I was ten years old before I knew it."

"Twenty four minutes," Pat said, again looking at her watch.

At the end of the time permitted, Roy had outlined his life as succinctly as he could, trying to capture his best parts but adding some of his *not so finer hours.*

"Do we go now?" he asked, happy to be finished talking about himself.

Pat shook her head. "I left time for Q and A period."

"I should have expected that."

Pat accepted the comment as a compliment. "So never married?"

"No."

"Never engaged?"

"No."

"Why not?"

"Why not?"

"That's my question."

Roy had to think. He wanted to get it right. "Never met the right lady."

"Ever been in love?"

Roy laughed. "A hundred times."

"Ten times then?"

"Yes, about that. I've never actually counted."

Pat turned to face Roy. She looked serious. "May I make a personal comment?"

Roy nodded.

"You remind me a bit of Albert Finney. Not so much the actor but a role he played in a movie some years back."

Roy chewed on his lower lip. He knew this was not just a passing comment from Pat. This was a test. A test he wanted to pass.

"You obviously mean Arthur Seaton in, *Saturday Night and Sunday Morning*. Hmm, I'm not sure I like the comparison. But fair enough, let's talk about it. How much time do we have?"

"Plenty."

"Well to start with I don't go drinking eleven pints of beer on a Saturday night. I don't live with my parents in a council house, and I most certainly don't shoot fat ladies with an air gun. I told you I'm in sales where I work. What I didn't tell you is that I'm Vice President of Sales and Marketing. I told you I live in a flat, but I own that flat and right now it's worth about a hundred thousand pounds. No mortgage. I paid cash for my car. *I* drive my life, Pat. I'm no Arthur Seaton."

Pat tried to smile. "Ooops! Are you mad at me now?"

Roy shook his head. "Absolutely not! I told you I wanted us to get to know one another. I just wasn't expecting it to be so down to earth."

Pat stood. "Well let's go see Ottawa, and when we get back you can ask me questions about myself. But I should tell you that . . ."

"Yes, I understand there are limitations, Pat." He tapped the side of his nose. "I was born during the day, not yesterday. For one, I don't think your name is Weston, and secondly I don't think you met Eddie in Turkey. In fact I don't think you've ever been to Turkey."

"Ready to go?" Pat asked, ignoring his comments. She reached out to take his hand. "Friends?"

"For a long time to come," he replied taking her hand in his. "For a very long time to come." At the door to the hallway, Roy leaned down and kissed her gently on her mouth.

She held the back of his neck, wanting to convey the right message. She winked as they separated. "No kissing in the street, okay?"

"When we get back?"

"Probably."

"Probably?"

"Probably means most likely. Did you know that?"

"I do now."

"C'mon," Pat said, pushing him through to the hallway, "lots of things to do and see."

Roy gestured for Pat to show the way. "You lead. I follow."

Pat nodded. "Now you've got it," she said. *Got him nibbling*, she said to herself.

Roy slumped into the kitchen table chair. "Well I'm knackered. You sure know how to see a lot of stuff in just a few hours."

Pat was putting on the kettle for tea. "Why thank you. I try to be organized."

Roy chuckled. "Organized? Heck I think you'd do well in the army: as a General. General Pat Weston—or not Weston, as the case may be."

"Quit your bellyaching. Tomorrow is really busy."

"I was impressed with both the National Gallery and the National Museum, but the one that really impressed me was the National War Memorial. And I must admit you sure know a great deal about that spy fellow . . ."

"Igor Gouzenko," Pat said.

"Yeah, the first Russian spy to come over to the west. Since he crossed over in Canada, does that mean he came *into* the cold?" He smiled. "It's almost as if it's part of your job to know about spies and all that stuff."

"Ha ha. Very funny." She was not going to let that discussion go anywhere.

Roy took the hint. "Can I take you out for dinner tonight?"

"We're eating in. I'm cooking. However, tomorrow . . ."

"Tomorrow it is. I'll pick you up at eight."

"Excuse me! You're right here."

Roy stood and walked over to her. He took her hand. "Tomorrow, Pat, I leave here at seven pm ready to go. I'll pick you up at eight, just like a real date. That should give you plenty of time, yes?"

"That would be nice. Very thoughtful of you, actually."

"I think of you a great deal lately."

"Quit with the BS, sit back down, and I'll bring the tea." She poured the tea with her back to him. She couldn't help but smile. They had truly enjoyed each other's company on the walking tour of Ottawa. *Careful now, Pat, careful . . .* she told herself, but the warmth she felt toward Roy was difficult to argue with.

Roy enthusiastically finished his tea and took a deep breath. "Okay I'm ready to kiss you now."

Pat choked on her last mouthful and had to cover her mouth. "What! You're ready. Am I supposed to jump?"

"No. Just letting you know."

She swallowed to settle her throat. "Well, Mr. Johnson, it does seem to me that there is one small issue here."

"Where there's a will, there's a way. What's the problem?"

Pat rested her hands on the table. "It's like this. You're way up there with your head in the upper stratosphere or somewhere, and I'm just a little shy of normal height down here in the real world. If you expect me to stand on a chair, forget it."

Roy nodded his understanding. "Not an issue," he said and walked to the sofa. He removed a cushion and placed it on the floor. Without waiting he lay down with his left elbow on the cushion and his head resting on his left hand. "Please join me, Pat."

"Hey, we're just . . ."

"Just kissing, Pat, just kissing."

She shrugged and carefully joined him on the floor. She lay down on her right elbow, now facing Roy—almost at equal levels. "Now what?"

Roy answered by reaching over with his right arm and pulling her toward himself. He started kissing her; gently at first and then with full passion. Initially Pat responded slowly and then put both of her arms around him and accepted his now wonderful embrace. When they parted, he turned her on her back and looked down to her. He stroked her face, tracing her eyebrows and then her nose to her lips. She kissed his finger as he touched her lips.

She smiled up to him. "We seem to have changed the scenario with you with the upper hand here."

"We can switch, Pat. Whatever you prefer."

She shook her head. "This is fine."

He kissed her again. "May I ask you a bit of a personal question?"

"You can ask."

"When you let Billy put his flick-knife in you blouse, did it scratch you?"

Pat laughed. "It's called a switchblade, Roy. Was it that obvious?"

"It was to me. Others may have been looking at your swollen face, but I noticed it."

"No comment on that. Why do you ask?"

Roy spoke seriously. "Well I'm not a doctor . . ."

"But you'll take a look, right?"

He shrugged.

Pat's eyes widened in disbelief. "You're a cheeky bugger, you are. Here I am lying on the floor in front of you and you want to do what exactly?"

"Check your sternum area for scratches. A sort of medical investigation."

"I don't believe this," Pat said, and then to his surprise she undid the top three buttons of her blouse. "Go on then, doc, tell me the bad news."

Roy looked at her chest as she held open the blouse revealing the top of her bra. He took a serious look. "Nope, I don't see any damage."

"But there was . . ."

"Maybe I should . . ."

"Maybe you should."

He carefully moved down and kissed her exposed skin, being careful not to actually touch her breasts. She held his head in place and he didn't move until she removed her hand.

"Feel better?" he asked.

She did up the buttons. "I'd have to say, yes."

"Me too."

She moved to get up. "Let's get supper going."

Roy didn't move. "Can you give me a minute?"

Pat looked at him and then rolled her eyes. "Are you telling me . . ."

Embarrassment was beyond him. He laughed. "Hey, I'm lying on the floor with a most beautiful lady, kissing her in special places and . . . well . . . and . . ."

"So do we need to talk about the weather to get you back from your disability?"

"On the contrary, Pat. Let's talk about the weather in order to cancel my *ability*."

They shared a laugh, and when Roy was 'disabled' they went to their separate rooms to change for supper.

Pat couldn't believe how the day had changed and spent some time getting ready for a wonderful evening. *He's ready to take the bait,* she smiled to herself.

Roy was happier than he had ever expected and he collected the two 'gifts' he had brought for Pat. He thought about it and put one back in the drawer.

Pat was working on supper as Roy entered the kitchen area.

"Pizza," Pat informed him.

"Great choice," Roy said enthusiastically. "Is there any Italian in you?"

Pat shook her head. "No, it's just easy. I'm no gourmet cook. If truth be told, I'm no cook at all."

"Can I kiss the cook?"

"No. But you can open a bottle of wine."

He opened a red and poured them a glass each. They toasted each other.

"I have a gift for you," Roy said, placing a folded envelope in Pat's hands after she had wiped them clean.

"Gee, you didn't have to gift wrap it so nicely, Roy."

"It's a business gift. I have another one for you which I'll present tomorrow night, if that's okay?"

Pat shrugged off the question and un-folded the envelope. She took out its content and gave Roy a big grin. "Your driver's license! That's clever."

"The one I lost, so to speak. The one I lied to the police about losing. The one that helped identify our kidnappers and send them to the slammer."

"Hey, that's great. Can I keep it?"

Roy nodded. "I think you had better keep it. I'm not used to lying to the police, so the further away it is from me the better."

Pat flipped the license in her hand. "Nice photo too."

"Too bad you'll have to keep it in your official file, eh?"

She slipped the license into the pocket of her apron. "Nothing official about me, big guy. And while you can't kiss the cook, I can kiss the wine sommelier. Get over here."

Roy did as he was told and they kissed nicely as he leaned down to reach her. She pushed him away as he moved in for more. "No distracting the cook," she winked at him.

They talked about everything and nothing as the pizza cooked and then ate it to great delight. Topping up their wine, Pat directed them out to the balcony. The sky was clear with only a few clouds moving slowly across the magnificent view.

Roy took a deep breath, taking in the freshness of the evening. "Very nice, Pat, very nice indeed."

Pat nodded. "It is isn't it?"

Roy turned to face her. "You're the nicest thing that's happened to me for, oh, I'd have to say weeks."

"Wow! You're such a smoothie, Roy. Why I'm just blown away."

"Yep," Roy continued, "about five hundred and sixteen weeks."

Pat thought that through. "That's almost ten years, Roy. Are you bull shitting me again?"

"No, it's been almost ten years since my roomy moved in with me. That was an important day in my life. She's a real sweetie."

Pat rolled her eyes in disbelief. "And what would she say if she heard what you just said?"

Roy thought for a while. "She's probably just say, meow!"

Pat punched him hard in his arm, spilling his wine. "You big shit, she's a cat!"

"Of course. What were you thinking?"

"What's her name?"

"Calpurrnia."

"Nice name. I like that."

Roy nodded. "Actually she's rather like you; not very big but with a heck of a personality. She doesn't carry a gun though."

Pat ignored the comment, taking a sip of her wine.

"I mean it though, Pat. The time frame, that is."

Pat smiled, walked into the apartment, put on some music and returned with the bottle of wine. She topped them up.

"Roy, I wish you wouldn't say things like that. I know I should be pleased to hear you say that and somehow respond in kind, but I find that sort of thing difficult to get through my thick skull." She chuckled. "Not that I hear such nice things all the time. In fact, if truth be known . . ."

Roy toasted her with his wine. "I understand that, coming out of the blue as it did. But it is what it is. Mostly I want you to know that I mean it, that's all. You don't have to respond in kind. Let's just listen to Gordon Lightfoot."

"Hey, you know Gordon?"

"I'm a huge music fan. I like all music: New Orleans Jazz, Classical, Opera, Oldies, Folk, you name it. Eddie was good enough to send me a tape of Lightfoot. Really very good music."

"Oh! Did he say anything about any of the songs?"

Roy shook his head. "No, should he have?"

Pat's mind quickly returned to the first time she and Ed had made love. Her favorite Gordon Lightfoot tape had been playing.

"No, just curious. He's never made it big in the U.K."

"Well he changed the subject of our conversation, didn't he? Why don't you point out the high spots of the city? It's quite a view you have."

Happy to change the conversation, she spent fifteen minutes outlining the many buildings and countryside that could be seen from the balcony. To no surprise of Roy, she was a fountain of knowledge capable of answering his most detailed questions. Her enthusiasm was obvious, and he watched her with awe.

When she was finished, she emptied the wine bottle into their glasses. She took a sip, put her glass down and reached over for his hand. "I do like you, Roy. In fact I like you a lot. I decided that at London airport, and in spite of my bad manners upon your arrival you have been a wonderful guest. Can we just keep things in slow motion? I'm just not accustomed to such generous compliments. I'm not intending to be rude, honest."

Roy kissed her hand. "Not an issue, Pat. You're the boss."

"Oh, God," she said, pulling back her hand. "Please don't call me that, okay."

Roy was now confused. "But Carolyn, and . . ."

"Exactly."

"Okay . . ." Roy said slowly, understanding the message. "That would be a do-not-ask, would it?"

Pat nodded, appreciating his response. "Yes, that would be a DNA."

"Got it. Any further DNA's, you be sure to tell me. I may be many things, but slow on the up-take is not one of them."

"One thing you're not, Roy, is slow on the up-take. Let's finish our wine and head in. Long day tomorrow."

"I'll save my questions about you for tomorrow?"

"Fine."

He took her hand and they entered the apartment to the comforting music of Lightfoot.

Roy kissed that top of her head. "Time for beds, then."

Pat nodded. "Well said. Please leave your door ajar."

"Just in case you want to sneak in on me?"

"For Robin to make his nightly prowl. He seems to think he runs the joint. Goodnight, Roy."

CHAPTER ELEVEN

SATURDAY, AUGUST 31ST, 1985 STONEBRIDGE MANOR, ENGLAND 1PM

Lord Stonebridge nodded into the phone. "Yes, Prime Minister, I agree, Ottawa is the best choice. Washington still filters more than needed, notwithstanding, I might add, your excellent relations with President Reagan." Having agreed with the outline of the plan, he put down the phone and pressed the intercom button. "Get me Miss Andrews please, and then patch us through to Ted Morden at CSIS in Ottawa: top priority please."

CHAPTER TWELVE

Saturday, August 31st 1985 Ottawa, Canada 6:30am

Roy tapped on Pat's bedroom door. "Tim Hortons coffee, milk only, nice and hot," he announced. He could hear Pat as she shuffled around in her bed.

The response was what he had expected. "It's six bloody thirty for crying out loud!"

"My clock is five hours ahead. Don't want to let the coffee get cold, do we now?"

"God forbid!" She paused. "Bring it in then."

She was sitting up in bed with the covers up around her neck. Roy gave her the steaming coffee.

"So where's yours," she asked.

"In the kitchen."

She took a sip and relaxed. "Well go get it. We can sort out today's agenda."

Roy moved quickly and enthusiastically to collect his coffee, and sat on the end of her bed when he returned. "You look very nice this morning," he said.

"Then you must be blind or stupid," she retorted.

"Then blind it is."

She asked him to open the window curtains and as he did the sun shone magnificently across the room changing the mood to bright and cheery. She covered her eyes to adjust. Roy sat down on the bed, waiting for orders. He didn't have to wait long.

"This is today's plan," Pat said, handing him a sheet of paper. He reviewed it quickly.

"Looks great! Boat cruise on the Rideau Canal, train ride through the Gatineau Hills, tour of downtown Ottawa, and then I treat you to dinner tonight. Sounds wonderful."

Pat smiled and took another sip of her coffee. "I think we'll enjoy it, and thanks for the coffee."

Roy stood. "Okay, I've fed Robin, cleaned out his litter box and read the newspaper. I'll take a half hour walk around the block and let you get changed and dressed in peace. Any chance of a good morning kiss?"

"Not a chance in hell, but thanks for the rest. I'll be ready in forty five."

Roy left the room leaving Pat smiling, knowing that her plans were well in hand.

Sitting in the back of the Rideau Canal cruise boat, Roy took a risk and put his arm around Pat. She didn't respond, which he assumed was a good sign. After a few seconds, she moved slightly closer to him keeping her eyes straight ahead. She leaned closer and whispered in his ear. "What do you want to ask about me?"

"Phew," Roy laughed, "I thought for a moment there, you were going to whisper sweet nothings in my ear."

"Don't kid yourself. Questions."

"Family?"

"Parents in Oakville, and one younger sister. She works at a travel agency in Toronto."

"Ever married?"

She chuckled. "Obviously not. Except the Ed thing in Paris." She didn't go into detail.

"Ever been engaged?"

"No."

"Why not?"

"Why not?"

Roy looked around. "Is there an echo here?"

"Maybe guys don't find me pretty," Pat shot back, "and maybe they don't like my personality."

"I think you're pretty."

Pat paused. "So what does that mean?"

"Pretty? It means . . ."

"I meant not commenting on my personality?"

Roy smiled. "Well you're the university grad. Didn't they teach you in biology to dissect issues and deal with them one at a time?"

Pat took a breath. "When you're dealing with a people's fundamental way of living, it's called anthropology!"

Roy bowed slightly. "I stand corrected. I always did get my ologies confused."

"Really? Well then there is zoology, the study of animals in their natural habitat or in captivity . . . Which reminds me, what do you want for breakfast tomorrow?"

Roy squeezed her closer. "You're wicked, young lady. But then I like wicked. But I like your personality; in fact all of them."

Pat shook her head. "No comment."

"Do you have any current boyfriends, other than me that is?"

She pushed away. "Hey, who said you're my boyfriend?"

Roy pulled her back and spoke quietly. "Well, let's see. We've been kidnapped together, we've lied through our teeth together, I watched you shoot a young man—for good reason, I might add. Further, we've kissed in special ways and we agree we like each other. Sounds like a girlfriend—boyfriend relationship to me."

"Yeah, well other *things* happen in such a relationship and that ain't likely to happen between us!"

"That would make us lovers, and I'm not there yet. If it's not boyfriend—girlfriend, then what?"

"How about a pain in the ass, or is that arse, bloke from England?"

"That could work. It's not very subtle, but it could work"

Pat rolled her eyes. "Alright, so you're my boyfriend. Feel better?"

He kissed her forehead. "Much."

She slid an inch closer. "Okay, it feels better for me too."

"And are there any other boyfriends?"

"No."

He pulled her closer. "Okay, tour guide, why don't you tell me all about the Rideau Canal?"

It was gone six o'clock when they returned to Pat's apartment, both excited about their day and similarly exhausted. As agreed upon, Roy showered and dressed for dinner and was out the door by seven.

Pat sat and thought for a while trying to get her head around what was going on. Things were now moving faster than she planned or had ever expected. She wanted to slow things down, or did she? She needed to speak to someone, and that someone was not easy to find. Neither her mother nor Carolyn would work. Her mother was just getting comfortable with her having a yet-to-be-seen English boyfriend named Ed. Another Englishman, another name . . . way too much. Carolyn was better, but she knew that Pat was involved with Ed, although not about the extent of their involvement. Talking to Ed was totally out of the question. What a mess!

She stood, *ah, to heck with it,* she told herself and walked into her bedroom with a plan of attack.

Roy stood at the door with a large bouquet of flowers. He handed them to Pat. "For my hostess and girlfriend, with thanks and fondness." He stepped back to take Pat in. "Wow, do you look beautiful, or what?" She was wearing a light blue summer dress with short sleeves and a low cut that showed off her figure to its fullest. For the first time since Roy had met her, she wore jewelry; earrings, a necklace, and a bracelet. Her eye makeup set off her green eyes, almost mysteriously. The high heels she wore enhanced her figure. Roy let out a low whistle. "You really do look great, Pat."

Pat twirled to show off her dress. "It's new," she said. "I'm glad you like it."

Roy nodded his approval. "It is beautiful, Pat, but I'm afraid Charley's dead."

Pat froze to attention. "What? Who's Charley? Get in here. Now!"

Roy stepped into the room, trying not to smile but instead keep a very straight face. "You know, Charley; he's dead."

Pat shook her head. "I don't know what the hell you're talking about. Who is Charley," she demanded.

Roy grinned sheepishly. "You're not going to like this."

"I'll decide what I like and don't like, Roy. Speak!"

"When I say 'Charley's dead', it means that your petticoat is showing . . . at the back."

Pat's head sunk to her chest, her shoulders relaxed, and she took time to reflect on her reaction. When she looked up, Roy was surprised to see her smiling. "You blokes and your bloody British language can sometime be a pain in the butt. And here we call them slips, not petticoats."

"So perhaps I should have said, Charley's slipped?"

Pat quickly adjusted the back of her dress, walked into the kitchen, refusing to acknowledge the comment. She put the flowers in a vase that was sitting on the kitchen counter.

"Am I that obvious?" Roy asked.

"I wouldn't say obvious," Pat replied setting the flowers on the coffee table. "I saw you do a double-take at the florist we passed yesterday and could almost see the bulb flash above your head. I also noticed the way you gently frowned when you saw the two young girls smoking and speaking unnecessarily loud as they walked along the street. Plus I noticed, as we crossed a busy street, you wanted to take my arm to guide me safely, but were too concerned that I may have taken offense."

Roy shook his head in surprise. "I am duly impressed. Was this from your training as a spy?"

Pat shook her head, not bothering to respond.

"Perhaps I meant to ask, was this from your training as a civil servant?"

Pat moved the flowers to the dining table. "Do you know what they are?" she asked.

Roy shook his head. "No, but I think they're very nice."

"Yes, they are. They're gladiolus, often called sword lilies, and they're one of my favorites. What a lovely pink. Thank you very much."

"At the risk of repeating myself, you look beautiful."

"Well it's a special night for us, so I wanted to look my best. Would you like a glass of wine before we head out?"

Roy nodded. "Maybe we could stay in, listen to Gordon Lightfoot and just kiss?"

"I opened a white. I hope you like it. It's bottled in Ontario, not far from where my parents live."

Roy twirled the glass of wine and held it to the light. "It has good legs," he said, and slowly took a sip. He washed it around his mouth and swallowed gracefully. "Good flavor and a fine finish. Yes, a good choice."

"God, almighty," Pat groaned. "Don't tell me . . ."

"I have no idea of what I just said, Pat. I saw it on a television show once." He took a larger sip. "But it does taste good."

Pat took Roy's hand and walked to the balcony window overlooking downtown Ottawa. Roy stood behind her, close enough to smell her wonderful fragrance. He slipped his arms around her waist and she placed her arms on his.

"Beautiful city is Ottawa. Lots of history and culture. Nice view isn't it?" Pat asked.

"Very, very lovely."

Pat nudged him with her elbow. "You're not looking at the city view; you're looking down the front of my dress. You're checking out my breasts!"

"Admiring, not checking out. I checked out your breasts—to use your expression—the day I met you at Ed's mother's house, and have been admiring them ever since. You have a lovely figure, Pat, and it's such a pleasure for me to be so close to you both physically and, if I may say so, emotionally. Just being close to you makes me feel special. I do hope one day I can kiss your breast and indeed I hope one day we can have sex."

Pat turned around to face him. "Roy, we will never have sex. Never! In fact it's impossible. Do you understand me?"

Roy staggered back slightly, at a loss for words.

Pat continued. "Sex is a noun, Roy. You cannot *have* a noun. Now your sex is male and mine is female, so we cannot *have* sex. If you're going to use slang, an idiom if you wish, for touching, kissing, licking, sucking, etcetera, etcetera, then let's use the much nicer expression; making love. Are you with me here, Roy?"

Roy turned her back to him put his arms around her and pulled her close. "Amazing, you're just bloody amazing." He kissed the top of her head. "Pat, one day I hope we can touch, kiss, lick, and do everything else involved in making love; including sexual intercourse. Is that correct English, if somewhat blunt?"

"Clear as a bell, Roy. Let's see how things work out, okay?"

"Looking forward to whatever happens, Pat. I do hope it comes to fruition, but I will never be pushy about trying." He hugged her tightly and held her close.

"Speaking of amazing, Roy. Either you have three hands, and your third hand is massaging the small of my back—and a little higher, or you have a Coho salmon in your pants swimming up-stream!"

Roy took a small step back to separate their bodies from touching below his waist. "Hey, I'm sorry. I didn't think you'd notice. I . . . er . . ."

Pat stepped back to re-connect them. "Not a problem. I'll take it as a compliment."

Roy kissed the top of her head. "Thanks. Let's put it down to practice . . . just in case the need arises into the future."

"Arises? Is that a play on words?"

He squeezed her tighter. "I like you so much, Pat."

"So tell me something?"

"Of course, Pat. Whatever you want to know."

Pat squeezed his arms to make it clear she was asking her questions in a friendly manner. "You're seven-feet tall, right?"

"Six-two, smarty pants."

"So you're seven-feet tall, sixty-two years of age . . ."

"I'm twenty-eight."

"You've got a good job. Own your own apartment—okay, flat. You have a nice car, probably paid for."

"Correct."

"You're not bad looking. You've a worldly type personality. Not overly educated, but very smart. Smart is often better in the real world."

"Thanks."

"So tell me, Roy: what are you doing here? What are you doing here with me in your arms? Shouldn't you be with some charming English lady, who's tall, blonde, pretty, well endowed physically, who speaks with a posh accent, and one that is just below the upper ranks of British society? And shouldn't you have *her* in your arms as you look over the view of Paris, London, or some exotic city in the world? Instead you're here with me, a five-foot-two . . . okay five-foot-one-and-a-half inches, a lowly civil servant, a Canadian even—whose accent sticks out a country mile in Mayfair or Soho. I'm glad you're here, Roy, but it does make me wonder."

Roy paused before he replied. "Well if you put it like that . . ."

Pat nudged him in his ribs. "Be careful how you reply, Mr. Johnson."

Roy kissed the top of her head. "Well to start with I like your three personalities. I . . ."

"My what!"

Roy continued. "I like you when you're running the show; the boss. You are clear-minded, very sure of yourself, and willing to give and take orders—especially give. Then I like you when you turn on your charm and have people almost eating out of your hand; as was the case with Billy . . . and me, of course. And finally I like you when you let me hold you like this, make *me* feel like the boss, when I know I'm not, and you have me feeling so comfortable, I never want to let you go. Additionally, if I may, you are very pretty and have a very sexy and beautifully proportioned figure."

Pat squeezed his arms tight. "Whoa, I wasn't expecting that." She turned to face him, stood on her toes and kissed him quickly. "Thank you. That was very nicely put."

"I like you big time, Pat. I really do enjoy being with you."

"You're a great guy, Roy. I like you too. Let's finish our wine and go have a great meal." She looked up at him. "And feel free to help me across a busy street any time." She picked up her wine and took a sip of. "Or any street for that matter."

Roy sipped his wine. "Not bad looking?" he asked, raising his eyebrows.

Pat shrugged and wiggled her head in thought. "Okay, good looking!"

He toasted her and gave her a quick kiss on her lips.

Lord Stonebridge said good bye to Ted Morden in Ottawa and switched the speaker phone on. "So how good a shot is Mr. Crowe, Miss Andrews?"

"Not as good as I am, sir," Carolyn replied.

Stonebridge understood. "It can't be MI6. The risk is just too great."

"I understand, sir. It's just . . ."

"Next time, Miss Andrews. You have my commitment."

"Thank you, sir. He's a better shot than most considering his limited training."

Stonebridge continued. "Good, that's good. Strange that Miss Weston was not into work today, especially when she is usually the one that is in on Saturdays."

Carolyn nodded. "Well she took yesterday off, it seems reasonable she'd take today off."

"Apparently so. If Ted gets through to Miss Weston tomorrow at eight a.m. Ottawa time and you get through at eight thirty, please phone me as soon as you have an up-date."

"Yes, sir."

They hung up.

Roy and Pat entered her apartment arm in arm, and kissed as soon as the door closed behind them. She stood on her toes and he had to bend down.

Pat pushed him away, giggling. "Turn on the tape," she said. "I'll get the wine."

Roy turned on the tape and pressed play. Pat had poured the wine and placed them on the coffee table.

She looked up at him. "I have two words for you, Roy: let's dance."

The difference in height only allowed them to shuffle around the room, and they clung to each other to compensate. Neither spoke while they danced, and they separated when *Black Day in July* started.

Pat sat and picked up her glass. "I want to thank you again for the birthday card and the lovely earrings you bought me, Roy, but you really shouldn't have."

"My mother has good taste," Roy said, sipping his wine.

"Peridot is my birthstone. I suppose you knew that?"

"Of course. Green earrings with your lovely green eyes; absolutely beautiful. Saw your birthday on your passport. You know the passport that doesn't have you in Turkey."

Pat smiled. "DNA, Roy."

Roy looked at the cushion on the sofa. "I could check your sternum area, but I suppose it would be a bit awkward with your lovely dress?"

"Very awkward. Perhaps I'll change . . ."

"Terrific," he interrupted.

"Perhaps I'll change the location," she continued. "I'd like us to go to my bedroom."

"Oh, God, yes," Roy managed, taking her hands.

She walked him to her bedroom door and turned. "Get down here, Roy. I want to speak face to face for a minute."

Roy quickly got down on one knee, their faces now level.

Pat put his hands around her waist and moved closer to him. "Look, there is an issue I must address."

Roy nodded, gulping in anticipation.

"You're a big man. You have big hands, big feet, and . . . well I'm just a bit nervous."

"Oh, Pat, it'll work out, I promise."

Pat grinned. "It's not the *out* bit I'm worried about, Roy."

Roy pulled her to himself and hugged her with all the love he could muster. "We'll work on it together, Pat. We'll go slowly and carefully."

Pat closed her eyes for a moment, building up her courage. "You do love me don't you, Roy?"

Roy smiled and kissed her briefly. "Like I've never loved before, Pat. I love you completely and for ever. And it's not because we're at your bedroom door."

"If I didn't think you loved me, Roy, we wouldn't be at my bedroom door. And if I didn't love you, we wouldn't be here either." She paused. "I'm not asking you to love me for ever; I just want it to be for real."

"Absolutely for real. Honest. In the morning, Pat, I'd like to tell you when I fell in love with you, but it's a bit of a story."

Pat smiled and nodded her understanding. "Okay, Roy. Let's go become lovers."

Pat took his hand and led him into her bedroom. He reached for her, but she patted him gently away with a wink. Quickly she lit two candles, one each side of the bed. She had him sit on the end of her bed, and turned to him in the subtle glow the candles offered.

"I have two other requests, Roy."

Roy nodded.

"First, I want you to realize I'm not, how can I say this; I'm not as experienced in the world of romance as you are. In your Brit-talk, that would be a huge understatement. Okay?"

He reached up and placed his hands on her dress, covering her breasts. "I love you so much, Pat."

She covered his hands with hers, pressing them into her now hardening nipples. "So I want our lovemaking to be very, special. Not just for me, but for you also, Roy. I want this to be the best kissing, touching, licking, and even sucking . . . etc. ever. Please?" She giggled as he pushed his thumbs against her nipples.

"Never better, Pat. It'll never be better."

"And I want you to be the leader tonight. I'll follow your lead. Undress me please, Roy."

CHAPTER THIRTEEN

SUNDAY, AUGUST 31ST, 1985 7AM

R oy opened his eyes to see Pat wide awake and smiling gently at him. She leaned over and kissed his nose. "How ya doing, big boy?" she asked.

"Never better, lover, never better."

"So listen," Pat continued, "you promised something special, and last night was super special . . . each time, that is." She grinned. "I do hope it was . . ."

"Pat, it was everything I was hoping for and then some. Even after you kept falling asleep, that is." He laughed.

"Nodded off, big guy, not asleep. You're tough on a young lady! So tell me when you fell in love with me, Roy." She added a second pillow under her head to hear his answer, and covered her breasts with the bed sheet to keep his mind to the question at hand.

"Couldn't we cover that off over breakfast?"

"No." Pat replied briskly. "Now is the time to 'fess up'."

Roy nodded. He knew when Pat was giving orders it was best to take them. "Okay, so it was a few weeks ago," he began, "and a friend of mine was over on a Saturday night and we were having a golden oldies night. It was great; we were playing some old Beatles', lots of the Stone's, even Cliff Richards . . ."

"Never heard of him," Pat interrupted.

"England's answer to Elvis in the early sixties. Good guy."

"Nice bloke you mean?"

"Okay. Nice bloke if you prefer. Anyway this Beatles' song was playing, and . . ."

"Hold it. Hold it," Pat interrupted, putting her finger to Roy's lips. "Was this *friend* a woman: of the female variety?"

Roy shrugged. "Anyway . . ."

Pat sat up, letting the sheet slip. "Just a bloody minute here, young man. Are you telling me you decided you loved me while on a date with a girlfriend?"

Roy's eyes moved to her breasts and then to her eyes. "You have beautiful breasts, Pat."

She quickly covered up again. "Well? Was this a date with a girlfriend?"

Roy rolled his head, thinking of the better answer. "Not exactly."

Pat closed an eye making it clear she did not buy that answer. "So she wasn't exactly a girlfriend, or she wasn't exactly a date?"

Roy grinned. "Exactly."

"Now listen here . . ."

"She was, is, my friend's ex-wife. She was feeling a bit sad, so we shared Chinese."

"Oh, my God!" Pat groaned. "You're telling me . . ."

"Pat, you're not letting me tell you!" He leaned over and kissed her gently on her lips. "I love you. Let me finish."

"Okay, lover boy, but it better be good."

"So this Beatles' song was playing, and suddenly the words struck home and I couldn't help but think of you, and bingo! I decided I loved you. It obviously caught me off guard because my friend asked me if I was okay."

"And?"

"I just told her I was in love."

"Oh, Jesus, help me understand men! Did she think . . . ?"

Roy groaned. "I'm afraid so."

"Christ all bloody mighty! So did you let her think it was her? Did you sleep with her?"

Roy gasped and swallowed to catch his breath. "Of course I didn't . . . but shit, you can't ask that."

Pat gave a sly grin. "Okay, I take the question back." She shrugged. "You answered it anyway."

Roy shook his head. "You are a very cheeky bugger. I'll have to watch what I say with you around."

Pat nodded gently. "What a nice thing to say. Thank you." She paused for effect. "Lie on your back and close your eyes please."

Roy did as he was told, hoping for something special. Pat quickly moved on top of him and crossed her arms on his chest, making sure her breasts were not visible to Roy. "So what was the song that so romantically convinced you I wasn't such a bad person after all?" Pat asked.

"I was hoping for . . ."

"Forget it."

Roy put his hands behind his head. "You're very beautiful, Pat."

"The song please."

"Would you like me to hum it?"

"Would you like me to connect my knee to your crown jewels?"

"*In my life*," Roy answered quickly.

Pat though about the words. "Isn't that someone looking back on their life, sort of an old person? You're not that old are you?"

"I think it's more someone comparing prior experiences to his true love. I don't think age was a significant reference."

"So you were comparing me . . ."

"Absolutely not. It just struck me that you are the love of my life."

Pat gulped at his words, closing her eyes to take in what he was saying. "You know, Roy, you could hurt my feelings if you're messing with me, and I'm not a good person to get on the wrong side of."

"Oh, Pat, I fully understand you're not a *good* person to annoy, and I want you to know that, notwithstanding the salesperson in me, I'm not a person to exaggerate."

Pat rolled off Roy and the bed, taking the top sheet with her to cover herself. "Okay, breakfast time. Move your ass."

"But, Pat, I want to ask you . . ."

"Ask me at the breakfast table. Now move it." She left the bedroom and entered the bathroom.

Roy watched open-mouthed, not capable of words. He shook his head, slipped on some clothes, and walked to the kitchen to put the kettle on for tea.

Roy pushed his plate away and finished his cup of tea. He wiped his lips clean with a serviette, ready to face the music. "So I was wondering . . ."

The phone ringing in the bedroom interrupted him. Pat shrugged. "Roy, I have to get that. It's my business phone."

Roy shrugged in defeat. "So who is it, the KGB?"

Pat winked at him. "Don't get smart now. We civil servants are always on the job." She walked quickly to her bedroom closing the door behind her as she entered.

She returned several minutes later, obviously with something on her mind.

"Is everything okay?" Roy asked uncomfortably.

Pat waved away the concern. "Sure. No problem. Just something I have to think about." She paused. "I'll have another call in a couple of minutes, so if you can hold off on your question?"

Roy nodded, fascinated by how she could control their time.

Pat reached for his hand. "I did want to say that last night was very special. You treated me wonderfully, and as you suggested things did work *out* okay. I was a little nervous when you asked me to pose in just my slip, petticoat if you will, and my high heels. At first it felt a bit kinky, but when you said I looked like a princess, and swept me off my feet. Well . . . it was just beautiful."

"It was wonderful, Pat. I think you are . . ."

The phone ringing in Pat's bedroom ended the conversation. She motioned that she would be a few minutes and left to take the call.

Ten minutes later Pat returned, visibly more relaxed. She sat at the table, and picked up her cup of tea. "Okay, big boy, what's the question of the day?"

"You scare me sometimes," Roy smiled. "I really do think you are an amazing person. Are you this way with all your boyfriends?"

"Is that the question?"

"No," Roy said, shaking his head, "that was just a statement. What I wanted to ask you . . ."

The phone rang in the kitchen. Roy threw up his hands. "Oh hell, I give up!"

Pat let the phone ring. "It's okay. It's my mother. I'll phone her back." She rested her hands on the table. "Go ahead."

Roy took a deep breath and quickly asked, "Will you marry me, Pat?"

Pat closed her eyes, letting the question sink in.

Roy spoke quickly. "I don't mean 'marry me' like I asked Carolyn. That was a statement of friendship. I mean will you marry me, marry me: husband and wife . . . or wife and husband if you prefer. I er . . . I er . . . Christ! I thought I had my head in gear to ask you, and now I'm just bumbling along. Sorry. Forgive me."

Pat smiled and chuckled as Roy stumbled. "Took your time in asking, didn't you?"

"What?" Roy gasped, not believing what he'd heard.

"Of course I'll marry you," Pat said slowly, "next May at Stonebridge Manor, courtesy of Lord and Lady Stonebridge."

"Oh, my God!" Roy gasped. "How did you . . . how could you?"

"The second call was Carolyn. I told her you were going to ask me to marry you, she checked with her parents and they agreed to host the wedding."

Roy combed his fingers through his hair, not quite believing what was happening. "Now listen, young lady, I'm sitting here almost wetting myself, nervous as hell about asking you to marry me, and you're in the next room making the nuptial arrangements!"

Pat grinned. "You know what they say; if you want something done, get a woman."

"I can't believe this," Roy groaned. "You . . . you . . ."

"I love you, Roy. That's all that matters."

Roy laughed aloud. "Of course it is, of course it is." He stood and walked to his bedroom, pointing at Pat. "Wait there please."

He returned in less than a minute. Standing in front of Pat, he offered her a jeweler's ring box. "My mother helped me pick it out. I know some girls prefer not to be identified as engaged—women's lib and all that—but I hope you'll like it."

Pat took the unopened box. "I'll like it and I'll wear it, even if it's made of brass." She opened the box and sat back in her seat. It was a solitaire that sparkled in the morning light. The stone was huge. She looked up at Roy. "You'd better not tell me this is a diamond."

"It's a diamond."

"Didn't I just tell you to . . . ?" Before she could finish, tears formed in her eyes and slowly trickled down her cheeks. "Please put it on my finger, Roy."

Roy placed it on the ring finger of her left hand, pulled her up and held her close. He started to sing.

"There are places I remember,
All my life . . ."

Pat hugged him, and they sang and finished the song.

"In my life, I love you more."

They held each other for some time, not speaking. When they separated, Pat looked up with a smile. "Roy, we have to go see Ed in Oakville."

"Hey, we can phone him, can't we?"

"I have to see him for business, Roy. And what better way to tell him about us than face to face."

"Got it!" Roy agreed.

"But you'll have to follow my lead. Okay?"

"DNA, correct?"

"Yes: do not ask. Thanks. Now let's pack."

They eagerly went to their bedrooms to pack.

When he got to the guest bedroom, Roy quickly started packing now looking forward to seeing his best friend, *me best mate*, to pass on the good news and ask Eddie to be his best man.

Pat sat the end of her bed, thinking through the next twenty-four hours. She knew things could get tricky. She wasn't worried, but she had to control the process. She started packing by sliding her hand under the mattress, pulling out her handgun and slipping it into her overnight bag. *First things first.*

Pat finished packing, made three phone calls, topped up Robin's food and met Roy, now fully packed and ready to go, at the door to the hallway. He had a permanent smile on his face.

"What are you grinning at?" Pat asked.

"I'm just wondering what Eddie will say when he finds out we're engaged."

Pat smiled at the thought. "What will he think of your being engaged? What with all your past girlfriends."

"He'll be surprised. But then he'll know why I asked someone as nice as you. And what about you? What are the chances he'll expect you to turn up engaged?"

"Two chances—slim and fat!"

"Terrific," Roy said, now enthusiastic about the opportunity to surprise Eddie, it having been the other way around for the past eighteen months. He bent and kissed her gently. "Let's go have some fun."

"Just a reminder," Pat said gingerly, "there may be things I say to Ed you may not agree with or understand. But I need you to . . ."

"No problem," Roy interrupted, "you're the boss."

She squinted at him with one eye closed. "I thought we'd agreed . . ."

"Just a turn of phrase, Pat, just a turn of phrase."

"Men," she mumbled, opening the door and stepping out into a new phase of her life.

CHAPTER FOURTEEN

5PM SAME DAY

Ed looked at his watch and shrugged. He wasn't used to having visitors on a Sunday evening. He walked to the intercom. "Crowe's Nest," he said.

"Hi, Ed, it's me, Pat."

"What a nice surprise, I'll buzz you in. Tea or coffee?"

"How about some wine?" Pat asked.

Ed wondered what was up. "Red or white?"

There was a brief delay. "Both please," Pat replied.

Ed pressed the button to open the door to the lobby on the main floor, still unsure what was happening. He took out a bottle of red and white but didn't open them. Instead he scurried around the apartment putting away newspapers and throwing the dirty dishes into the dishwasher. He combed his hands through his hair and waited for the knock on the door. It was not the gentle four-knock rap that Pat used as a bit of an identifier. He was not worried, but curious. He stood to the side of the door and opened it.

"Bloody Hell," he exclaimed, stepping backwards into the room. Roy's wide grin and Pat's nervous smile caught him completely off guard. He looked each of them in the eyes and knew exactly what he was about to be told. His mind struggled to think straight as he took a deep breath.

"Are you going to invite us in, Eddie, or do we stand in the hallway all day?" Roy asked, totally enjoying himself.

"Come in, come in, come in," Ed mustered, shaking hands with Pat then Roy. He motioned them into the apartment, still grappling with the situation.

Pat looked Ed straight in the eyes. "So I'm not worth a hug now?" she asked.

Ed laughed off the question and gave her a full and solid hug. "My number one hero is always worth a hug."

"That's heroine, Eddie," Roy corrected him.

"Just a civil servant," Pat said. "Over-worked and under-paid."

Roy took the keys from Pat, and turned to Ed. "I'm told I have to go to the car and get our bags . . . and that I have to take at least half an hour."

"That assumes we can stay-over," Pat added.

"Go get the bags, Roy," Ed said, now visibly relaxed and in charge of his emotions.

Roy left with a wave of his hand.

Pat sat on the sofa, holding her hands on her lap, covering her left hand. "You're not mad at me are you, Ed?"

Ed walked to her and took her left hand in his. "That's a beautiful engagement ring, Pat. My very best wishes and congratulations." He sat across from her in the love seat.

"Well are you?"

Ed shrugged. "Why would I be mad at you? Just because we were lovers a few weeks ago, and agreed to have a year together? Just because you are now marrying my best friend, and just because I suppose I'll be asked to be best man? And just because a few weeks ago we were unofficially a *married* couple in Paris and made international headlines! And now you're marrying the bloke that asked Carolyn to marry him! Why would all that make me mad at you?"

"You can be a real a jerk, Ed," Pat said, holding her head in her hands. "Don't rub it in, okay?"

"Pat, let me make this absolutely clear. I am probably the third happiest person in the world right now, and I only wish I could have been part of getting you and Roy together."

Pat looked up, smiling. "It gets worse, Ed."

"You mean it gets better."

Pat took a breath to relax. "We're getting married at Stonebridge Manor. Carolyn is my Maid of Honor."

Ed grinned and laughed aloud. "Does that mean I can't bring a date?"

Pat didn't respond immediately. She knew he was probably hurting inside at the thought of her and Roy's wedding being held at the Manor. When she did respond, she had to laugh. "Do you know that I once told Carolyn that I loved you? In retrospect, I think she probably dropped the phone."

Ed gulped, not sure what to say.

"I'm not stupid, Ed," Pat said nicely. "I know you're in love with each other and I've known for some time. That doesn't change my feelings for you. I love you in my own silly way, and always will. I just hope . . ."

"Always, Pat. In my own silly way . . ."

Pat reached into her purse and pulled out a tape. "Please play this, Ed. I had planned on mailing it to you with a letter, but this is easier." She grinned. "It's sometimes better not to put things in writing . . . you never know, do you? I want to thank you for pulling a Simon and Garfunkel on me."

Ed shrugged, clearly not understanding the message.

"Just play the first song; and then press 'pause'."

Ed pressed the 'play' button and sat.

Without speaking they listened to *I Am A Rock*. Ed knew the words, but took them in more than he normally would. When it was finished, he pressed 'pause'.

Pat spoke clearly and sincerely. "That was me, Ed. That was me before I met you. I was a 'rock' and proud of it. Now don't say anything, just press 'play'."

Ed did as he was told.

Bridge over Troubled Water played gently in their silence. Ed winked at Pat when the words *Sail on Silver Girl* were sung. She nodded her thanks. The song ended and for a few moments neither spoke. Pat broke the silence.

"So that is what you've been to me, a bridge into a new life. And that was before Roy made it all even better. Thank you, Ed. Please keep the tape, and play it from time to time. I'll never be able to listen to those two songs again without thinking about you . . . and us."

Ed smiled his thanks. "They'll always be up there with Gordon."

"One other question, Ed. And this is very important to me. Please be honest with me."

"The answer is no, Pat. The answer to your question is a definite no!"

"You don't even know the question, for God's sake . . ."

Ed interrupted quickly. "Yes, I do. You want to know if I've ever told Roy we were lovers. No, I have not and never would."

Pat nodded her thanks.

Ed continued. "Which doesn't mean he . . ."

"That's different, Ed. It's not what he knows, or guesses, or assumes. I just wanted to know if you'd talked about us in that fashion."

Ed shook his head and crossed his heart.

Pat stood as tall and as erect as she could. "Good. Now's that's over, let's have a glass of wine."

Ed opened the red and poured them each a glass.

Pat took a sip. "And by the way, I'll sleep in your guest room and Roy will sleep on the sofa. Please don't argue with me, we've made up our minds."

"I've learned never to argue with you, Pat. Your wish and all that."

Pat toasted his comments. "I've taught you well, Ed. I've taught you very well."

Having gone over the wedding plans, such as they were, the three finished off their glasses of wine with a toast of good wishes from Ed.

"So are we going to the Queen's Head?" Roy asked enthusiastically.

Ed looked nervously at Pat. "That creates a bit of a problem," he said.

Roy shrugged in ignorance.

"I can't go there," Pat said.

"You've been barred from a pub?" Roy asked, not sure he was hearing right.

Ed shook his head. "Not barred."

"I'm afraid it's a DNA, Roy," Pat explained.

"DNA?" Ed wondered.

"Do not ask," Roy clarified. "I accept the fact that in marrying Pat, I have to get used to DNA's. Something I am more than willing to accept I might add."

Pat stood. "You two go for a beer, just give me a minute." She stepped into the guest room and closed the door. Two minutes later she returned and stood by the table. She looked into her hand where she held a small sheet of paper. With some authority, she spoke.

"You two blokes go to the boozer. You go by Shanks's pony, using your plates of meat and no skiving off on the way, yeah? Have a butcher's at the birds, but no chatting 'em up. The beer ain't dear, so three pints each, yeah? If you need to see a man about a dog, you go up the apples, have a Johnny Riddle, then down the pears. While you're having a grand time and I'm on me Todd, I'll hoover this place and I have to give some people a tinkle. We don't want no cock-ups with Old Bill, so phone when you're ready and I'll pick you up, drive you home, and your father's brother's name is Robert. When we get home we'll have a bit of a knees up, a bit of how's your father, a cuppa char and we'll all be dead chuffed!" She grinned. "Whatca fink of that then?"

Ed and Roy looked at each other in amazement, unable for a while to speak.

Roy spoke first. "Gawd luv a duck! Brilliant! You're awright me old china, there's no flies on you, sweetheart."

"Cor blimey, she knows her onions does our Pat," Ed said. He looked at Roy and motioned to the door. "C'mon, sunshine, before your missus changes her mind."

Pat held back a tear as she hugged them both. "Have a good time blokes, and thank you both for changing my life so wonderfully." She pushed them toward the door and turned away so they wouldn't see her cry.

They didn't speak until they were in the elevator. Roy turned to Ed with a questioning smile. "A bit of how's your father?"

"Methinks she knows not of what she speaks," Ed laughed, shaking his head.

"Well if you don't tell her, neither will I."

"Deal."

They shook hands.

They walked slowly to the Queen's Head enjoying the evening air and each other's company.

"I know it's obvious," Ed said, turning to Roy, "but you have a wonderful person in Pat. She certainly has a mind of her own . . . luckily you just do as your told."

Roy laughed. "Yeah, right. It's going to be an interesting life. She's not really going to hoover your place is she?"

Ed slapped Roy on his back. "Not a snowball's chance in Hell! She just wanted to use that silly British phrase."

Roy nodded and walked a few steps. "Which silly British phrase?"

Ed rolled his eyes. "May you have an interesting marriage, Roy."

Roy shrugged in ignorance and they walked on.

Ed stopped half a block from the pub and turned to Roy. "I should tell you, Roy, and I know Pat would be okay with this now. The reason she can't go to the Queen's Head is because as far as they know she is dead."

"Dead! Bloody Hell."

"Her apartment, just around the corner, was blown up shortly after I got back from Turkey. She and an unidentified male died in the blast. That was the official story anyway."

Roy closed his eyes and shook his head in disbelief. "The plot thickens. And the unidentified male was who?"

"Unidentified."

"Sure, sure. The cheque's in the mail and I'll love you in the morning."

"I'll buy the first round," Ed said, not responding to Roy's comment.

They stood at the bar sipping their beers. Ed introduced Roy to Seana, the recently hired bartender. She shook hands with Roy and commented with a laugh on having yet another strange accent in the Queen's Head. In his usual perfect manner, Roy expressed his pleasure in visiting his good friend Eddie in Oakville.

"Eddie?" Seana asked with a smile.

"Edwin to his mother," Roy added as Ed stood and shrugged at the conversation he had no intention of joining.

"Let's have a seat," Ed suggested motioning to the seats under the window by the side door.

"Nice looking lady," Roy said motioning to Seana. "You ever asked her out?"

Ed shook his head. "No. Let's talk about your wedding not my personal activities, shall we?"

"Hey, Eddie, my boy, you have to get out more. And I don't mean working on all your super secret stuff. You need more female friends, it's only healthy . . ."

He stopped talking as Stephanie who was serving their area interrupted. "Another beer gentlemen? Evening, Edwin," she said with a smile.

Ed rolled his eyes. "Now look what you've done," he groaned as Stephanie waited with a smile. "Two more beers please, Stephanie." Stephanie nodded and headed to the bar.

Roy gave Ed a wink. "Hey, two good looking young ladies here, Eddie. One blonde and one brunette. Don't you think . . ."

"Your wedding, Roy?"

The conversation turned to the wedding plans. Ed sat and listened to what few plans were already in place. He relaxed as he heard Roy speak so enthusiastically about his wedding that a week ago would have not even have entered Ed's mind as a possibility. He looked over Roy's shoulder and his relaxation disappeared. Stephanie and Seana were walking together toward them, with their two beers on Stephanie's tray.

"Here you go, gentlemen," Stephanie said, placing the beers on the table.

Seana leaned forward and spoke quietly. "So, Ed, are you still coming to our party next Friday? Steph and I are hoping it's still on you social agenda."

"Of course," Ed replied with a grin. "Same place? Same time?"

Stephanie nodded. "You got it. And remember, no date. Lots of young ladies there. Just you and a bottle of red wine."

They turned and headed back to the bar.

Roy's eyes followed them, and then he turned to Ed. "I think I've just had the wool pulled over my eyes."

Ed pulled a Gallic shrug. "Vhat can I say? They like my funny accent."

Roy shook his head and picked up his fresh beer. "Two good looking ladies, one bottle of red wine, and one Eddie Crowe? Never!"

"So, your honeymoon plans?" Ed asked, getting the conversation back on track. Behind Roy, Stephanie and Seana gave Ed the thumbs up.

Ed waved his thanks to the ladies as he and Roy left the pub.

CHAPTER FIFTEEN

MONDAY, SEPTEMBER 1ST, 1985 8:30 AM

E d shook hands and hugged them both as Pat and Roy left for a visit to her parents.

"Good luck and keep me up-to-date on everything," Ed said. "Some of us have to get to work you know."

With promises to drive carefully, Pat and Roy left arm in arm.

Quickly cleaning up the breakfast mess, Ed sat and scanned the newspaper. Not a lot of good news, and all the bad news seemed to take the lead. A knock on the door detracted him. *What did they forget,* he wondered. He opened the door to Carolyn, and for the second time in 24 hours he was caught completely off guard.

"Good morning, Mr. Crowe. May I come in?" She was obviously enjoying the moment.

Ed stepped back to let her in noticing that she had no luggage, not even a handbag. He peered each way down the hallway. "Is my mum hiding somewhere?" he asked, closing the door.

"Don't be so suspicious, young man. And don't I at least get a welcome hug?"

Ed took her in his arms trying desperately not to show his emotions. He failed. Carolyn held him tight, knowing what he was going through.

"I don't know what to say," Ed blurted.

Carolyn looked up at him. "Yes you do."

He kissed her on her forehead. "Yes, I do. I love you, Carolyn. It's wonderful to see you. I love you. I'm nervous why you're here. I love you. But I have to get to work in about half an hour."

"No you don't, Ed. Pat has looked after that. You're not expected to be back to work until next Monday. Incidentally, when I met her and Roy downstairs she slipped me a key which, I suspect, fits your front door. Comments?"

Ed thought for a while. "Hmm. Did she say anything about the key?"

"Two words. Any idea what they might have been?"

Ed responded quickly. "Never used?" He hoped he knew Pat well enough to think like her.

She smiled. "Very good answer. Now stop talking and kiss me properly."

Ed did as he was told.

"We need to talk," Carolyn said as they sat across from each other at the kitchen table.

"Can we make love?" Ed asked.

"No. Either I, or we, have to be ready to leave at 9:30."

"That's less than half an hour."

"My point exactly."

Ed gave up hope for a fun morning. "How can I be of assistance, Miss?" Using her code name changed the tone of the discussion.

Carolyn smiled her appreciation. "Thank you for that, Mister. Your country needs you; I'm glad or sad to say."

"Shall I pack?"

She shook her head. "Not this time. You need to agree to the plan before we leave. Time is short, the plan is dangerous, and you'll need to bring a gun."

Ed chuckled. "I don't have a gun."

"Look in the freezer portion of your fridge."

Ed got up to look. "A gift from the Boss no doubt," he said. The gun was there, along with ammunition. He placed the gun in the cupboard along with tea bags and coffee. "She does have her ways," Ed quipped. "This brings a new interpretation to the weaponry expression of 'freeze'."

Carolyn refused to acknowledge the comment. "Have a seat. Let me explain where we're at, what we need you for, and why I would personally prefer you passed on this one."

"Because you love me?"

"That is definitely part of it. But let me explain without interruption. Time is running out."

Ed waved her on.

"Your friend, Mike, the pig, wants a deal. He's offered us the opportunity to catch, in Britain, one of Columbia's biggest drug dealers. If it works out, he gets a recommended lower sentence from the Crown Prosecutor. The plan is simple. He arranges to meet with the dealer, in person, to buy a quarter of a million pounds worth of drugs. That'll be worth ten times the amount on the streets of Britain. Steps are already in place. The news media in Britain have been told that Mike has escaped, and there's non-stop havoc in the House of Commons. The PM doesn't know about the plan, so she's taking the brunt of it during Prime Minster's Question Period—and she is not amused, in fact she's madder than hell. The Minister in charge is staying out of the House and dodging the media. Talk is he's soon to be demoted to the back-benches. The meet is being set up for tomorrow, in lovely St. Albans of all places. We can't use Mike. That's out of the question. He's safely locked in a stately home in the country. Two guards, MI6, twenty four hours a day."

Ed nodded his understanding so far.

"We need a new Mike. You're him." Carolyn raised her hands to stop Ed's questions. "Hear me out." She paused and took a deep breath. "You meet with the drug lord and his two companions. They will be armed and that cannot be changed. You will have a bag with the money and Pat's gun. It's actually a stolen gun from Buffalo, New York, not traceable to anyone in Canada. The actual plan of attack— and I do mean attack—is being worked out as we speak. The other people involved directly will be CIA, no Brits. We can't go shooting people willy-nilly; they have different rules. That's why it's MI6, and not Scotland Yard. To be perfectly frank we're doing the Yanks, and ourselves of course, a favor. Their drug problems are way worse than ours. The limousine arrives downstairs at 9:30." She reached into her purse handed him a photo. "I know you saw him very briefly in Bradford, but these are the prison photos of Mike. As you can see, he has no shirt on. Charming looking chap, I'm sure. His vital stats are on the back. Questions?"

Ed scratched his forehead. "Does Pat know the plan?"

"No. Why?"

"She wouldn't be amused. She doesn't think much of my skill with guns."

"And?"

"And she wouldn't want to lose their best man in a shoot-out. Bad omen."

"We don't plan on losing you."

"Promise?"

Carolyn crossed her heart. "I promise you that it's not in the plan."

Ed reviewed the photos and information. "I don't look at all like Mike. He's taller than me."

"Mike's never met the Columbian before. Make-up does wonders. Beside we can add an inch in height easily."

"He's bald for Christ's sake."

"And your point is?"

Ed wondered if the next point was worth mentioning. "He's got tattoos all over his arms, back and neck; Swastikas for crying out loud!"

Carolyn shrugged. "Temporary tattoos. Rubbing alcohol: now you see them, now you don't."

"I thought you didn't want me to take this on?"

"I'm talking to you in your role as a consultant with MI6, not as a friend and certainly not as the man I love."

"Could I meet him again to learn the language of drugs?"

"You will."

Ed thought a moment. "Oh, God! The penny just dropped. You mean . . ."

"That's what I mean."

"He's being held at Stonebridge Manor!"

"Bingo!"

Ed stood and walked to his bedroom. "I'm in. Give me ten minutes."

Seven minutes later Ed returned from his bedroom with a carry-on bag and a skip in his step. Putting the gun and ammunition in the bag he turned to Carolyn. "Ready when you are, Miss Andrews."

"Oh," Carolyn said, with her hand to her mouth. "Did I say the limo would be here at 9:30? I meant to say 10:30."

"You bugger."

"I wonder what we might do to kill an hour, Mr. Crowe?"

Ed dropped the bag, walked to Carolyn and took her in his arms. "Let's say we begin by my undressing you and I start to kiss your beautiful breasts?"

"Now there's a thought," she said, taking his hand and leading him back to his bedroom.

An hour later they were in the limousine heading to Hamilton Airport. They sat next to each other holding hands.

"You should visit more often," Ed remarked, squeezing her hand.

"Perhaps I should," Carolyn replied. She turned to him and kissed his cheek. "Are you mad at me about Pat and Roy? Having the wedding at the Manor, I mean?"

"Should I be?"

"Please don't answer my question with another question, Ed. It's important to me."

"No, Miss Andrews, I am not mad at you and have no right to be mad at you. I think the location is wonderful. I suspect there will be way more guests from Roy's side than Pat's, even if it was to be held in Canada." He looked her in the eyes. "Besides, I'm sure there will be more weddings at the Manor in the next one-hundred years."

"Maybe," she shrugged. "Yes; probably."

"Perhaps even your own children's?"

Carolyn moved closer to him. "Put your arms around me, Ed. Tell me how much you love me."

Ed did as he was told.

CHAPTER SIXTEEN

TUESDAY, SEPTEMBER 2ND, 1985, THE INN, ENGLAND 9AM

The flight had been uneventful. Other than making coffee for themselves and the pilot and co-pilot, they relaxed. Ed knew enough about the operation not to have to ask Carolyn any further questions, and he didn't want to talk about it anyway. Instead they talked about Pat and Roy's engagement, about how happy they were to be part of the wedding, and how neither of them would ever had expected that Pat and Roy would become a couple. They held hands, kissed from time to time and enjoyed each other's company at forty-thousand feet. They could not have been happier.

They got little sleep on the plane or at the MI6 Inn that was just a few miles from Stonebridge Manor. They were too excited to care about sleep. Breakfast was hot tea and cold toast, which they shared with a variety of birds as they sat on the veranda of The Inn. Carolyn listened and watched the man she loved as he identified the birds, some by their calls only. In the fifteen minutes they sat enjoying their surroundings, Ed identified six different birds. Carolyn could have sat there all day, but the gentle 'cough' from the driver ended that dream. Reluctantly they grabbed their bags and walked to the waiting limo.

Lady Stonebridge was waiting at the front door of Stonebridge Manor. She was obviously relaxed, holding a cup of tea and sipping from it slowly as the limo with Ed and Carolyn pulled up.

Lady Stonebridge nodded her welcome. "Good morning, my dear, and a good morning to you, Mr. Crowe. I was expecting you. Please come in. Tea is available in the sitting room."

"We don't have a lot of time, Mother," Carolyn said, kissing her mother on her cheek.

"You never do, dear. But Mr. Crowe likes his tea, don't you Mr. Crowe?"

"Tea and good company, Lady Stonebridge," Ed replied, following her into the sitting room.

Carolyn rolled her eyes, never sure what her mother would want to talk to Ed about. She followed them into the sitting room and poured for Ed and herself.

"We have a special guest at the Manor," Lady Stonebridge said, expressing no pleasure. "But then I imagine you both know that already. A not very nice looking character, I might add."

"Looks like he's from Neasden does he, Mother?" Carolyn asked, referring to the area of London where Lady Stonebridge had been born.

Lady Stonebridge ignored the comment.

"More like from Kilburn, Lady Stonebridge?" Ed asked, endeavoring to level the discussion.

"Yes, probably more like Kilburn, Mr. Crowe. But one shouldn't generalize should one?"

They finished their tea without further commentary and after a quick conversation on the weather, Ed and Carolyn headed upstairs to Lord Stonebridge's office.

Lord Stonebridge and Mr. Cooper were happy to see them both, but were visibly nervous about the matter at hand. As was expected, Lord Stonebridge had them sit and took command of the discussion.

"I confess some concern regarding this action," he said. "Too much over which we have no control. We're not used to dealing with the CIA in this sort of arrangement. They want this man, and they want him now."

"Way too much unknown," Mr. Cooper agreed.

Carolyn was straight to the point. "Then let's send Mr. Crowe home after a decent lunch and we cancel the meet. If it's too late to cancel, then arrest the man at the airport for importing drugs. Sounds simple to me."

Lord Stonebridge tapped his desk with his knuckles. "Good idea, Miss Andrews, but he's not carrying the drugs with him. He's not that stupid. The drugs are already in the U.K. somewhere. He's just delivering them to our man as the first of many such drops. Meet your customer, so to speak. They would never meet again, at least not in the exchange of goods and money. And, no he won't be delivering drugs personally. He'll take the money, give our man an address for the pick up and disappear. The money will stay in the U.K. and be used in the years ahead; strictly cash. No bank accounts, no trace."

Carolyn continued. "Why wouldn't he simply take the money and run? Why leave the drugs anywhere? It doesn't make a lot of sense."

Mr. Cooper shook his head. "This is a business deal. No drugs and 'Mr. Columbia' is dead before he leaves the country. It's that simple. No, the drugs will be somewhere. But it's him we're after, not the drugs. He's the prize."

"Why, Mr. Cooper," Ed chipped in, "it sounds like you've done this sort of thing before. I never pictured you as a drug cop."

Mr. Cooper shrugged. "Drugs, top secret documents, embarrassing photos, they're all the same. Quick exchanges of envelopes in a dark alley are a thing of the past. One has to change with the times."

Lord Stonebridge pressed a button on his phone and ordered tea. "Let's think it through over a nice cup of tea."

The tea was delivered along with some biscuits. The break allowed everyone to relax and clear their mind.

"What think you, Mr. Crowe?" Lord Stonebridge asked, his feet now resting on an open drawer of his desk. "The meet is set up for 6 pm tonight, so we don't have a lot of time."

"I'd hate to come all this way and not be of use to be honest. Having said that, I'm not sure why I'm your man on this one."

"Well let's see," Lord Stonebridge responded. "You started it all with Miss Weston in Paris. You know our man is being held under 24 hour protection right here in the Manor, and besides you're Canadian, not British—for this purpose anyway, certainly not American. You can safely head home after the meet and carry on your regular life while the British media will ask questions that require some level of honesty in response. The story will be that our prisoner will have been involved in the exchange—through the co-ordination of Scotland Yard and the CIA and the bad guy will be shipped to the US as soon as legally possible."

"And the Commissioner of Police is on-side, sir?" Ed asked, wary of their previous meeting.

Mr. Cooper answered. "He gets their man and also gets the credit. He's looking forward to turning him over to the CIA. A touch of professional pride I suspect."

Lord Stonebridge raised a hand of warning. "But he doesn't want any gun-fire involved. He's very nervous about that."

"Perhaps Mr. Crowe is also," Carolyn added quickly.

"As we all are," Lord Stonebridge agreed. "As we all are." He turned to Ed. "Mr. Crowe?"

"I'm game," Ed said.

"Please don't use that expression," Carolyn added quickly. "It creates the entirely wrong thought process."

The rest agreed and re-filled their cups. Once settled back in their seats, they started reviewing the details of the plan.

Sunnydell Lane, St. Albans.
5:45pm

Walking from the A405 through the tree-lined path to Sunnydell Lane seemed totally out of sync with the operation at hand. Ed took in the English countryside surroundings and inhaled a deep breath of the fresh air. Sunnydell Lane was on the outskirts of St. Albans, literally minutes from farmland, country estates, and lush forests. But here he was carrying a quarter of a million pounds in cash in a small bag and a Smith and Wesson, 45mm, 6 round, double action revolver tucked in the back of his belt. Since the money and the revolver were out of sight, his presence would not normally have turned heads. However his shaved head and well tattooed arms and head were not the local flavor. He didn't see anyone looking at him from the windows of the well maintained houses, but he would not have been surprised if he was being watched by more than one set of eyes. He had wanted to wear long sleeves, but was advised against it. The less he wore the more comfortable his guests would feel. That was the message from Mike, and it a seemed reasonable point of view.

The meeting with Mike had been short and to the point. There were no secret passwords to remember, just an address and a time. Ed stopped in front of the designated house and looked at his watch; it was both the address and the time. Wearing a wire was out of the question, although Carolyn had raised hell over the lack of one. It had been the only time he had seen Lord Stonebridge over-rule her, almost to the point of reprimand. Mr. Cooper was comfortable with the gun, which was to be expected. But not a wire. A wire would mean police.

It was the largest house on the lane. It was detached, while the others were semi-detached. Along both sides of the front garden were large evergreen trees which blocked any view from the neighbors. Ed opened one side of the double gate, walked the sixty feet to the door and rang the bell. The Big Ben sounds from the chime made him smile. Perhaps they would offer him a cup of tea, he wondered. Maybe not!

The door opened with no one in sight. Whoever opened it was standing behind it, out of view.

"Step in," the voice said calmly with a strong American accent.

Ed stepped in, not turning to see the voice.

"Put the bag down in front of you, and don't move," the man ordered. Ed did as he was told.

The man was over six feet tall, casually dressed, with an old-fashioned American brush-cut. He dropped to his knee and searched the bag. To be certain everything was acceptable he ripped open the bottom and cut into the sides with a sharp knife. When he was comfortable there was no wire, he flipped through the stacks of money, sniffing several stacks. Satisfied, he stood in front of Ed, slipping the knife into a leather sheath attached to his belt.

"Hands up," the man said, motioning Ed to spread his legs.

Carefully and diligently he searched Ed's body. Ed closed his eyes when the man felt Pat's gun, but he said or did nothing to acknowledge it. Surely Mr. Cooper couldn't be that correct, Ed thought. It didn't make sense, but the man carried on searching for what Ed was sure was now a wire of some kind.

When he was finished the man stood in front of Ed, now up close. "Open your mouth," he asked. Ed opened his mouth as wide as he could. The man looked inside, and nodded satisfied.

"Now give me your watch," the man demanded, stepping back. Ed slowly took off his watch and gave it to him. "I'll return this when you leave," he said with a smile and slowly, very slowly, slid it on his left wrist next to his own watch. The motion was slow enough to have Ed follow his move, and his heart jumped at what he saw. Printed on the man's wrist, now uncovered by his own watch, was: DEA/CIA. Ed's watch now covered the printing, but the message was clear—the man was a US Agent. Ed closed his eyes for a second, struggling to think what could be gained by the Columbian pretending to have a US Agent in the process. It didn't make sense, it had to be real. For reasons he couldn't explain, Ed was now more nervous than he had been before. Against every wish in his head, his bladder was now making itself known.

"Follow me," the agent ordered, picking up the bag of money and leading Ed into a large reception room to the left.

The room was large and sparsely furnished. At the far end of the room were doors to the garden. Through them the sun was setting, reducing Ed's view of the two men who stood in front of the doors. The agent dropped the bag in front of the heavier-set man to the left and turned to face Ed.

There were now the three men, six or seven feet apart, with the Columbian in the centre, obviously the boss man. Against the sun, Ed could only pick out a sun-tanned skin and a heavy head of slicked-back hair. He wore a light-covered suit and held his hands in front of him, no doubt to show he was not armed. The agent and the man to Ed's right both had their hands behind their backs, the message obvious. Ed went half way and held his hands by his sides, his fingers spread against his legs.

"You can call me Miguel," the Columbian said. "Something like Mike, si?"

"Good evening, Miguel," Ed replied. He looked around. "You have a nice house."

"A nice house," Miguel laughed. "Yes, I have a nice house. In fact I have many nice houses, but not this one. This is not mine. I borrow this house." He laughed louder. "Yes, I borrow this for free."

Ed shrugged, not sure he wanted to continue the conversation any longer than he had to. The house was now surrounded by four cars and fifteen casually dressed CIA operatives. None could be seen and no-one would move on the house until Ed closed the double gate and jumped into an ambulance that would pull up in front of him. He just needed the location of the drugs. Without the drugs no crime had been committed, not in Britain.

"I don't wish to seem rude," Ed said, "but could we settle our business and let me get to the package you have for me." He pointed to the bag of money. "My end of the bargain is complete, and I do have a business to run."

Miguel looked at the agent, who nodded that everything was in order. "Perhaps, Mr. Mike, perhaps," Miguel said, taking a step toward Ed and moving his hands to his sides. He chewed on his lower lip. "Tell me, Mr. Mike, talking about business, what is an acceptable ratio of EBITA to net sales?"

Ed's bladder started to take over, and he had to hold back the pressure as best he could without peeing himself. "Miguel, I don't have the time for such discussions, I . . ."

But it was too late, all three of the men had their guns drawn and pointed at Ed. He licked his lips, now hoping for some help from the agent, but nothing was happening. "Well if you must know," Ed said, moving his hands slowly toward his back, "I would have to say I have no fucking idea."

Ed grabbed for his gun, just as the bullet hit him on the side of his head sending him backwards. A second later his bladder gave way. As he fell he heard three more shots expecting them to hit him. He hit the floor feeling the wetness of his urine, unbelievably embarrassed at the thought of what he looked like. He gathered his wits, rolled over and pulled out his gun. As quickly as he could he lay flat facing the men in a prone position, somehow managing to have his gun hand supported by his left arm. He had been trained to do it, but it seemed to happen automatically. Blood ran down the left side of his face forcing him to close his eye. He felt faint, adjusting his right eye to bring reality into picture.

What he saw scared him. Miguel and the third man were flat on the floor, blood oozing from each of them. The agent sat on the floor against the wall, groggy but moving and holding his left arm that appeared to be hanging on by muscles and sinew. He looked at

Ed, struggling to hold back the pain. He whispered more than spoke. "United States, Drug Enforcement Agency, Agent McGill. Get out of here and phone the cops."

As McGill spoke, Miguel moved and ever so slowly pushed himself up on one arm. It appeared to Ed to be in slow motion, as his mind began to slip. He knew he wouldn't last long. Then the horror of what was happening struck him. Miguel had recovered his gun and was raising it to shoot, not at Ed but at McGill.

With every effort he could muster, Ed slipped off the safety, aimed at Miguel and fired. As he collapsed, with the last burst of energy he pulled the trigger again.

In the dark distance of nowhere he heard shouting voices, the sound of glass breaking; and then nothing.

Senior CIA Agent, Michael Kashty looked around the room, dropping his gun to his side. "Holy Fucking Hell," he exclaimed, "Holy Fucking Hell."

Ed's 'get-away' ambulance drove across the grass to get to the front door. This was to be the Paramedics busiest of days, with more bullet wounds to treat than would be expected in many years of service in their St. Albans community.

Lord Stonebridge and Carolyn rushed into the room, pushing aside the CIA agents that tried to stop them. Carolyn walked to Ed, knelt by his side and took his hand. The paramedic working on him nodded to Carolyn with a quick smile. "He'll be fine," he said, "just a headache from hell when he wakes up."

She shook her head. "He peed himself again," she said.

Lord Stonebridge put his head in his hands, needing all of his strength of character to hold back his anger.

CHAPTER SEVENTEEN

THURSDAY,
SEPTEMBER, 4TH 1985
10AM

H is head felt like it was in a vice. Hoping it would help, he opened his eyes. It didn't; it got worse. At the end of the bed Pat stood with her arms crossed and a cold look on her face.

"You pissed your pants again," she said.

"Thanks for enquiring about my health," Ed replied, trying to laugh.

"I know more about you health than you do, more than I want to by the way." She came to the side of the bed and took his hand. "How are you doing?"

"You tell me. I have a bit of a headache. Never had a hangover like this, I'll tell you."

Pat looked at her watch, reached over to a side table and gave him a pill and a glass of water. "Take this. It'll make you feel better."

Ed swallowed the pill. "So where am I?"

"In The American Hospital in Paris, away from London, and a guest of the U.S. Government. Better than they treat their own citizens I might add. Private health care, what a crock of . . ."

Ed interrupted. "Can we chat about politics later? What happened? Why are we here? Why are you here? In fact, what day is it?"

Pat took his hand again. "I'll tell you the basics, Carolyn can fill in the details. She's asleep in the next room, probably in a state of exhaustion. It's Thursday. I'm here because I flew back to London with Roy on Tuesday to announce our wedding and for me to meet his family. No sooner had we arrived when you attended the meet and everything went wrong."

"Everything?"

"Okay, not everything. You're alive and so is the DEA guy. He's two rooms down drinking coffee."

"That's a relief," Ed said, feeling the pill doing its job. "The other two?"

"Brown bread. Dead as dead can be."

He closed his eyes. "Oh, shit." He waited a couple of seconds to recall what he could. "Did I . . . ?"

Pat nodded very slowly. "I don't want to sound flippant but you done good. Both bullets hit him. I'd say what you did was something to *Crowe* about." She smiled and squeezed his hand. "Agent McGill thinks you're a regular hero. I tried to convince him otherwise, but you know how pushy and stubborn those Yanks can be."

"Thanks. You're all heart." Ed smiled. "Where's Roy?"

"Back in London. I'm heading back in an hour or so, courtesy of the United States Air Force. On a jet bomber no less."

"I appreciate what you're doing, Pat. Does Roy know?"

"No, he does not and we can't tell him. He thinks I'm here on a quick bit of work while in London. Let's keep it that way."

"Yes, of course."

"By the way, I have a bone to pick with you." She arched her eyebrows.

"Shoot," he grinned.

"Very funny." She squeezed his hand. "You didn't tell me Roy was rich. You didn't tell me he owns an eighth of the company he works for. You didn't tell me he lives in one of the fanciest parts of London. You didn't tell a lot about your best mate, and I suggested he was a sort of Arthur Seaton."

Ed laughed aloud, but stopped when the pain in his head returned. "Arthur bloody Seaton! Good Lord. What did he say?"

"He told me he wasn't in the habit of drinking eleven pints of beer."

"And?"

"And I love him whoever he is, whatever he is. And just as important he loves me, and he won't stop telling me so."

"That's nice," he paused. "You know he suffers from ailurophilia, do you?"

Pat's face turned white and her mouth dropped. "No I don't, and I don't know what it is either."

"Hmm," Ed pondered.

"Details, Ed, or I'll hit your bloody head with my shoe."

"Ailurophilia," Ed said, licking his lips to take his time, "is the love of cats."

"You bastard," Pat said, pointing at him. "I'll get you for that." She turned to leave.

"Pat," Ed called after her, "you know I . . ."

She turned at the door. "Yes, I know . . . and I love you in my own silly way. I'll wake up Carolyn. Don't play smart-ass with her. She's a bit on edge." She closed the door quietly as she left.

Carolyn entered the room five minutes later with a cup of tea. "No coffee allowed," she said, "as if Americans know how to make tea." She put the cup on the side table and sat toward the end of the bed. "How are you doing?" she asked.

"I hope I'm feeling better than you look, Carolyn." Her eyes were bloodshot and without make-up the darkness under them was accentuated. Her hair, instead of lying softly around her face with well attended bangs across her forehead, was pulled back tight into a bun at the back.

She sat up straighter. "Friends don't always need tell friends the truth. Isn't that the new way?"

"I never thought I'd see you with a council-house facelift," he offered, not taking Pat's advice.

She untied her hair, shook her head, and quickly fluffed her hair. "Sexy enough for you?"

"I dreamt of you for two days," he said, smiling.

"No you didn't. The doctor said you were in a state of unconsciousness and your brain wouldn't let you dream. Basically you were close to death."

"Okay, maybe you're right, but if I could have dreamed I would have dreamt of you."

"If that is supposed to make me feel better, you don't know me very well, Ed."

Ed nodded in agreement. "Let me try again, Carolyn. I love you so much; I even tried lying to make you smile. Please smile. Smile for a couple of minutes and *then* you can tell me off for what I did wrong."

She moved up the side of the bed, kissed him quickly on his lips, and smiled.

Ed took her hand and kissed it. She remained smiling for what seemed like several minutes, but was in fact just thirty seconds.

She raised her voice slightly to gain control. "You did nothing wrong, we did it wrong. We didn't do our homework properly and look what happened. My father is beside himself, Mr. Cooper is livid, and I'm not sure my mother will ever forgive my father and me."

"Any good news?"

"Mrs. Thatcher is happy that we got our man and earned brownie points with the U.S. Of course she doesn't know you were shot. If she did I suspect my father would be out of a job."

"Am I correct in assuming that Mike is an accountant?"

"Exactly."

Ed shrugged. "But I didn't know the answer anyway."

Carolyn nodded. "That's not the point. Maybe Mike wouldn't have know either, but his response wouldn't have been 'I have no fucking idea', would it?"

"No. Sorry."

She kissed his hand. "What would you have said, if you had known he was an accountant?"

"I would have mumbled something about not being my field of accountancy, and suggested a question on U.K. taxation."

Carolyn laughed. "And what do you know about that?"

"Nothing, but surely neither would Miguel have known what more to ask."

"Good point. But whatever. What happened happened."

"What happened?"

Carolyn took a deep breath. "Miguel shot you when you went for you gun, then Agent McGill shot Miguel, and to top it off the third man and McGill shot each other. I assume you remember the rest?"

Ed nodded. "Pat said I hit him both times."

Carolyn nodded.

"Well?" Ed asked.

"Once in the head: then in the shoulder. You didn't need your second shot."

"Shit," Ed muttered.

Carolyn put her hand to her heart. *"Liberty's in every blow, let us do or die*; Robbie Burns."

"Okay, I'll buy that. My mother would be proud of you." He reached up feeling the bandage around his head. "And me?"

"Thick skin and big bones, you'll get by. You'll have to re-grow your hair longer. There will be a nasty scar."

"And Mike?"

Carolyn smiled. "Well there's the good news. The official story stayed the same, except that Mike shot the two men, there was no McGill, and instead of Mike giving authorities the opportunity to catch the bad guys, he shot them—with an illegal gun." She grinned.

"He's back in Broadmoor Prison, in solitary confinement by choice and scared for his life. It breaks my heart."

"You're a tough lady, you are," Ed mused.

"Me? Pat wants to drive up to Yorkshire and serve him breakfast in his cell. You'll never guess what she wants him to eat?"

"I think I can."

"Go on then," she giggled.

Ed winked. "She wants him to eat crow."

"Bang on! What a wonderful lady she is."

They enjoyed a good laugh together and Ed could see Carolyn relax, back to her old self. "So where do we go from here?" Ed asked, knowing the future had to be discussed.

"Well, we sneak you back into England . . ."

"Sneak me back?"

"Well," Carolyn continued, "the Police Commissioner, Sir Robert Newton, is not amused at two dead and two wounded, certainly not in lovely St. Albans."

"Maybe I should stay away."

"Certainly not! My father, Lord Stonebridge that is," she took a bow, "is looking forward to seeing you in good health. Besides," she winked, "a Lord trumps a Sir anytime."

"Ouch! You can be wicked."

"Speaking of which," she whispered, "when we get back to the Manor I want us to go to our special place to make love. And that," she announced, "is an order!"

"What I have to do for England," Ed groaned. "But England expects . . ."

"And you better do your best, young man, or we'll do it all over again until you do."

"I love you, Miss Andrews."

"God, I love it when you call me that." She leaned forward and kissed him.

She jumped back quickly as the door opened and Agent McGill entered the room. His left arm was in a solid sling which made it impossible to move the arm in any way. He held out his right hand to Ed. "Thanks for saving my life, buddy," he said enthusiastically. They shook hands with McGill gripping Ed's hand like a vice. "In addition to saving my life," he continued, pumping Ed's hand, "I get to return to the U.S. of A., and am no longer undercover. A good day all around I'd say."

Ed recovered his hand. "My pleasure, but the thanks are all mine, I'm sure."

McGill continued, speaking fast and energetically. "Hey, so we're blood brothers. Can I call you Ed? My name's Lawrie. Lawrence at birth after my father. Scottish, of course. So what are you Ed? The other lady, the Canadian; some lady! She spent some time telling me why George Washington was a traitor to his birth country. Makes sense if she's correct, but don't ever say I said so."

Ed sat absorbing all the questions, while Carolyn standing behind McGill, smiled at their guest's enthusiasm. "What am I?" Ed asked aloud, turning his mind to the interesting question. "I guess I'd have to say that I'm British by birth, English by nature, and Canadian by choice. How does that sound?"

"Pretty damn good to me," McGill nodded. "What do you think, ma'am?" he asked, turning to Carolyn.

"Sound pretty damn good to me too," she agreed. "Although it's been said you can take the English out of England, but you can't take England out of the English."

"Hell, that ain't too bad now is it." McGill said. "Speaking of which," he said, speaking slower now, "that English gent that came in the room with you, ma'am, was a true gentleman. As soon as he knew I was alive, he was there to help me. Held my broken arm in place until the medics arrived. And I can tell you, he didn't know I was one of the good guys. He started speaking to me in Spanish, for God's sake. I'd like to thank him personally. Can you arrange that, ma'am?"

Carolyn felt a lump in her throat hearing such positive comments about her father. "I'll see what I can do. Why don't you leave me a business card and the next time I see him, I'll let him know your thoughts." She paused. "Although maybe a favor?"

"You've got it."

"When you file your report, perhaps you could . . . ?"

McGill nodded. "Consider it done. What shall I call him?"

Carolyn shrugged with a smile. "Just call him 'the English bloke'."

McGill struggled to get two business cards from his wallet using only his right hand. "'The English bloke' it is. I like that. I sure hope you'll let his boss know what a fine man he is."

She pondered the thought of phoning Mrs. Thatcher to pass on his comments. "I'll see what I can do."

He handed Carolyn his card and shook hands with Ed as he gave him a card. "Phone me sometime, blood brother. Hands across the border and all that never did anything but good." He left the room as enthusiastically as he had entered.

Carolyn turned to Ed for advice. "You don't think I was too pushy do you? I mean my about father and all."

Ed sat up in bed, feeling better by the minute. "No I most certainly do not. I didn't know your father did that, which was rather good of him. And I certainly didn't know he spoke Spanish."

"Oh, we're not just a lot of pretty faces, my family," she said, holding her head just a little higher. "Good breeding; that's us."

"Really?" Ed quizzed. "And how many languages does your mother speak?"

"Two," she replied proudly.

Ed looked at her questionably. "And they are?"

"I'm leaving now," Carolyn said walking to the door.

"And they are?" Ed asked again.

"English and Cockney," she answered defiantly, "and we're all proud of her." With her nose in the air she left the room, closing the door.

Ed called after her. "Dun a bunk she did, and 'ere I wuz hoping for another cuppa o' Rosie Lee!" He leaned back into the pillow laughing and happy. He closed his eyes. The pill was taking its full effect and within two minutes he was asleep.

The throbbing in his head woke him. Carolyn was sitting by the side of the bed holding his hand.

"Time for a pill," Carolyn said, getting a glass of water and handing it to Ed with the pill.

He swallowed the pill, drinking the entire glass of water. "So what happened to the drugs?" Ed asked, relaxing into the fluffy pillows.

"They were in a luggage locker at Watford Junction train station, still are."

Ed sat up. "Still are? Okay I'm confused."

Carolyn sat on the bed and lowered his voice. "Well as it turned out some smart-thinking person had the idea of leaving the drugs where they were. McGill knew all the details, so we knew exactly where they hidden. Now he's officially dead, so this smarty assumed that if we kept an eye on the location, someone from the drug cartel would come and get them; it would be just a matter of time. The time-lock runs out next week, so we'll wait and see. If someone comes looking, we grab them; Scotland Yard, that is. Then we'll have the drugs, plus a low-level soldier under arrest and hopefully he can be convinced to talk."

"Hey, that was a great idea," Ed said, nodding. "So who was the sneaky one with the idea?"

Carolyn rubbed her chin and looked to the ceiling for the answer. "Hmm, now who might that super intelligent person have been?"

"Well aren't you miss clever clogs," Ed said. "Amazing what an Oxford education can do for you. Well done, Miss Andrews! I think it's time for a congratulatory kiss!"

"Correct you are," she said and leaned over to kiss him gently on his forehead. She stood back quickly as the door opened and Lady Stonebridge entered the room. To Ed's amazement Lady Stonebridge was wearing a 1960's nurse's uniform with a badge that read 'Andrews, R.N.'

"My God, Mother, what are you doing here?" Carolyn gasped.

Lady Stonebridge waved a file in her right hand. "I'm here to take Mr. Crowe home, my dear, home to the Manor. The doctors have agreed it is medically acceptable, and we'll be transported by Air Ambulance, leaving in about an hour."

"But, Mother . . ."

"The decision has been made, my dear. Please don't question me on this. I will nurse him at the Manor and Dr. Stevenson will oversee everything."

Carolyn raised a hand. "Mother, you haven't been qualified for years as a nurse, you cannot just . . ."

"Yes, I can." Lady Stonebridge cut her off sharply. "Now Mr. Crowe," she said looking at the chart in the file, "You cannot drink alcohol for ten days. Do you understand?"

Ed nodded. He didn't want to get between the two combatants, and the thought of resting at Stonebridge Manor was more than acceptable.

"And further, Mr. Crowe," Lady Stonebridge continued, "no sexual activity for six weeks."

Carolyn turned her back and covered her face. "Mother! I er . . . I . . . I . . ." She gave up.

Ed looked at Lady Stonebridge, speechless and helpless.

"I'm just 'aving you on, laddie," Lady Stonebridge said with a shrug a smile. "Just a wee joke between friends."

"Forgive my mother, Ed," Carolyn begged. "It's the power of the uniform! We obviously need a doctor in the room to bring balance."

Lady Stonebridge walked to the door, feeling totally in control— her favorite role. "I'll be back in ten minutes with a wheelchair." She turned to Carolyn. "Please have him dressed and ready to go."

"Mother!"

Lady Stonebridge raised her hand. "I asked you to get him dressed, my dear, not to dress him." She smiled sweetly. "And please put his socks on for him. He is not to bend down." She waved the file as some form of proof and left the room.

Carolyn gathered Ed's clothes from the closet and laid them on the bed. She turned her back.

"Aren't you going to help me," Ed asked. "I'm not sure I can manage my trousers on my own." He grinned.

"If you fall down, I'll help you. God helps those . . ."

Ed looked around. "I'm not sure he's in the room. I suspect the conversation between you and your mother may have embarrassed Him."

"Get dressed, Ed."

Sliding out of bed he carefully slipped on his trousers and shirt. He pulled up the zipper on his fly. "Barn door's closed," he said.

Carolyn had him sit on the bed and she sat on the chair to help him put on his socks. She slipped them on slowly, almost methodically. When she was finished she kept her head down, unnecessarily adjusting them.

"Penny for your thoughts," Ed said quietly, knowing something was bothering her.

She looked up at him, almost in tears. "I saw a story the other day about a man who hurt himself, and his wife had to help him on with his socks every day for weeks." She sniffed back a tear. "After he was better, his wife continued to put his socks on for the rest of his life; as a message of love." She wiped her eyes. "Recently she put them on for the last time. He died. She put the socks on him at the funeral parlor. How sad is that, Ed?"

The message got to him and he had to cough to clear his throat. "That is sad, Carolyn, but a very nice reminder of how easily love can be shown to overcome problems in this sometimes hectic world. I think the lady was a champion."

"Well don't get any ideas!" she said, pushing his feet away, and standing up. She took his hands in hers. "We've known each other for less than eighteen months, Ed, and look what's happened. We're friends and lovers. This is the second time you've come close to death since I sponsored you into the department. Your best friend is marrying a girl he barely knows, after he asked me to marry him. The lovely lady he's marrying is your . . . your what, Ed?"

"My very special friend." Ed answered quickly.

"Yes," she smiled, "your very special friend. You're his Best Man, and I'm her Maid of Honour. They're getting married at Stonebridge Manor, the location where my mother was expecting me to marry my long-time boy friend; and her best friend's son, I might add." She took a breath. "And here you are with a serious head wound, as bald as an old man, and I have to help you put your socks on." She grimaced. "Is this what we want, Ed?" Before he could answer, Carolyn felt more than heard her mother enter the room.

"Am I interrupting?" Lady Stonebridge asked, quietly.

"No, Mother, I was just telling Ed how much I love him."

"Then don't let me stop you, dear" Lady Stonebridge said, not moving.

Carolyn smiled and squeezed his hands. "Ed, I love you so very much and look forward to you holding me in your arms again; and the sooner the better."

"Very nice, dear," Lady Stonebridge smiled. "Mr. Crowe?"

Ed leaned and looked around Carolyn. "Me?" he asked, pointing to his chest. "Why, I didn't know I was party to this conversation."

Lady Stonebridge moved closer with the wheelchair. "Don't push your luck, Mr. Crowe. We're still mother and daughter, isn't that so, Carolyn?"

"Yes, Mother, very much so," Carolyn laughed. "Let's get this patient home."

"Are you ready, Mr. Crowe?" Lady Stonebridge asked, rolling the wheelchair toward Ed.

"Yes, ma'am." Ed replied.

Lady Stonebridge pointed to her badge.

"Yes, Nurse Andrews," Ed corrected himself.

Nurse Andrews smiled broadly. "Now you've got it," she said.

CHAPTER EIGHTEEN

FRIDAY, SEPTEMBER 5TH, 1985 STONEBRIDGE MANOR.

E d woke to the sound of Carolyn entering his bedroom with a cup of tea and a pill. She sat on the side of his bed and handed him the tea while popping the pill in his mouth. The bed was the largest Ed had ever seen and the room was almost as large as his apartment in Oakville.

"Be a good boy and take your medicine" she said. She was wearing shorts with a Toronto Maple Leafs T-shirt.

"You look beautiful this morning, Carolyn," Ed said reaching for her hand. "Why don't you join me in bed and we can make mad passionate love?"

She shook her head. "Not here. Not now." She squeezed his hand. "Nurse Andrews could drop in at any minute, and how would that look? Me taking advantage of her sick, bald, and lucky-to-be-alive patient."

"Maybe we could put it down to physiotherapy? Sort of rehabilitation?"

"Nice try, lover boy. Another time."

"Promise?"

She took the empty tea cup and walked to the door. "Just keep your mind on our making love." She winked. "Sooner rather than later"

"I love you, Miss Andrews."

"God, I love it when you call me Miss Andrews," she said opening he door. "Oh, and by the way, Mother has invited your mother to tea this afternoon along with Pat and Roy. Cars will pick them up and run them home."

"But . . ."

"I know, I know. Too late now. Mother had no intention of having you in a sick-bed in England and not letting your mum see you."

Ed put his hand to his bandaged head. "But what do we tell her about . . . about everything? Bloody Hell!"

Carolyn shrugged. "We'll have to sort something out."

As she was leaving the room, Nurse Andrews entered the room. "Did you tell him?" she asked.

"Yes, Mother," Carolyn answered heading down the hallway. "He's pleased as punch."

Nurse Andrews closed the door. "My daughter can be very sarky at times. Have you noticed that, Mr. Crowe?"

"I can't imagine where she got that from," Ed replied, raising his eyebrows in amazement.

"Probably from her father."

Ed nodded. "Probably."

"Now, Mr. Crowe, would you please tell me your home phone number."

Ed answered slowly, wondering what the point was. He then answered a variety of questions about his youth, his schooling, his friends, and his family. He finally understood that the goal was to ensure his memory was not adversely affected by the wound to his head. Nurse Andrews took notes of his answers, visibly pleased with the results.

"Now some quotes, please," nurse Andrews said. "I start them, you complete them."

Ed nodded.

"A horse, a horse . . ."

"My kingdom for a horse."

"All the world's a stage . . ."

"And all the men and women mere players. They have their . . ."

Nurse Andrews waived him off. "It was the best of times . . ."

Ed grinned. "When I met and fell in love with Carolyn."

Never one to miss an opportunity, her final question caught him off guard.

"Why haven't you asked Carolyn to marry you, Mr. Crowe?" She put her hands behind her back, knowing it would not get a quick response.

Ed closed his eyes to think through the answer; an answer acceptable to Lady Stonebridge—it was she who was asking the question, not Nurse Andrews—yet an answer that would be acceptable to Carolyn. October, 29th 1989, The Sun Inn, Little Kimble, a village he had never visited, that is where and when he was going to ask Carolyn to marry him. As much as Carolyn told him often, not often enough for his liking, that she loved him, he was not at all certain she would accept his offer: indeed he suspected she would ever-so-nicely say 'No'. The thought almost made him cry, but he screwed up his eyes to recover. He licked his lips, trying desperately to come up with an acceptable answer. He was rarely stuck for words, but he was now. But he needed an answer. He quickly shook his head, feeling the bandages move slightly as he did. The answer appeared from nowhere.

"I will when the sun rises over The Sun and the DOA are equal to zero," he said, now smiling. He hoped she wouldn't press him for details.

Lady Stonebridge took a gentle breath and nodded. "It *will* happen then. That is all I need to know. Bear in mind, Edwin, that Carolyn is a very persuasive young lady. She has a habit of getting her way in a fashion that belies her objectives. Make sure you are equals, Edwin. She has a great deal of charm."

Ed fully understood what she meant, perhaps summed up in his DOA's—Days Of Agony: days he had to wait to even ask Carolyn to marry him. He further understood that by calling him Edwin, she was speaking as the mother of the person he loved, not as a nurse and not as Lady Stonebridge. He thanked her as she left the room and closed the door behind her.

The door quickly re-opened. "And don't forget your mother is coming for tea," she said with a wide grin.

Ed looked around the walls of his temporary hospital room and at the hundreds of books in the shelves. An idea popped into his head, and with a self-satisfied look he slipped off the bed and headed to the shelves.

Lady Stonebridge had set the table for tea in order to recognize Pat and Roy's engagement. Lord Stonebridge was seated at one end of the table, with herself at the other end. Pat and Roy sat on one long side and facing them were Ed, Carolyn, Ed's mother, and Mr. Cooper. Pat was unusually shy, quite out of character. Roy, however, was his usual out-going self, thanking the Stonebridges for hosting 'the very happy couple' at their first opportunity to review the wedding plans, set for May 7th, less than ten months away. Having mentioned, for the tenth time, what a wonderful person Pat was, he ignored her kicking him in the shins for the third time.

Lady Stonebridge thanked him for his generous remarks and proceeded to lead the way for the after-tea planning session.

"As you can appreciate," she said, keeping her eyes away from Carolyn, "we do not host many weddings at the Manor, so it will be our pleasure to share in this most joyful gathering of friends and families."

Carolyn smiled bravely, but died a little inside.

Ed nodded agreeably, kicking Carolyn under the table.

Lady Stonebridge continued. "I have a draft agenda for the day; two actually—depending on the weather. After tea, perhaps, we could review it to make sure it covers everything?"

Everyone nodded.

With all in agreement, Lady Stonebridge waived for Miriam to serve tea—starting with Pat and Roy.

As the discussions about weddings circulated around the table, Ed leaned to Carolyn and quietly said, "I've decided not to make that date in October 1989."

Carolyn stiffened up, wondering what Ed was up to. She was determined not to let his comment disturb the conversations around them.

"Really," she said, reaching for the milk, "that is disappointing."

"Yes," Ed continued, reaching for the sugar that he did not use but allowed him to lean closer to Carolyn, "I've decided to ask that question of you, May 7th next."

Carolyn smiled sweetly, and turned to Ed's mother to pass her the milk. She took some time to catch up with Mrs. Crowe on how she was doing, agreeing that Pat and Roy made a wonderful couple. Ed waited for her to turn back to him, but to his surprise she stood up and got everyone's attention.

"As Maid of Honor and Ed as Best Man, we would ask that you excuse us for just a few moments. We will return in just a few minutes." Ed stood; nodding as if he was aware of what was happening and followed Carolyn through to the butler's pantry. Carolyn asked Miriam to go to the cellar and bring back a bottle of her father's champagne. As Miriam left, Carolyn turned to Ed.

"You were saying?" she asked.

Ed took her hands. "Carolyn, I love you. You know I love you. Your mother knows that I love you. Roy knows I love you. My mother knows I love you. Christ, even Pat knows that I love you." He swallowed to catch his strength. "October, 1989, is more than four years away for crying out load. No matter what your answer is, I'm going to ask you to marry me at Pat and Roy's wedding. I'm sorry, Carolyn, I simply must."

Carolyn pulled him toward her, wrapping his hands behind her back. "And I love you, Ed, as much as I could ever love anyone." She stood higher and kissed him. "May 7th, 1986 it is."

"And that will be a 'yes' or a 'no', Carolyn. Postponing your decision is not an option."

Carolyn smiled. "Well aren't you getting pushy all of a sudden, lover boy?"

"Yes, my dear, I am."

Now giggling, she tapped gently him on his chest. "Hmmm, this could be interesting."

"Oh, it will be, Miss Andrews, it will be."

"You make me feel so good when you call me Miss Andrews," she said kissing him again. "Now let's get the champagne in there and toast our wonderful friends' engagement."

Ed opened the bottle of champagne as Carolyn walked around the table handing out glasses. The cork popped with a bang and everyone cheered. He held the bottle high. "Ladies and gentlemen, this is indeed a special occasion. Carolyn and I are so proud to have been asked to stand up for such a wonderful couple that fell in love so quickly and fully, all within the past year."

Roy nodded his head and took Pat's hand under the table. Pat smiled, wondering where Ed was going. It was soon apparent.

"While I fill the glasses, ladies and gentlemen, Carolyn will say a few words about Pat, and when finished I will briefly add some comments about my friend Roy and the up-coming special day; May 7th 1986!"

"What a wonderful idea," Lady Stonebridge exclaimed. "If only your best man had been so dashing; isn't that so, dear?" she said, looking at Lord Stonebridge.

Carolyn almost froze in her spot. She filled Mrs. Crowe's glass slowly, giving herself time to think what she could say about Pat; at least with this audience.

Her mind ran at full speed, capturing everything she could not say. *Pat was a member of Canada's spy network; she had shot at least two men, one in the head who had died instantly; she was at one time in love with Ed, and had told Carolyn so; and to make it worse, Carolyn didn't even know Pat's real surname!* Ed was in for an earful!

Lord Stonebridge and Mr. Cooper looked at each other and each hoped for the best.

Carolyn held up her glass to toast. "Ladies and gentlemen, it is a great honor to speak about, and to, my new friend, a friend who has given me the pleasure to be her Maid of Honor." Her mind was racing. "Now we all recognize Pat as the true Canadian who represented Prime Minister, Brian Mulroney, in Paris recently in reminding the world of the events in France during the last war. Indeed she was a television heroine to thousands, if not millions, across the world of television." *So far so good.* She took a breath. "Now there is always a price for fame, and my dear friend had to pay a price for her fifteen minutes of fame. She had to pretend to be married to Mr. Ed Crowe!"

There was laughter and clapping around the table. Ed bowed to accept the comment.

"In real life, of course, she is wiser and more selective in her choice of a life-long partner." She nodded at Roy. "Pat is a senior advisor in the federal offices of Export Development Canada, and has only recently been promoted to recognize her excellent work. She graduated from the University of Toronto, with honors, and is an expert on North American history, a fact that many Americans learn when she helps them better understand their own history." *What else, what else?* "I have had the pleasure of working with Pat on several joint ventures and I can say quite honestly that a nicer, more diligent, more sincere person, I have not met." She raised her glass and toasted Pat with clinking of glasses and cheers throughout.

Roy leaned over and kissed Pat on her now more relaxed cheek. Pat nodded her thanks and made a note to herself to give Carolyn a big hug for dodging the bullet.

Ed now took the floor, a refilled glass in hand. He tipped the glass to Roy in recognition.

"My friend, my best mate . . . ," Ed began, and then proceeded to speak highly of their friendship since age sixteen, and the success Roy had enjoyed in his working career rising from a boy on the printing floor to the vice-president of sales of one of Britain's largest printing firms. There was applause when Ed took a breath, and then he continued.

"Now next May 7th will, of course, be a very special day for all of us. In addition to celebrating the future of such a wonderful couple, it will allow their friends and families, from both sides of the Atlantic, to meet and make new acquaintances for life."

Carolyn looked up at him smiling, while kicking him under the table to end his words. Ed carried on.

"Now May 7th has other special significances which some of you may not be aware." The now solid kick from Carolyn didn't stop him. "It was on this day in 1915 that the German Navy sank the RMS Lusitania, turning many then pro-Germany Americans against Germany. Isn't that correct, Pat?"

Pat smiled, appreciating Ed's historical knowledge. "Yes," Pat agreed, "killing 128 Americans, as it turned out."

Ed acknowledged her input, and carried on. "But of greater importance than the 1915 event will be a *much* more current and topical event that will be remembered next May 7th. Does anyone know what that will be?"

Shrugs and shaking of heads abound, except for Carolyn who held her head in her hands.

"Are you alright, my dear?" Lady Stonebridge asked.

Carolyn sat up. "Yes, Mother. I was just thinking what could be of such importance to distract the conversation."

Ed raised his hand in explanation. He spoke slowly, capturing *almost* everyone's attention "Well you see, ladies and gentlemen, on Saturday May 7th 1986, we will be celebrating the historic forty-first anniversary of the surrender of Germany in the Second World War. Now that is truly historic, and the other side of the coin from 1915, if you will."

The celebration was immediate and loud. Lord Stonebridge ordered a second bottle of champagne, Pat was applauding wildly, and Carolyn almost broke down in tears.

Mr. Cooper nodded approvingly. "Yes, of course. And it didn't go into effect until the next day. Well done, Eddie. Well done."

With the second bottle of champagne empty, Lady Stonebridge stood and took charge.

"Now if Pat and Roy would join me and Mrs. Crowe in the rose garden we will set tentative plans for the wedding." She turned to Lord Stonebridge. "I assume you and Mr. Cooper will want to talk business?" and not waiting for a reply she turned to Carolyn for comment.

"Ed and I will get out of the way, Mother. I think he needs a nice stroll in the fresh air."

"So be it," Lady Stonebridge agreed. "Now, Mrs. Crowe, if you would fill in for Roy's parents, I will fill in for Pat's parents and we will get the plan in place."

With the orders given and received, the room was emptied for Miriam to clean up.

Carolyn took Ed's arm as they walked beyond the rose garden and into the acreage leading up to their favorite spot, leaving behind the voice of Lady Stonebridge directing the actors for the main event.

Carolyn squeezed his arm. "You had me scared there for a while,"

"Yes, I know."

"Am I so pushy that I need reminding of it?"

Ed kissed the top of her head. "Not pushy, Miss Andrews, just a controlling charm that seems to get its way almost every time."

"Hmm, I see. That's not all bad is it?"

"Not at all, Miss Andrews, not at all."

They walked on through the gate in the hedgerow that separated the kept grounds from the woods higher in the grounds. She stopped and took his hand.

"What did your mother say about the accident in Paris story?"

Ed grimaced. "Well as Mr. Cooper tells it, when he explained the details of my being in Paris for a travel convention and how I fell from a bike into the side of a bus, she responded monosyllabically."

"Really?"

"Very clever."

"And her word was?"

"Whatever."

"Whatever?"

"That was her response." Ed laughed. "Of course she didn't believe a word of it. But then why should she? She knows your father is the head of MI6. She knows you travel all across the world. And Pat and I being 'married' in Paris makes everything questionable."

Carolyn nodded. "Yes, of course it does. I suppose she's too wise to ask questions that she knows she won't get an honest answer to. What else did she say?"

"She asked me just two questions, both of which I answered monosyllabically."

"Pray tell?"

"She asked me if I was happy, and then she asked if I was in love with you."

"Oh! I hope your answer was 'yes'."

"No."

"Your answer was 'no'?"

"No."

"Okay, smarty-pants, what was your answer?"

"Absolutely."

Carolyn squeezed his hand and they walked on, now entering the woods with the view of Stonebridge Manor hidden by the shrubs and trees. Upon reaching a large oak tree, Carolyn stopped behind it, now fully out of sight from the Manor. She pushed him against the tree and kissed him.

"That was nice," Ed said, holding onto Carolyn. "What a lovely day this has been."

Carolyn looked up at him with a wide smile and a wink. "Yes, a very *special* day I would say."

He knew there was a message in her wink. He closed his eye for just a moment to think.

"Blooody Hell," he gasped, gently holding her away to face her. "It's your birthday! Carolyn, I am so sorry. I must be going mad. Please forgive me. Why didn't anyone say anything? Oh, God!"

Carolyn hugged him and held herself as close to him as she could. "No matter, Ed. At my age . . ." she laughed into his chest. "Besides, my parents didn't want to take anything away from Pat and Roy's special day."

"I feel so guilty," Ed mumbled, kissing the top of her head.

"There will be cake when we gat back," Carolyn said, now moving gently away from Ed. "But there is a price to pay, Edwin William."

"You name it. I'll pay the price!"

"I want you to make love to me, Ed."

"Here?"

"Yes."

"Now?"

"Right here and right now." She started undoing the buttons on his shirt. "I want you to undress me slowly and kiss me and touch me all over, and then I want you to tell me ten times how much you love me while you make love to me."

"Ten times! Once a minute?" Ed grinned, unzipping the back of her dress.

She looked up and smiled. "Ten times; once every two minutes."

Ed did as he was told.

Carolyn enjoyed the best birthday gift she had ever received.

Leaning against their now favorite tree, they held hands, not wanting to rush back to the Manor. Carolyn kissed Ed's hands. Ed told Carolyn, for the eleventh time in thirty minutes, that he loved her.

They had never been happier, and wouldn't find such happiness for a long time to come.

CHAPTER NINETEEN

FRIDAY,
SEPTEMBER 12ᵀᴴ, 1985
6PM

E d walked into the Queen's Head at his usual time. It was Friday and he was expected. No one would have expected him to be wearing a bandage that covered most of his head. In fact he didn't need a full-head bandage, but he preferred wearing it rather than having a smaller bandage that showed he was all but bald, still with less than two week's hair growth. He waved and smiled at the looks and nods of acknowledgement that he received.

"Hello, Edwin," Seana said. She and Stephanie were sitting at a high table to one side of the bar. Seana was enjoying a long-stemmed drink and Stephanie had her usual beer. Obviously not on duty tonight, Seana was wearing a green summer dress and Stephanie was wearing a red blouse with a black knee-length skirt.

"What happened to you?" Stephanie asked, as she ordered a Double Diamond for Ed.

He joined them with a bow. "You should see the other guy," he joked.

"Really, what happened?" Seana asked.

"Well I was facing these three armed drug mafia guys, and . . ."

"Yeah, yeah," Stephanie interrupted. "That's a problem every travel agent has to overcome every so often. Probably fell asleep at his desk!"

Mary delivered his drink and Ed took a sip toasting his hosts. "So where are you two ladies headed tonight? If I may say so, you both look very lovely. Even better than in your regular Queen's Head shirts," he added quickly.

"You may say so, Edwin," Stephanie answered with a smile, and returned his toast.

"Actually, Ed," Seana added, "we are going out for a very special evening with a very special friend."

Stephanie nodded at Ed. "A friend who needs some female companionship, or so we were informed by his English mate." She spoke quietly. "That would be you!"

"Oh, my God" Ed exclaimed. "Really?"

Seana nodded. "Really. But there are some rules. No talking about Manchester United, Chelsea, West Ham, the World Cup, the F.A. Cup, or any other 'footie' matters."

"And," Stephanie added, "no talking about cricket or any of its funny stuff like 'leg before wicket', 'ozat!', 'silly mid-off', and the rest."

"Okay," Ed agreed. "No talking about shoes and purses and we've got a deal."

Seana and Stephanie looked at each other, thought for a while and reluctantly nodded in agreement.

"Greek or Italian?" Seana asked.

Ed bowed again, this time a tad lower. "With such charming company, the food will be the least of the evening's enjoyment. But given the greater choice of wine, let's go Italian."

"Que sera," Stephanie said.

"Que sera, sera," Seana added with a wink and a smile.

"Bottoms up," Ed added, making sure he didn't look down.

As they were leaving the pub Peter, the Bar Manager, called Ed over holding the phone in the air. "For you, Ed. Sounds rather English, posh like."

"Crowe speaking," Ed said into the phone.

"Miss Smarty, speaking," Carolyn replied.

"Carolyn. What a pleasant surprise. You got me just in time. I was just heading out for supper with two young ladies."

"Sure you were," Carolyn laughed. She then spoke more cautiously. "Listen, you don't have to respond. I wanted you to know the results from Watford Junction." Ed immediately knew she was referring to the drugs. He covered his other ear with his hand to better hear her over the noise at the bar. "So we waited and watched and a couple of days ago the drugs were picked up. We, we being Scotland Yard, followed the trail and today six people were arrested for a variety of crimes. *Plus* we found more drugs and some weapons. Overall a great catch."

"Well done, Carolyn!" Ed replied enthusiastically. "Oh that Oxford education."

"But the best news . . . guess the location of the house they used as their base?" Ed could hear her quietly chuckling.

"Surely not?"

"Surely yes. It was in Neasden! My mother doesn't want to talk about it. Look I have to go. I'll phone you Sunday. I love you, Ed."

"Likewise," Ed said.

"Excuse me?"

Ed covered the mouthpiece with his hand. "I love you, Miss Andrews, and always will."

"And don't you forget it, Edwin William. Speak to you Sunday. Kiss. Kiss."

Ed replaced the phone and caught up with Stephanie and Seana. "Sorry about that," he said. "Just an update on the drug stuff I was telling you about."

"Yeah, right," Seana replied.

Stephanie laughed. "You should write a book, Ed. With an imagination like yours, you'd do well writing fiction!"

After a relaxing Italian inspired meal the three new friends sat on the patio of a local favorite restaurant. They were sipping their second bottle of wine and finishing their desserts, or 'afters' and 'puddings' as Ed insisted on calling them.

Seana and Stephanie were planning their next day trip to the U.S., Niagara Falls, New York. Plans were set for the Outlet Mall, Target— which they insisted on pronouncing Tarjay—and Tops grocery store. As promised they did not mention shoes and purses, although they were high on the list of things they intended to buy. With the Canadian dollar at 75c US, Ed couldn't understand why they would go so far to shop. Up to this evening he had never heard of 'retail therapy' as a reason to shop, but recognized on certain issues in life, the two sexes lived in different worlds. Intuitively, he preferred his, but kept his opinion to himself.

Ed was looking into the restaurant watching the television above the bar where the Toronto Blue Jays were playing against the New York Yankees in Yankee Stadium. The Blue Jays were having a good year and since it was baseball, he felt he was living up to his side of the bargain.

He topped up their glasses, draining the bottle. Leaning back into his chair allowed him the opportunity to think through where he was at in life. In the eighteen months since Mr. Cooper had asked him, as an employee, to visit Turkey with a goal to locate hotels and tourist spots that Mr. Cooper could recommend as safe and comfortable, next to nothing was the same. He no longer lived in Kensal Rise in London working as a travel agent, but lived in Oakville, Canada as both a travel agent and a part-time consultant with MI6. His best friend was engaged to his special friend and now ex-lover. He was in love with the daughter of the head of MI6, the same lady that his best friend had asked if she would marry him—in front of both Ed and his mother. He thought her response; 'that she couldn't say yes,' was one of the nicest expressions he had ever heard. What would she say to him when he asked her to marry him, at his best friend's and ex-lover's wedding, next year? He didn't want to think too long on that!

He had seen peopled killed, and had recently shot and killed a man himself. He frowned at those memories but knew it was, in his new world, the right things to have seen and to have done.

He felt even worse about forgetting Carolyn's birthday; and he knew that made no sense. He was looking forward to speaking to her at greater length on Sunday.

Stephanie shaking his knee brought him back into the real world. "Wake up, Edwin," she laughed. "Are we so boring that you're going to fall asleep on us?"

Ed gestured his apologies. "Sorry. Just pondering life in general."

Seana moved closer to the table. "So tell us, Ed, talking about books, what book do you have by the side of your bed at night?"

Ed grinned. "A book on birds."

"Birds!" Seana gasped.

"No, no, no," Stephanie laughed. "He's English. That means it's a book about girls. Probably scantily clad girls at that."

Ed laughed out loud. "The book is Roger Tory Peterson's Field Guide to the Birds East of the Rockies. Nothing naughty about that, ladies."

Seana tried another question. "Okay, let me ask you this. Which book, fact or fiction, have you read lately that you would recommend as a great read?"

"'The Dreaming Suburb', by R.F. Delderfield," Ed answered quickly. "It's about the people that live in a London suburb between the World Wars. And you, ladies?"

"A book on Philosophy," Seana replied.

"A book about international spying. CIA and all that," Stephanie added. "What are you up to tomorrow, Edwin?"

Ed shrugged. "Nothing much. Just making sure I don't bump my head on my desk again."

"Good," Seana said, excitedly. "Here's the deal. We want you to join us on our trip across the border tomorrow. On the drive down, during lunch in the U.S., and on the drive back we want you to read us the beginning of your chosen book. But not the bird book! We don't want a family history of the Crowe family now do we?" She chuckled. "Future trips the three of us will take will allow Steph and me to read our books. Sound like a deal?"

Ed sat up straight in his chair. "Wonderful idea! I'm honored to be part of the team."

They all shook hands.

"We'll pick you up at eight-thirty tomorrow morning," Seana said as they stood to leave. "And don't worry, we know your address. We're not in the habit of having dinner with 'blokes' we know nothing about."

"The name Edwin helped," Stephanie grinned. "How could you not be a good guy with such an English name like that?"

"That's me," Ed agreed, "just a boring old travel agent."

AUTHOR'S NOTE

This novel is fiction but is based, in part, on actual events.

The actions of the Vichy government are now well documented, but it went unmentioned in French history until July 1995, when President, Jacque Chirac publicly recognized the events that occurred.

He said, in part:

> *"France, the homeland of the Enlightenment and of the rights of man, a land of welcome and asylum, on that day (July 16th, 1942) committed the irreparable. Breaking its word, it handed those who were under its protection over to their executioners."*